TWO CORINTHIANS

TWO CORINTHIANS

Carola Dunn

Walker and Company
New York

First published in the United States of America in 1989 by
Walker Publishing Company, Inc.

Published simultaneously in Canada by Thomas Allen & Son Canada, Limited,
Markham, Ontario

Library of Congress Cataloging-in-Publication Data
Dunn, Carola.
Two Corinthians / Carola Dunn.
p.   cm.
ISBN 0-8027-1087-5
I. Title.
PR6054.U537T8   1989
823'.914—dc20   89-16446
CIP

Printed in the United States of America
10 8 6 4 2 1 3 5 7 9

=== 1 ===

WITHOUT RAISING HER eyes from Cushing's *Exotic Gardener*, Claire Sutton absently tucked a vagrant lock of light brown hair into the loose knot at the nape of her slender neck.

"Claire, you are scattering hairpins again!" snapped her mother. "I wonder you will be so careless. It is as well you are an old maid for you would drive a husband to distraction, I vow. And you may fidget with your hair for ever without the least improvement in your appearance. I am sure you have something better to wear than that old brown rag."

Only a slight tightening of her sensitive lips showed that Claire had heard Lady Sutton's disparaging rebuke. However, the third occupant of the shabby parlour dropped her needlework and flew to the defence of her sister with a toss of her blonde curls.

"That is unfair, Mama! If she is not married, it is because none of the gentlemen she meets are interested in anything beyond Papa's horses."

"Don't be pert, Elizabeth," said Lady Sutton sharply. "Your sister had her Season in London, and a great disaster it was. Nor is yours likely to be more successful if you do not learn to curb your tongue. Not that I think your father should waste his money on such an ungrateful child. With a third son starting at Cambridge this autumn there are better uses for it."

"But Mama, I am twenty! My come-out has already been postponed twice!"

Claire's quiet voice forestalled the approaching storm.

"Lizzie, I must find some more briar roots before this thaw ends. Will you walk with me?"

Having girded up her loins for battle, Lizzie was reluctant to abandon the field. Clair read the mutinous sparkle in her blue eyes.

"Do come, it is a beautiful day for midwinter. Pray excuse us, Mama." Claire rose swiftly to her feet.

"I will not have you wandering about the neighbourhood dabbling in the mud, Claire. Claire! People are already saying that you are peculiar. I forbid you to take your sister with you."

Lady Sutton's harangue faded as Claire gently closed the door behind them. The sisters went up the stairs to dress for walking.

"I know it is worse than useless to protest," said Lizzie penitently. "Only I cannot bear it when she abuses you so. I do manage to pay no heed when I am the target, I promise you, but it will be the outside of enough if I cannot go to London next month."

"You shall go, dearest, and neither Papa nor our brothers shall be called upon to make any desperate sacrifices. I could not think it right to go against Mama last spring, or the year before, however specious her excuses. A death in the family, even though both were *very* distant cousins, must have put us in the wrong. But if her only reason now is lack of funds, why, I have plenty thanks to Godmama. I am eight and twenty, sufficiently ancient to be your chaperone without raising too many eyebrows, should Mama decide not to accompany you."

"Claire, you darling! I should have known I could trust you." Lizzie flung her arms around her tall, slender sister in a hug that sent the last few hairpins flying. "When shall we leave? We must have time to order new gowns before the Season begins. And where shall we stay? At your house at Bumble's Green?"

"No, that is too far out of the city. I shall rent a house in the centre of things. When we return from our walk, remind me to write to my lawyer about finding a place."

"You will not forget. I know, if no one else does, that your absentmindedness is all for show."

She smiled at Lizzie's exuberance. "Hush, you will give me away." With her fine, straight hair tumbling about her shoulders and the vagueness in her grey eyes replaced by a glow of amusement, Claire's face showed a piquant beauty which was more than mere prettiness. The glow faded as they entered the chilly, north-facing bedchamber they shared. She shivered. "Put on your warmest cloak and boots," she advised. "Thaw or no, it is still January."

"You know I never feel the cold. I am better padded than you." Lizzie patted her rounded hips cheerfully. "Though I wish Mama would allow us a fire in here, for your sake. Here, sit down and let me pin up your hair properly. If it falls down while we are out you will get it caught in the thorns."

A few minutes later, the two girls slipped down the back-stairs to a side door. Claire wore a short cloak of dark brown wool with a hood. Her sister was elegant in a blue pelisse, fitted to her softly curvaceous figure, and a matching bonnet which was the last word in fashion as far as the nearby town of Banbury was concerned. If the pelisse was worn at the hem and elbows, and the bonnet carefully constructed by her own nimble fingers, it was not apparent from a distance.

The side door was the shortest route from the house to both the gardens and the stables where Sir James Sutton kept his much sought-after hunters. As Claire and Lizzie started down the gravel path in the pale winter sunlight, their father came towards them. With him were their eldest brother, Edward, and another gentleman whom they guessed to be a customer. The three were deep in discussion of equine pedigrees.

"Good-day, Papa," the girls murmured, stepping aside.

Sir James nodded curtly as he passed, neither looking at them nor pausing in his conversation. The customer cast an appreciative glance at Lizzie's blonde comeliness. Edward dropped back to greet them with a scowl.

"Must you go about looking like a servant, Claire?" he demanded petulantly. "You put the whole family to shame. And you're the only one of us who can afford to dress decently."

"Gammon!" snorted Lizzie vulgarly. "I happen to know that your coat was delivered only yesterday from that tailor in London, what's his name? Nugee, isn't it? And that waistcoat must have cost a fortune."

Edward glanced down at the purple brocade, lavishly embroidered with gold thread, and had the grace to look a little disconcerted.

"And very odd it looks with riding boots and breeches," added his younger sister. "At twenty-six you ought to be capable of deciding whether you want to be a dandy or a sportsman."

"Impertinent chit! I've a mind to tell Mama..." His voice trailed away as Lizzie left him without ceremony.

Claire had wandered on as soon as she realised that her brother, as usual, had nothing to say that was worth listening to.

"Edward is a popinjay!" said Lizzie decidedly as she caught up. "I am not precisely sure what a popinjay is, but it sounds right. I cannot wait to go to Town. I shall find someone to marry right away so that you can go and live in your little house and never see the rest of the family again."

"Oh no," cried Claire in distress. "I knew I ought not to have told you my plan. I shall never be happy if you rush into marriage only to rescue me. You must wait until you find a man you can love, however long it takes."

"I'm not at all sure I believe in romantic love. It is all very well in a novel, but sadly impractical for daily use. If I catch a husband who is agreeable, and not a popinjay, and who does not ignore me as Papa does, then I shall be perfectly satisfied."

Claire had long ago given up hope of finding romance herself, but her sister's prosaic dismissal of the idea dismayed her. She resolved to impress upon Lizzie the foolishness of a hasty match.

They reached the garden shed, and Claire went in to fetch a basket and a trowel. An ungainly youth dressed in home-spun stood by the rough wooden table. Tufts of ginger hair topped his broad, flat face, which wore an expression of despair as he regarded the clay flowerpot held in his large hands. The despair changed to joy when he saw Claire.

"I bin sorting them pots, Miss Claire. Big uns here an' little uns there like you said. On'y this un be middling an' I don' know where to put it."

"Let's find a special place for middling ones," Claire said gently. "I think there is room on that shelf. You are doing an excellent job of tidying my mess, Alfie."

"Ex'lent, Miss?"

"Good. Very good. Now where is my basket? Miss Lizzie and I are going to find roots."

"I come an' help?" the lad begged.

"Not today, Alfie." She was loath to disappoint him, but she wanted to talk to her sister without interruptions. Alfie tended to become utterly absorbed in studying a tree or a rock or a fence post, and it took constant urging to make him keep up with them. "You can help me best by finishing here," she assured him. "I shall need those pots when I bring the roots home. And then you must carry in some coals for Cook."

"I don' like Cook," he muttered.

"Alfie, you promised."

"Promised I do what you say an' what Miss Lizzie say. *Will* do, Miss Claire. Don't like Cook, will carry coals for *you*."

"Thank you, Alfie. Now, remember to put the middling pots on this shelf. You are a great help to me."

She left him beaming as he carefully set the pot on the shelf. He was slow, but he was not an idiot, and since she had rescued him from a life of tormented misery as a scul-lery boy he had been devoted to her and Lizzie. He followed their simple directions with a literal-minded patience and thoroughness which occasionally brought unexpected re-

5

sults. She smiled as she remembered the time she had set him to dig over a flowerbed. She had come back some time later to find it twice as large. Alfie had been quite disappointed to learn that she did not want the entire lawn dug up.

Claire slung her basket over her arm, and she and Lizzie set out. They crossed the park beyond the kitchen gardens, past the paddocks where grazed the stallions, mares, colts, and fillies which were both Sir James's passion and his livelihood.

Claire and Lizzie walked on with the brisk stride of countrywomen until they left the Sutton estate to enter pasture and cropland, crisscrossed with hedges of hawthorn and hazel. A pair of speckle-breasted thrushes flew up from a cluster of crimson haws as they passed; the hazel bushes were bare, stripped of nuts long since by squirrels and thrifty villagers.

Here and there scarlet hips showed where wild briar roses had flowered in June. Claire took her sharp knife and cut a thorny, dead-looking main stem several inches above the ground, then dug up the root and put it in her basket.

She passed by the next few rose vines, leaving them to delight the eye and nose next summer, before taking another. The local farmers and landowners were used to her depredations and waved indulgent permission if they happened to see her at it. She knew their indulgence was tinged with pity and some derision. Lady Sutton was right to say that people thought her peculiar. Still, come July her rose garden would draw admiring visitors from as far away as Oxford.

Her basket filled, she hurried to join Lizzie who sat patiently on a stile, holding the bunch of green-veined snowdrops and yellow aconites she had gathered as they wandered.

"What a charming sight," Claire said, conscious of her own muddy gloves and hem. "I wish I could paint."

"They will look pretty embroidered on a cushion cover, do you not think? Like a mediaeval tapestry."

"Certainly, but you are the charming sight I referred to, goose. Is it not odd that I, who am timid and fearful, should enjoy so active an occupation as gardening, while you, the lively one, prefer embroidery?"

"I daresay everyone needs some contrast in their lives," said Lizzie wisely as she jumped down into the winding lane.

Claire was following when a carriage swept around the bend, startling her. She stumbled, slid down the bank, and landed in a crumpled heap at the bottom, dropping her basket.

The driver had seen the mishap and pulled his team of four superb bays to a snorting halt some yards beyond them. Handing the reins to his companion, he descended from the box and hurried towards them.

His many-caped greatcoat was open and it was obvious to Claire from her glimpse of his clothes that he was a gentleman. Feeling foolish, she took Lizzie's hand and scrambled to her feet. As soon as she put her weight on her ankle, agonising pain shot up her leg and a wave of dizziness overcame her. Though she clung to Lizzie she felt herself sinking, until strong arms caught her up, lifting her easily off the ground.

"I fear she has injured herself," a concerned voice said close to her ear.

Through a whirling mist she heard Lizzie answer. She strained to make out her words as consciousness slipped away.

It must have been a brief swoon, for she was still in the stranger's arms when awareness returned. After making such a cake of herself, she did not want to face him. She kept her eyes closed and tried not to stiffen as he lifted her into his carriage. Then Lizzie was pulling off her boot, and it took all her self-control not to moan aloud.

"It is dreadfully swollen already. What shall I do?" Lizzie sounded frightened and Claire wanted to comfort her, but her head was swimming again.

7

"I daresay it is only a sprain," said the man's deep, reassuring voice. "They can hurt as much as a break, I believe."

"Surely she ought to have come 'round by now?"

"She is probably feeling lightheaded."

"I hope she did not hit her head."

Claire forced herself to open her eyes. She looked up into a handsome face full of solicitude. The gentleman had dark hair, tousled, touched with grey at the temples, dark eyes, a patrician nose whose haughtiness was belied by sensitive lips. Faint lines about his mouth gave him a slightly cynical air, but despite those and the greying hair, she thought he could not be much above five and thirty.

"She is awake!" cried Lizzie. "Thank heaven. Is it very painful, Claire?"

"Yes...No...It does not signify," she whispered feebly. "My basket?"

"I'll get it, don't worry. Only I cannot move without disturbing you."

"Slade shall fetch the basket," said the stranger.

Claire became aware of a small man dressed in the fastidious black of a gentleman's gentleman, sitting on the opposite seat. The carriage was luxuriously upholstered in supple leather, dyed dark blue. She was unhappily certain that the mud on her gown must have transferred to the seat, and since she was leaning against the stranger, with his arm supporting her, his clothes must also be suffering.

"It does not matter," she murmured as the valet rose to his feet with a resigned look.

"Yes it does," Lizzie contradicted. "You will doubtless be confined to your bed for a few days and unable to collect more roots. Pray make sure you find them all, Slade, and the trowel and knife as well."

"Roots, miss?"

"Rose roots. They cannot have fallen far from the basket, so you will see them."

"Yes, miss."

The handsome gentleman turned a look of amused enquiry on Lizzie.

"You are a gardener, ma'am?"

"Not I. Embroidery is my forte. Claire, you are shockingly pale. I am sure your ankle is hurting."

"It throbs a little. As long as I do not move it is not too bad."

The valet scrambled back into the coach, setting the basket on the floor.

"Thank you, Slade," said the gentleman. "And now I must direct the coachman, Miss...?"

"I am Elizabeth Sutton. Our house is just a mile or so along this lane."

He knocked on the roof and called, "Peter, drive on!"

"It is very kind of you to take us up, sir," Lizzie said as the carriage started off.

"The sooner your maid's injury receives attention, the better, Miss Sutton. You are Sir James's daughter, I presume? I was on my way to purchase a mount from him."

"Yes. I am glad we do not take you out of your way. But Claire is my sister, sir, not my maid."

He looked down at Claire with surprised interest. She felt a hot flush of embarrassment rise in her cheeks as she quickly closed her eyes and wished she had not so soon abandoned her feigned swoon.

"I beg your pardon, Miss Sutton," he said, a note of amusement now colouring the deep voice. "These are your gardening clothes, I collect?"

Bravely she opened her eyes. She read sympathetic understanding along with the amusement in his gaze, and nodded. The motion, slight as it was, somehow transferred itself to her ankle and the pain shot up again. She bit her lip, holding back a cry.

Lizzie squeezed her hand. "We are nearly home, dearest," she said. "It is lucky that your carriage is so well sprung, sir, for it jolts hardly at all."

"Lucky indeed, Miss Elizabeth," he responded smiling.

Her head on his chest, Claire noticed the vibration of his speech and realised she could feel his heartbeat and the rise and fall of his breathing. It was a shockingly intimate position, but she did not dare move. She was grateful for the warmth of his body and the comfort of his strong arms protecting her from the inevitable swaying of the coach.

Who was he? A wealthy man, to judge by his vehicle, though of course it might not be paid for. A sportsman, if he meant to buy a horse from her father. The coat against which her cheek was pressed was smooth, of Bath cloth she guessed. His linen was snowy white. His neckcloth, though neat, was simply knotted. Better dressed than the average country squire, yet no dandy, he must be a member of the Corinthian set, Claire decided.

More important, he was a true gentleman, kind and considerate even when he had thought her a servant. This was the sort of man she wanted Lizzie to fall in love with and to marry.

The carriage turned in between familiar gate posts and pulled up before the manor. Slade let down the step, hopped out, and scurried to knock on the front door. The unknown Corinthian carefully lifted Claire and carried her into the house, followed by Lizzie with the precious basket. The butler hovered, clucking at them anxiously.

"Golightly, send a groom for Dr. Farrow at once," ordered Lizzie, taking charge. "Sir, will you be so good as to carry my sister above-stairs?"

He was nodding his willingness, when Alfie charged into the hall. Seeing Claire in the arms of a stranger, he raised his fists, his face thunderous.

"What you done to her?" he demanded. "Leave her be!"

"If you want to take a poke at me, lad," said the gentleman calmly, "wait until I have set your mistress down."

"Alfie, Miss Claire has hurt herself," Lizzie hurried to explain. "You must fetch some coal from the shed and take it up to our chamber. Then ask one of the maids to light a fire. Do you understand? Take some coal up and ask Molly to light a fire."

"Un'stand, Miss Lizzie. Miss Claire be all right?"

"She will be fine, Alfie. Hurry now and have a fire made up in our chamber."

Lady Sutton, sweeping into the hall, heard these words.

"What do you mean by ordering a fire in your chamber, Elizabeth? It is quite unnecessary. Heavens, Claire! What disgraceful scrape have you landed yourself in this time? You will be the death of me, I vow. Sir, I beg you will not allow my daughter's shocking behaviour to disturb you."

"Miss Sutton has hurt her ankle, ma'am." The stranger's composure was unimpaired. "If you will allow me to carry her up, I shall return at once to present myself in due form. I am George Winterborne. Sir James is expecting me, I believe."

Lady Sutton gasped. "Lord Winterborne! Of course, my lord! But pray put Claire down, I am sure she can walk up, the silly girl."

"No, she cannot, Mama," interrupted Lizzie firmly. "If you will follow me, my lord, I shall show you the way."

With a nod to her exasperated ladyship, Lord Winterborne strode after Lizzie.

Claire wanted to die of humiliation. She ought to be used by now to being scolded in front of strangers, she told herself, but she still found it difficult to bear, impossible to ignore. And somehow it was worse because this stranger had been so kind and understanding. Now he must think her a ridiculous old maid. She avoided meeting his eyes as he laid her gently on her bed.

"Thank you, my lord," she whispered.

"I wish you a speedy recovery, Miss Sutton," he said, then turned to Lizzie. "Will your servant remember the fire, or do you suppose your mother has rescinded the order?"

"He will bring it," Lizzie assured him. "He obeys Claire and me without question, and will take no notice of anything Mama tells him. I do not mean to be rude, my lord, but as soon as you leave I can make Claire more comfortable."

He grinned, looking almost boyish. "Then I shall go down and explain matters to her ladyship. May I have your abigail sent to you?"

"We have none. We help each other."

"Admirable," he murmured, and departed.

Soon Claire was in her nightgown and under the covers. Alfie and Molly came, and a fire burned merrily in the small grate. Dr. Farrow arrived, diagnosed a bad sprain, and promised that it would heal quickly if she did not put her weight on it for a few days. He bound her ankle and left laudanum, but she discovered that as long as she kept still it only ached a little. Lizzie brought their favourite book of poetry and read to her. She was warm and comfortable and beginning to be drowsy, when Lady Sutton burst unannounced into the chamber.

"Elizabeth, I cannot imagine how you managed it, but Lord Winterborne complimented me on your pretty manners. He admired your appearance, also, and your care of your sister. I do believe Claire's clumsiness may be turned to good account for once."

"Who is he, Mama?"

"How shockingly ignorant you are, child! Why, he is the Marquis of Bellingham's heir. He is one of the most eligible gentlemen in the country. Rich as Croesus in his own right, and he will inherit I know not how many estates. You must try if you can catch him, Elizabeth. I have persuaded him to spend the night here, and you shall sit next to him at dinner."

"But he is quite old, Mama."

"Not a day over six and thirty, and handsome into the bargain. What more can you ask? Besides, you will do better with an older husband to hold the reins. I depend upon you to set your cap at him."

"Rome was not built in a day," murmured Claire.

Her mother rounded on her. "I will not have you interfering in this, miss! Just because you could not bring any gentleman up to scratch in an entire Season, there is no reason to suppose that your sister cannot make an impression upon Lord Winterborne that will at least bring him back. He already admires her, after all. Now, let me see what you have in your wardrobe that will be suitable."

As they searched through the meagre collection for the least shabby dinner gown, Claire mused on the extraordinary fact that for once she agreed with her mother. Lord Winterborne would be a splendid match for Lizzie.

= 2 =

A SCOWL TWISTED Lord Pomeroy's usually affable features as he urged his chestnuts onwards. His lordship's groom, Abel, perched up behind the swaying curricle, hung on for dear life. He disremembered when he'd last seen his even-tempered master driving in such a neck-or-nothing style, just like the veriest whipster!

"Eight years!" muttered his lordship. "And I still love her, the devil take her!" he groaned. "I am altogether too honourable a gentleman!" he castigated himself savagely. "I ought to have taken her into my arms years ago and kissed her till she set the date."

They reached the top of the long, steep hill down to the little town of Banbury. It was early yet, but January days were short and already the setting sun glinted on windows in the valley below. Cotswold stone turned to mellow gold, and snowy roofs glowed rosily. Abel closed his eyes and wished he had had the sense to join his lordship's valet, Pinkerton, in the travelling chaise. He should have known that after near a week knocking back bad brandy in that hovel of a tavern, his master was in no fit state to drive.

Lord Pomeroy heard his faithful servant moan. Grinning, he glanced back at his pale companion, and slackened their headlong pace. Though his own life might not be worth living, he would not risk his horses' legs on the icy slope.

Abel had accompanied him on many a wild race without turning a hair: if he thought they were going too fast for safety, he was undoubtedly right.

Half an hour later, as the last light faded from the sky, the curricle came to a halt before the pillared portico of an imposing manor. Abel jumped down and took the reins from his master.

"We leave for Tatenhill the day after tomorrow," said Lord Pomeroy, swinging to the ground with the grace of an athlete. " You can travel with Pinkerton."

"Oh no, m'lord! Druther go wi' your lordship, for ye're a top sawyer, be ye in never such a dudgeon."

His lordship clapped the wiry young groom on the shoulder. "You're a brave man," he said with a wry smile, "or a foolish one."

Abel watched him run up the steps to the front door, his tall figure imposing in his many-caped greatcoat. He shook his head.

"A rare dance that Miss Hartwell led you, m'lord!" he muttered to himself as he led the chestnuts towards the stables.

Lord Pomeroy, handing his curly-brimmed hat and gloves of York tan to the butler, allowed a footman to divest him of his greatcoat, revealing a close-fitting coat of russet superfine, pale yellow waistcoat, and beige inexpressibles. Even after five days spent trying to drown his sorrows, his fair hair was unruffled, his cravat impeccably creased, and no speck of mud marred his glossy Hessians.

"Is my sister at home, Braithwaite?"

The butler beamed. It was a pleasure to serve a gentleman like Lord Pomeroy. Never overly familiar, but he always remembered your name just as if you were a member of the Quality.

"Her ladyship is expecting you, my lord," he said.

Lady Caroline Carfax, a matronly blonde some five years older than her brother and equally easygoing, sat by a roaring fire in the Crimson Drawing Room, her head bent over a Gothic novel. She looked up as his lordship entered, and beamed. He bowed over her outstretched hand.

"Bertram! I have been expecting you this age and had given up for today. It grows dark so early these winter af-

15

ternoons. Have you seen Louise?"

"My niece goes on famously," his lordship assured her briefly. "How are the boys?"

"Oh, scarlet fever is a wretched business. We have been unable to entertain for fear of infection, but they are out of quarantine now and will go back to school shortly." Caroline had noted his discomfort at the mention of her daughter. "I hope Louise has not been troublesome? I am well aware that she is the veriest hoyden, so you need not scruple to tell me all."

"If she has been in the briars these last few days I have not heard it. She was well and happy when I saw her."

"It was a prodigious kind of Lord Daniel to take her in for the Christmas holiday. Miss Hartwell must have been relieved not to be charged with her."

She looked at him questioningly, but he did not respond. He was staring into the fire with a look of utter despondency, his broad shoulders slumped.

"Bertram, is it not settled yet?" she demanded.

"Yes, it's settled," he told her in a voice of gloom. "She is to marry Winterborne."

"Winterborne? Lord Daniel? Oh Bertram, I am so dreadfully sorry! How could she treat you so after you have been faithful to her for so long!"

He shrugged. "You must not blame Amaryllis. She has changed—we have both changed over the years. After all, we did not see each other for six years! She loves him, and you would not wish me to be married to a woman who loves another."

"They are betrothed, then."

"If they are, they have me to thank for bringing them together." He laughed hollowly. "They had quarrelled, and she told him she was to marry me. Then she refused me, and I could not bear to see her unhappy, so I went and told him. Or at least his brother, George Winterborne."

Lady Caroline clasped her hands and gazed at him with glowing eyes. "How utterly chivalrous you are, my dear!"

she crowed. "It is just like something out of a novel. Of course I am sorry that you are unhappy, but perhaps if you have both changed so much you will recover. After all, you were only two and twenty when you first asked for Miss Hartwell's hand, and you were engaged for two whole years without ever setting a date for the wedding. And I daresay if you had exerted yourself these past six years you might have found her sooner. You have not been abroad all the time!"

"Are you trying to persuade me that I never really loved her, Caroline? You'll catch cold at that."

"Of course not." Her ladyship had the grace to look a little conscious. "Only that you were a mere boy when you fell in love, and now you are thirty and much better able to choose what will suit you. And you must choose soon, Bertram," she added anxiously. "I had a letter from Mama only yesterday saying that Papa is fretting. He is far from well, you know, and it would relieve his mind greatly to know that his heir is settled with a wife."

"You need not tell me that he is in queer stirrups. I suppose I shall have to spend the Season doing the pretty to all the eligible young ladies. The thought makes me shudder. Half will be outrageous flirts and the other half milk-and-water misses without a word to say for themselves. I believe that is why I first loved Amaryllis—she was neither coy nor forward but totally self-possessed."

"Perhaps I can find you a bride beforehand so that you can enjoy the Season in peace," said his sister thoughtfully. She was about to go on when the door opened and her husband entered. "James! See, Bertram is come, is that not delightful? He brings word that our dear Louise is well."

"Servant, Pomeroy," Viscount Carfax nodded to his brother-in-law. A quiet, stern-faced gentleman of middle height, he was dressed with propriety but with none of Bertram's fashionable flair. Their relationship was cordial but distant, and upon his arrival the conversation turned to indifferent matters.

Braithwaite appeared bearing a silver tray with a pair of

decanters. Lord Pomeroy accepted a glass of Madeira and forgot his sorrows and his prospective search for a bride in a discussion of the bloodlines of foxhounds and the price of corn.

Later, when they went up to change for dinner, Lady Caroline assured her brother that he need not put on his London finery.

"We dine *en famille* tonight," she explained. "Indeed, as I said, we have not entertained this age, but I have in mind to plan a dinner party while you are with us. There is someone— there are some neighbours I should like you to meet."

He looked at her suspiciously. "I am expected at Tatenhill," he said. "I cannot stay beyond tomorrow." ⋅

"Then you must give us some of your time on your way to London next month. Perhaps I shall be able to rescue you from the horrid fate of spending the Season hunting for a wife."

"Who is it?" he asked with a resigned sigh.

She glanced down the hallway. Lord Carfax was closing the door of his dressing-room behind him.

"A Miss Sutton. She is eight and twenty, or thereabouts, so she has quite put missishness behind her."

"A trifle long in the tooth to remain unmarried! An anti-dote is she? Squint? Crookback? Laugh like a hyena?"

"Certainly not!" said his sister indignantly. "I will not claim that she is a beauty, and I believe she did not *take* in Town, but she is very well-looking, I assure you."

"What's wrong with her then? Come on, Caroline, out with it."

"Well, she is a trifle unconventional. Nothing too dread-ful, I promise. She behaves with perfect propriety, but per-haps a little *oddly*."

"So you would wed me to an eccentric!"

"Say an original, rather. There are not a great number of unmarried young ladies available, Bertram, who are neither flirts nor insipid! You will not expect, I suppose, to fall in love again? I am persuaded that Miss Sutton would make you a perfectly unexceptionable wife."

"I assume her birth is acceptable, or you would not suggest her. Sutton... Not Sir James Sutton of the Sutton Stables? They are near Banbury as I recall."

"His elder daughter. They are an old and respected county family with aristocratic connexions."

"Penniless, I daresay?"

"No, she has a handsome fortune from her godmother. Two thousand a year, I have heard, which is not to be sneezed at! Not that you will have the least need of it when you inherit Tatenhill. I do not consider that an inducement, particularly as you were willing to take Miss Hartwell with nothing. But if you do not care to meet her, I shall invite her next week instead of waiting on your return."

Bertram grinned at her pout.

"No need to get on your high ropes. It can do no harm to meet her, so long as you promise me you will not so much as hint to her of your intentions!"

"I promise." She stood on tiptoe and kissed him. "And now I must run and change my dress, for Carfax likes to sit down to dinner on time. You will not mention this to him?"

"You cannot expect me to encourage you to keep secrets from your husband," he said severely.

"Bertram, you would not tell! Oh, you are roasting me. I never knew such a tease!" she complained, and pattered off in high good humour.

The weather held clear and cold two days later when Lord Pomeroy set out for his ancestral home at Tatenhill in Staffordshire. Abel was relieved to find that his master once more handled the ribbons like the top-o'-the-trees Corinthian he was. He drove to an inch, to be sure, but with cool competence rather than reckless abandon.

It was dark by the time they reached their destination; the windows of the great mansion glowed with a welcome promise of warmth and comfort. It was impossible not to feel a certain pride in being heir to such magnificence, but Bertram did not think of this place as home. Between Eton, Cambridge, and the diplomatic service, he had spent little enough time at his family's country seat since his early youth. He was not yet ready to settle down and take from his ailing father the burden of running the great estate.

If only he had been able to bring a bride home to share his new responsibilities—but Amaryllis was lost to him for ever.

The Earl and Countess of Tatenhill were quite as distressed as he had expected to hear his news. Also as expected, they accepted it without discussion or recrimination. With a new sensitivity, Bertram realised that he had never heard his parents air their differences, and though devoted to each other in an undemonstrative way, they must surely disagree on occasion.

He had never argued with Amaryllis. She had quarrelled bitterly with Lord Daniel, and yet in the end she had chosen him. He had been mistaken in her; she was not the cool, collected creature he had fallen in love with so long ago. The last thing he wanted was a life of emotional turmoil, and for the first time he began to look upon her rejection of his suit as a narrow escape.

Lord Tatenhill, with the gout which had plagued him for years now creeping painfully from joint to joint, wanted nothing so much as to see his son settle down with a wife. He had managed to attend Queen Caroline's trial last year, but the effort had exhausted him and he was now a semi-invalid. Bertram accepted with quiet acquiescence his orders to get himself betrothed by the end of the Season.

He would do so for his mother's sake, if not his father's. He had been shocked to see how tired and worn she had become recently, and it would be unconscionable to add to her burden by not doing his utmost to bring home a bride.

Surely it would not be difficult for the wealthy heir to an earldom to find a quiet, well-bred female willing to accept his hand, if not his heart!

Not a week later, a suitable young lady was presented to his attention, nay, forced upon it. He had spent the interim mostly on estate business with his father's land agent. Riding home that evening after visiting a tenant farmer, he found a large and antiquated travelling carriage preceding him into the stable yard.

The faded baronial crest upon the door instantly warned him that his Aunt Dorothy had arrived.

When he entered the house, the butler informed him in a sepulchral whisper that Lady Harrison was accompanied on her visit by the eldest Miss Harrison and by Mr. Harrison.

"I have taken the liberty, my lord," he went on, "of ordering a footman to wait upon Mr. Harrison. I trust your lordship will agree that it would be unwise to expose a chambermaid unnecessarily to the young gentleman's—ah—attentions."

Lord Pomeroy, all too aware of his cousin Horace's reputation as a loose fish, heartily concurred.

He went upstairs to change out of his riding clothes. Pinkerton had laid out his most soberly elegant evening dress: black swallowtail coat, snuff-brown waistcoat trimmed with black satin, and matching brown pantaloons. His lordship grinned, instantly recognising this as a response to his cousin's tendency to overadornment. To complement this attire, he tied his neck-cloth in a simple knot of his own invention and accepted from his hovering valet a plain diamond stickpin.

When he entered the drawing-room where the family was gathered before dinner, he did not at once notice Horace Harrison. Lady Harrison had chosen to wear a particularly virulent shade of royal blue. Though short, she was stout, and the quantities of bows, rosettes, and rouleaux that embellished her gown turned her into a sphere. It was some moments before Lord Pomeroy had eyes for anyone else.

"Horace never gives *me* a *moment's* worry," announced his aunt's piercing voice, covering the sound of his arrival.

Correctly assuming this to be an indirect attack upon him, he was unsurprised to hear his mother defending him.

"I'm sure no one could have a better son than Bertram," said Lady Tatenhill firmly.

"Mama, this tribute unmans me!" A smile in his blue eyes, he bowed gracefully over her hand, then turned to his relatives.

"How do you do, Aunt. Your servant, Cousin Horace."

"Servant, Cousin."

The Honourable Horace Harrison did not subscribe to the discredited George Brummell's creed that a gentleman should dress with unobtrusive elegance. His hair was frizzed up to add inches to his height; the shoulders of his peacock blue coat were grotesquely padded and the waist nipped in, in an unsuccessful attempt to remedy an unimpressive figure. His waistcoat was silver, embroidered with purple butterflies, and seven gold fobs dangled from his watch-chain. His weak chin was entirely concealed by a huge, elaborate cravat adorned with a large amethyst surrounded by diamonds.

Paste, thought Lord Pomeroy. Horace's pockets were notoriously to let.

"And this," announced Lady Harrison in stentorian tones, with a wave of her pudgy hand, "is your cousin, Amelia."

His lordship became aware that the third member of the family was also present. Dressed in a pale pink muslin round gown which left her goose-fleshed arms bare, Amelia Harrison curtsied nervously to her imposing cousin.

"You have not seen Amelia since she was seven, Pomeroy," his aunt informed him complacently. "She is grown into a charming young lady, is she not? She makes her come-out this Season, and we have every expectation of a brilliant match."

Bertram bowed again, politely but a trifle impatiently. Amelia appeared to be precisely the type of insipid female he had successfully avoided for the past eight years, with the aid of his long-standing engagement to Amaryllis Hartwell. Now that protection was at an end, and he knew without a shadow of doubt that Lady Harrison would make every attempt to foist off her mousy schoolroom miss upon him.

And Caroline was expecting him to do the pretty to the eccentric Miss Sutton! Nonetheless, it was with the greatest relief that he departed a week later to return to the Carfaxes'.

At least Miss Sutton might prove amusing, and anything must be better than another day with his overbearing aunt, her silent daughter, and her coxcomb of a son.

= 3 =

IMPATIENT WITH THE pace of his luxurious travelling carriage, George Winterborne left it to follow him up the Great North Road. It was a perfect way to try the stamina of the black gelding, Orpheus, which he was thinking of buying from the Sutton Stables, and he would reach Northumberland days earlier. He was not such a dandy that he could not live out of a saddlebag, and without the aid of his valet, for a while.

He had had to spend a couple of days in London on business after he left his brother's house, and then the detour via Banbury had added another delay. Of course, a letter would have told his father the news long since, but he wanted to bear it himself. The opportunity to deliver such joyful tidings, to see the shadow lift at last from the marquis's face, was not something to be surrendered in the interests of mere speed.

After a night in Newcastle, he turned inland. This border country of rugged hills and moors, north of Hadrian's Wall, was very different from the lush, gentle landscape of his own estate in Dorset. His blood sang to its grandeur. Here his ancestors had driven back the Scots' raids time and time again over long centuries of feuding. It was his home, and in spite of the deeply drifting snow he set out confidently along lanes which were little more than cart tracks.

Orpheus seemed scarce to notice his rider's considerable weight as the miles vanished beneath his long stride. It had been worth going to Banbury on his way; he would certainly purchase the horse when he returned to the south. It would be amusing to see Sutton's pretty, pert daughter again, and he must remember to enquire after her odd, quiet sister's recovery.

They stopped to rest at noon in a tiny, greystone hamlet where my lord was recognised at once in the taproom of the whitewashed inn, recognised and welcomed and fed, and sent on his way warmed by good wishes as much as by the fire. The Marquis of Bellingham owned much of the land hereabouts. He was a fair master, and his genial heir was a prime favourite with one and all.

His mount was tiring when at last he trotted past St. Cuthbert's Well. The crumbling ruins of Bellingham Castle were silhouetted on the skyline. Below it on the hillside, facing south with its two wings spread like open arms, the long, low house sprawled across the slope.

Lord Winterborne rode straight up the long drive and drew rein in the rose garden in front of the house, sheltered by the wings to east and west. At this season nothing was visible but carefully pruned stumps, half buried in muddy straw, but this had been his mother's favourite place. When he thought of her, he could almost smell the heavy perfume of the dark red blooms she had loved best, the lighter fragrance of pink and yellow and white.

She had told him when he was six years old, when his brother was nothing but a squirming scrap of newborn humanity, that he must always take care of Danny. He had tried, and he had failed, and she had died not knowing that in the end he had succeeded after all.

"Mother," he said aloud, "it's all right now. Danny's happy now, I helped him win the woman he loves. I took care of him, Mother."

Feeling like a sentimental fool, he turned Orpheus towards the stables.

Lord Bellingham, seated at his desk, looked up as his tall son entered the library unannounced. For a moment he simply enjoyed the unexpected sight of his firstborn, the broad-shouldered, well-muscled figure, the arrogant nose so like his own, the dark hair and eyes that reminded him of his beloved wife. At thirty-six, George had lost the slimness of youth and gained a few grey streaks at his temples. The marquis ran his hand through his own thick white hair, put down his pen, and rose to clasp his son's hand in both his.

"Forgive my dirt, sir. I have ridden from Newcastle this day, but I could not wait to give you my news. Father, Danny is to marry again!"

His face pale, the marquis sank back into his chair, looking suddenly old. George cursed himself for his abruptness. Daniel's first marriage had been disastrous, ending in the scandal of divorce; he ought to have made it plain that his news was good before blurting it out like any rattle-tongued windbag.

"You will approve his choice, sir," he assured his father over his shoulder as he hurried to pour a glass of brandy from the decanter on a side-table. "Here, take this. True, she has no portion, but her breeding is impeccable, and I can vouch for her being a delightful young lady."

A little colour was creeping back into Lord Bellingham's cheeks as he sipped at the brandy. "Who is this paragon?" he asked drily.

"The Honourable Amaryllis Hartwell. I daresay you knew her father?"

The marquis threw back his head and guffawed. "Hartwell's daughter! Well matched, a scandal for a scandal! What has Miss Hartwell been doing since the viscount ran off with the Spanish ambassador's daughter?"

"Running a school, and most competently," George answered with some indignation. "And I wish you will not laugh, sir. Daniel is so changed, so happy, you would not know him. They are very much in love."

"Creampot love! Marriage with even a younger son must be preferable to the life of a schoolmistress."

"She might have had the heir to an earldom. Tatenhill's heir, young Pomeroy, offered for her and was refused."

"So she says!"

"You are too skeptical, sir. I had it from his own lips not a fortnight since."

At last the marquis began to allow himself to believe. "Danny is happy?" he asked softly.

"Happy?" George laughed aloud, joyous, triumphant. "That is too poor a word. He is like a man released from a dungeon after ten years without a glimpse of the sky. She has given him back his youth. I tell you, Father, almost I think to look for a wife myself!"

"Then she has my blessing! You should have married and produced an heir long since!"

"Danny's example was scarce encouraging, sir. I'd no mind to suffer the horns as he did, and I never met a woman worth the risk."

"What of the child?"

"Amaryllis knows Isabel is not Danny's daughter, yet she loves her as dearly as he does." Suddenly alert, George studied his father's face. "If you could bring yourself to acknowledge Isabel as your granddaughter... He wants a reconciliation. He wants your blessing, your presence at his wedding."

"The estrangement was not all on my side," said the marquis harshly.

"I know. He felt he had let you down. In his humiliation, he could not face you. But now..."

"I wish your mother were alive." Lord Bellingham leaned his forehead on his hand, hiding his face.

George knew he had won and did not press his point. "No more than I wish it, no more than Danny does," he said in a gentle voice. "Would that I might hope to find her equal!"

"I shall write to him. George, thank you."

With a light heart, George went up to his chamber to change out of his riding clothes. It would be at least two days before his carriage arrived with his luggage and Slade, but the closets in his dressing-room held an assortment of cast-off clothing. He did not suppose that either his father or the widowed cousin who ran his household would object

27

if his dress this evening was not in the first stare of fashion.

To his utter disgust he was quite unable to fasten the pantaloons made for him by the best tailors in London not five years since.

Turning to a rack of coats, he chose one that he remembered as being fairly loose fitting, not that he had ever cared for coats so tight he needed help in donning them. With a struggle he pulled it on, then leaned forward to adjust the cheval glass. There was a ripping sound as the coat split down the back.

George groaned. He stripped to the buff and pondered his reflexion in the mirror, turning and twisting like a debutante before her first ball.

It was no use pretending he was still a slender Adonis, but he was not yet ready for a Cumberland corset! There was no flabbiness, he decided with relief, poking and prodding at himself. He had always led an active life, riding and walking in the country, sparring with Gentleman Jackson, and dancing till dawn in Town.

There were other activities that had helped, no doubt, to keep him fit. None of his many mistresses, high-born or low, had ever complained of a lack of ardour on his part.

He heard the door of his dressing-room open, followed by a ladylike shriek. The door slammed shut.

"George!" came an indignant voice from without.

He seized a crimson brocade dressing gown, wrapped it around himself, and went to the door. Outside stood a tiny, wispy lady of late middle years, wearing a quilted sacque of plum-coloured satin which would have been the height of alamodality some thirty years ago. Mrs. Tilliot, once companion to the marchioness and now mistress of the house in all but name, did not believe in new-fangled fashions; somewhere in the wilds of Northumberland she had found a dressmaker to cater to her whims.

Grinning, George swept her into his arms and kissed her cheek soundly, eliciting another shriek.

"Put me down at once, you great bear!" she scolded, twinkling at him. "Indeed, I beg your pardon for walking in on you. I meant to check that all was set to rights, and I thought you were still with Bellingham in the library."

"You are welcome at any time, dear Tilly. Since you are here, perhaps you can advise me." He explained his predicament.

Mrs. Tilliot tutted and clucked and gave it as her considered opinion that neither coats nor inexpressibles might be successfully let out to accommodate his expanded figure. She bore off the wrinkled clothes from his saddlebag, promising that his father's valet would quickly produce something presentable from the heap.

"We must hope your carriage will arrive tomorrow," she said as she left. "These will do for tonight. Our only guests will be the vicar and Mrs. Gates and their daughter, and Mr. Bowe, the lawyer from Hexham. Miss Gates and Mr. Bowe are betrothed."

George remembered Miss Gates as a pretty young woman with whom he had enjoyed a mild flirtation on his last visit. Doubtless her engagement ruled out that harmless pastime. He anticipated a dull evening.

Neither Miss Gates's discretion nor her presumed affection for her future husband were proof against the attractions of the handsome, dashing, rich and titled Lord Winterborne. She brought to bear on him her full battery of coy glances, fluttered eyelashes, rippling laugh, and flirted fan.

George encouraged her. Better the man should know the worst before the knot was tied, he thought cynically.

Before he left Bellingham a week later, a letter arrived from Lord Daniel in response to his father's overture. Jubilant, the marquis announced that he would follow George south in a month or so. Besides Danny's wedding there was Prinny's coronation to be attended, and he expected to enjoy the Season with a lighter heart than any time these ten years. Mrs. Tilliot, too, looked forward to renewing her acquaintance with old friends she had not seen this age.

Even the constant rain which began when he reached York and continued throughout his journey could not dampen George's high spirits.

He received a royal welcome from the Suttons. Sir James was delighted with the price he offered for Orpheus. When Lady Sutton pressed him to stay indefinitely, until the roads were fit to travel, he was confirmed in his belief that she was yet another matchmaking mama. After the caustic way she had spoken of Miss Sutton in his presence, it was clear that she intended him for Miss Elizabeth.

Nothing loath, he prepared to indulge that young lady in a flirtation, without any intention of letting it lead him to parson's mousetrap.

He found it extraordinarily difficult. They met in the drawing-room before dinner, taken early in the country fashion, and Lady Sutton took care to leave them alone together at one end of the room. His opening salvo, an admittedly commonplace remark that she was even prettier than he remembered, was met with a merry laugh.

"This is a new dress, and there is something about a new dress that makes one feel pretty," Lizzie said dismissively. "I have you to thank for it, my lord. Mama only bought it because she wants me to impress you. She hopes that you will decide to marry me so that she does not have to bother with giving me a Season."

Nonplussed by her frankness, his lordship made a quick recover.

"And dare I hope that you, too, wish to impress me, Miss Elizabeth?"

Lizzie considered the question with a serious face. "It cannot be denied that you are the most eligible gentleman I have ever met," she admitted. "And I like you, because you were so kind to Claire. But as for setting out to impress you, Claire says it is shockingly vulgar to set one's cap at a gentleman, whatever Mama says. I do not know you well enough to have fallen in love with you yet," she added apologetically.

George fell back on an enquiry as to Miss Sutton's health.

"She is perfectly recovered, thank you. She will be down

to dinner, but she always comes late because it gives Mama less time to snipe at her. Oh, I know why I am prettier now than last time we met. I expect I was quite haggard with worry over Claire's ankle."

"Of course, that must be it." Grinning, Lord Winterborne gave up the attempted flirtation and decided to enjoy her artlessly enchanting conversation.

He was rewarded by her delight at learning that he meant to spend the coming Season in London.

"I hope we will see you there," she exclaimed. "It will be much more comfortable if we have at least one acquaintance."

"Surely Sir James and Lady Sutton have a wide acquaintance among the ton."

"Papa knows any number of sporting gentlemen, of course, but he never bothers to introduce us to them, and when he goes to London he only goes to buy and sell horses at Tattersall's. And I do not think Mama will go with us. She thinks it a waste of money for me to have a Season." Lizzie explained about the postponements, and how Claire had promised to take her to Town this year regardless of their mother's opposition.

"I am glad to hear it," said George, "for the ton would be the loser by your absence."

Again the compliment was wasted on infertile ground. Lizzie ignored it completely. She was looking at him as if she had never seen him properly before.

"I don't know how it is," she said in a puzzled voice, "but I feel I can tell you anything. I promise you I do not usually bore strangers with tales of family quarrels. I beg your pardon, my lord."

Touched, he took her hand and pressed it. "I am honoured by your confidence, Miss Elizabeth," he said gravely. "You may be sure I shall not repeat to Lady Sutton anything you choose to tell me."

"I am glad of it," she responded, her sunny temper restored, "for though I do not care a groat for Mama's scolding, I know it distresses Claire, however hard she pretends it does not."

At that moment, Claire drifted into the room, a faraway look on her face.

"Good evening, Mama, Papa," she said in a soft voice, sketching a curtsey to her parents.

Sir James went on talking to his two older sons as if his daughter did not exist.

"You are late as usual," said Lady Sutton automatically.

Claire turned towards George and Lizzie, and he thought he saw a spark of recognition and even welcome in her grey eyes. Then her gaze was unfocused again, as if she was looking through him to some unimaginable vision beyond. Again she curtsied, with a murmured, "How do you do, my lord," then turned as if to seek a seat far from everyone.

He stepped towards her and she hesitated.

"I am glad to hear you are quite recovered from your fall, Miss Sutton," he said, smiling down at her, wondering why she looked like a doe at bay.

Despite her obvious unease, her low voice was composed. "I must thank you for rescuing me from the effects of my clumsiness, my lord."

"I fear I startled you, coming round the bend at such a speed. While I hesitate to boast, I am accounted something of a top sawyer and I have a deplorable tendency to show my paces whether I have an audience or not. Something like one of your father's horses galloping round an empty field, I suppose."

She smiled, her eyes lit with amusement. For a startled moment he recognised the delicate beauty animation brought to her fine features, then her face was blank again as her mother took her arm.

"Claire, you must not interrupt his lordship's conversation with Elizabeth," scolded Lady Sutton. "I despair of ever teaching you the niceties of social intercourse. Pray excuse her, my lord, her head is for ever in the clouds."

George began a protest, but Claire was borne off willy-nilly. As he turned back to Lizzie, dismissing her lacklustre sister from his mind, he heard Lady Sutton's piercing whisper.

"Did you not see, ninnyhammer, how he took her hand?"

Lizzie's whisper, on the other hand, was nicely judged for his ears alone.

"Let us pretend," she said with a wicked sparkle, "that you are in truth courting me. Then it will be one in the eye for Mama when you leave without coming up to scratch."

His lips twitched but he said severely, "Where did you learn such vulgar expressions?"

"From my brothers, of course. Do say that you will do it, it would be beyond anything great."

"You have a vindictive mind, Miss Elizabeth." George was grinning openly now. "Very well, I will fall in with your infamous scheme, since you have already deflated my fragile ego by telling me you have no desire to impress me. Ah, dinner is ready, I believe. I wager your mama means you to go in on my arm?"

Her dimples were delightful. He had no aversion to staying a few days to hoodwink her ladyship.

Lying in bed that night, as Slade bustled about setting his clothes to rights, Lord Winterborne tried to make sense of his reactions to Lizzie. She was amusing company, yet he had had many an amusing flirt before and she was unlike any of them. Though she was at least fifteen years his junior, she was no schoolroom miss, yet she had a childlike enthusiasm and innocence which reminded him of his niece, Isabel.

Avuncular, that was how he felt. Like an indulgent uncle, or perhaps an older brother, for after all he was only fifteen years or so older.

The thought of Isabel brought Danny to mind. A contented smile spread across George's face as he dwelt on his brother's new happiness. Then he sat bolt upright.

"The devil!" he groaned.

Slade jumped.

"My lord?" he enquired nervously.

"Never mind. I have just put two and two together and come up with an answer I cannot like. Are you finished in here? Good-night."

"Good-night, my lord." The valet bore off his lordship's boots for blackening, shaking his head in foreboding.

George, too, shook his head in foreboding.

His hostess had announced at dinner that the family was to dine with neighbours, the Carfaxes, on the morrow. Lady Caroline Carfax's letter of invitation had mentioned that her brother was visiting, and it had naturally included the Suttons' guests, if any. Lady Sutton, looking smug, hinted that Lord Winterborne might find in the brother some competition for Elizabeth's attention.

This had not worried George since his pursuit of the young lady was not serious. But it had just dawned on him who the brother must be.

He knew Lord Carfax slightly from his London club. He had met Lady Caroline a few times in Society, but she was a year or two older than he, and he did not know her well. She had been married before he went on the Town, and whatever his faults he did not poach on other men's preserves; Danny's life had shown him too clearly the damage that could be done.

From Danny to Isabel to Isabel's little schoolfriend, Louise Carfax. The trail led inexorably to Louise's uncle, Bertram Pomeroy, whose betrothed Danny had stolen out from under his nose. Lord Pomeroy could not be expected to be overjoyed to see his successful rival's brother. Moreover, Louise had broken her arm while in Danny's care, so that Lady Caroline was equally unlikely to extend a warm welcome.

George looked forward to an uncomfortable evening. He even wondered whether, discretion being the better part of valour, he ought to cry craven and run.

No, he had promised to aid Lizzie's scheme to discomfit her overbearing mama, and he wanted to see again the mischievous twinkle in her blue eyes. It was odd, then, that the last thought he had before he dropped off to sleep was of grey eyes—dreamy, distant grey eyes which looked through him as if he were not there.

= 4 =

"I WISH I had not allowed you to talk me into meeting your eccentric Miss Sutton," growled Lord Pomeroy to his sister.

"You cannot hide behind Miss Hartwell's skirts any longer," she pointed out. "I do not understand how a diplomat—and a buck of the first stare!—can be so bashful at making the acquaintance of an inoffensive young woman."

"I am not bashful, merely suffering in anticipation of an evening of intolerable boredom."

"Hush, now, here they come."

A glance in the mirror over the fireplace assured Bertram that his blue coat clung unwrinkled to his broad shoulders and his cravat, in a spirit of irony tied in a *trône d'amour*, was perfection itself. He turned an imperturbable face towards the door.

"Sir James and Lady Sutton," announced Braithwaite. "Miss Sutton, Miss Elizabeth Sutton and Lord Winterborne."

Bertram did not hear the rest of the names, nor notice the lady his sister intended him to woo. His shocked gaze was fixed on the face of the one gentleman above almost all others that he least desired to meet. Lord Daniel's brother!

Lady Caroline bustled forward with a warm welcome, followed more staidly by her husband, giving Bertram a chance to regain his composure. He greeted Sir James and Lady Sutton with punctilious, if abstracted, courtesy, carried through the introductions by his innate good manners. His bow to the young ladies was elegant, his smile charming, his attention elsewhere.

"Servant, Winterborne."

"Pomeroy," the older man nodded acknowledgement.

Bertram noted with annoyance Lord Winterborne's expression of sympathetic understanding. With all the self-possession at his command, he looked him in the eye and said, "I trust your brother is well?"

"I believe so," responded Lord Winterborne with noncommittal cordiality. "Have you recent news of your niece?"

Lady Caroline interrupted. "I forgot to tell you, Bertram, that my poor little Louise broke her arm. She is back at school, and I received an excellent report of her recovery from Miss Hartwell. Oh dear!" She looked flustered as she realised that that name was best not spoken in present company.

"Pray introduce me to the rest of your guests, Caroline," requested Bertram in a perfectly steady voice, turning to the two young men who hovered nearby.

He quickly wrote off the young Suttons as a popinjay and a country bumpkin respectively. It was beneath him, however, to put on a display of aristocratic superiority. For several minutes he civilly responded to their remarks on London tailors and hunting the Shires, until each accused the other of boring him.

At that point he excused himself, murmuring something about paying his respects to the Misses Sutton. He left them staring at him in astonishment, united in the conviction that their sisters were unworthy of his attention.

If there was any family resemblance, he thought, then they were right.

Winterborne was talking to the younger girl, a pretty blonde. Judging by their laughter, she was the kind of flirt he abhorred. Miss Sutton was sitting by herself, turning pages of a book of prints with an abstracted air. Her appearance was unexceptionable, if colourless after Amaryllis's vivid beauty. Still, he could not expect everything, as Caroline had pointed out, and she had a quiet dignity which pleased him. He went to sit beside her, all too aware of his sister's approving glance.

The book was one he had given to Caroline upon his return from Italy.

"I fear woodcuts, however artistic, do little to convey the picturesque charm of Venice and Florence, Miss Sutton," he said with a smile.

"No?" she asked warily.

He launched into a description of the beauties of the cities of Italy, interspersed with amusing anecdotes of his diplomatic travails in that country. She listened for the most part without comment, but occasionally she asked an intelligent question and she smiled in the right places. He was feeling quite in charity with her, when he noticed that he had lost her attention.

Following her apprehensive gaze, he saw that Lady Sutton was glaring at her. The glare changed to an ingratiating simper when her ladyship realised she was observed, and she promptly approached them.

Her daughter's face closed as if a shutter had slammed shut.

"Claire, whatever are you thinking of to monopolise Lord Pomeroy so selfishly! You have allowed him no opportunity to speak to Elizabeth."

"I assure you, ma'am, it is by my own choice that I remain at Miss Sutton's side."

She looked at him disbelievingly. "You will find my younger daughter an enchanting creature, my lord," she persisted. "Elizabeth, pray come here at once."

Bertram turned with a shrug of apology to Miss Sutton, only to find that she had risen and was drifting away aimlessly. He noted that she was tall and slender, like Amaryllis, but really, her behaviour was distinctly odd.

Miss Elizabeth was looking rebellious, as if she had every intention of ignoring Lady Sutton's request. Then Winterborne whispered something in her ear. She smiled, nodded, and moved to join her mother.

Lady Sutton immediately made an excuse to leave Bertram and Elizabeth together. Bertram wondered whether she was unaware that Winterborne was the better catch. No, doubtless she meant to play them off the one against the other. She would catch cold at that, for he had not the least intention of dangling after the younger daughter and was far from certain that the elder was any more to his liking.

He reminded himself that the alternative was the Marriage Mart.

"I beg your pardon, my lord," said Elizabeth.

He looked at her blankly, certain that his reminder had not been muttered aloud. Was the whole family fit for Bedlam?

"For wanting to cut you," she explained in a friendly fashion. "Lord Winterborne said it would be shockingly rude in me to refuse to speak to you only because Mama commanded it. When someone orders you in such a way, does it not make you want to do precisely the opposite?"

"It is many years since anyone has ventured to attempt it," he said drily.

"Of course," she sighed, "you are a man, and a nonpareil into the bargain."

"Who told you that?" Despite himself, he was pleased at the coveted accolade.

"Lord Winterborne said that you are an out-and outer, which means, I collect, that you excel at sport. And I can see for myself that you are slap up to the echo. Your dress makes Lord Winterborne look casual and my brother Edward like a positive counter-coxcomb!"

Bertram laughed. He might have suspected flattery, but there was no guile in her blue eyes, nor would a calculating young lady have announced her desire to snub him.

"I shall not be so unreasonable as to hold you responsible for your brother's aping the dandy set, Miss Elizabeth. Your own dress is vastly becoming."

"You exaggerate, sir, but it is not too bad for a Banbury seamstress, I think." Lizzie looked down complacently at her new blue muslin. "Mama would have had it flounced and ruffled, but Claire ignored her instructions. She said simplicity becomes me better."

"She is perfectly correct." Bertram was surprised, since Miss Sutton's own gown was a shapeless beige creation giving little hint of her figure beneath.

"Claire is always right," said Lizzie with conviction.

Before he could follow up this intriguing remark, dinner was announced. He knew Caroline intended him to sit by Claire, but Lady Sutton somehow contrived that both he and Winterborne took in Lizzie, while her sister trailed behind with her brothers.

Conversation at the dinner table was unexceptionable and dull. Sir James's only topic was horses, and though his wife had two subjects, they were household management and the brilliant achievements of her three sons. Stuck between her brothers, Claire sat in silence, and even Lizzie seemed subdued by the proximity of her parents.

At last the ladies withdrew. Though his brother-in-law's port was excellent, Bertram was ready to follow them after a single glass, hoping to further his acquaintance with the young ladies. However, the Sutton males were impervious to hints. Their sole collective aim in life appeared to be to see the decanters emptied of every last drop of ruby liquid. Restrained by good manners from leaving without them, Bertram sat fuming with impatience.

He could only be grateful that Lord Winterborne was comparatively careless of the dictates of good breeding. After a muttered exchange with his host, that gentleman rose to his feet.

"Coming, Pomeroy?" he asked without further explanation.

They left the topers to the unfortunate Lord Carfax.

"The advantage of being heir to a marquis rather than a mere earl," commented Bertram lightly as they made for the drawing-room.

"The advantage of knowing from experience that in the morning they will remember nothing of this evening, not even my lack of courtesy," George said, grinning. "I gathered from the increasing blankness of your expression and shortness of your answers that you wished to join the ladies."

Bertram's response was guarded. The last thing he wanted was to find himself in competition with Lord Daniel's brother. "The Misses Sutton are unusual young ladies," he proposed. "You have known them long?"

"I first met them a fortnight since, when I came to purchase a hunter. You must come over and give me your opinion of him. As for your opinion of the ladies, yes, they are unusual. Miss Lizzie is delightfully unaffected."

Bertram swallowed a sigh of relief. If George was taken with Lizzie, that left him a free field with Claire.

"I have it on the best authority that Miss Elizabeth is an enchanting creature," he said drily.

"Her mother, I take it. Devilish vulgar woman, and bullies them both unmercifully, or tries to."

Lizzie was seated at the pianoforte, playing a Mozart minuet with a deft lightness of touch, while Claire turned the pages for her. The gentlemen went to join them at the instrument. When Lizzie finished the piece they provided polite applause, and she rose to sweep a grand curtsey, laughing.

"Do you play, Miss Sutton?" Bertram asked Claire.

"A little, but I am beyond the age when I am required to show my paces, my lord."

A little startled at this set-down, he chose not to take offence. "Then do allow Winterborne to turn the pages, and we may have a comfortable cose."

Without demur she joined him on a nearby sofa. Once again he found himself talking of his travels, this time of the concerts he had attended in Vienna. Her occasional interjections showed common sense and intelligence but were so diffident and inoffensive that he decided he had misheard her remark about showing her paces. Perhaps Caroline was right and she would make him an acceptable wife in spite of her deplorable family.

Not that he was by any means ready to declare himself. His father was not so unreasonable as to refuse him time to recover from Amaryllis's defection. Nor would the earl expect him to find a new bride before the start of the Season, and he must allow a month or two thereafter for him to fix his interest.

Lord Pomeroy did not suppose for a moment that in this case fixing his interest would prove necessary. Miss Sutton was on the shelf and could only be delighted to snare so eligible a husband.

Throughout his complacent musing he continued a description of Beethoven conducting a Viennese orchestra. This was now interrupted by Braithwaite's entrance.

"Lady Harrison, my lady," the butler announced in a voice of doom. "Mr. and Miss Harrison."

"Aunt Dorothy!" moaned Caroline, meeting Bertram's appalled eyes. "I thought you said she was fixed at Tatenhill."

"She claimed to be lending Mama her support at this difficult time." Bertram knew very well that his aunt's sole aim in life at present was to see him hitched to his cousin Amelia.

It was too late for explanations. Lady Harrison swept past Braithwaite and bore down on her niece.

Her ladyship was more voluminous than ever in a travelling costume of puce *gros de Naples* adorned as usual with a multitude of bows. Behind her trailed Amelia, in a sadly crushed carriage dress of most unsuitable pink muslin. She looked half frozen. And then came Horace, sporting today a waistcoat in startling shades of scarlet and green shot silk.

Bertram saw Lizzie's blue eyes turn to that item of fashionable apparel with a look of unholy glee.

With a word of apology to Claire, he went to greet the newcomers. Caroline was suggesting hopefully that they must want nothing more than to retire at once after their journey.

Aunt Dorothy glanced around the room, her inquisitive gaze hardening as she noticed Lizzie's presence.

"Later, Caroline," she said impatiently. "Pray make me known to your guests."

Lady Sutton acknowledged the introductions with a stiff nod, while she eyed Amelia's mousy hair and pale face with an appraising stare. Satisfied, she summoned Lizzie and presented her.

"I daresay she is much of an age with your daughter, ma'am," she went on complacently. "I am for ever telling her how lucky she is to be fair, since blondes are the fashion."

Lady Harrison glared at Lizzie's golden curls.

"Surely Miss Elizabeth is past her first Season," she reciprocated, and followed up with a second body blow. "Dear Bertram has been waiting these several years to see his little cousin make her bow to Society."

Bertram fumed silently. It was the outside enough for his aunt to link him thus with poor Amelia, but she had done it so subtly that he could not object. He noticed that Lizzie, awake on every suit, was enjoying the exchange while Amelia looked as if she wanted to crawl into the woodwork.

"Allow me to present Miss Sutton to you, Aunt Dorothy," he said to distract Lady Harrison from the combat.

As Claire made her curtsey, he realised too late that he had handed his aunt the victory. Lady Sutton was the unhappy mother of a spinster daughter of eight or nine and twenty.

Fortunately, Claire was preoccupied, seemingly unaware of the undercurrents and her mother's disgruntlement. She turned to Lady Caroline.

"Of course we will leave, ma'am," she said in her soft voice. "Your relatives must have first call upon your attention, and besides, we have several miles to go and it grows late."

Lady Sutton cast her daughter a furious glance which promised future retribution, but she was not so lost to all sense of propriety as to insist on staying, particularly where she had been bested. However, she did manage to get something of her own back. She beckoned forward Lord Winterborne, who stood in the background listening with a look of sardonic amusement, and introduced him as her house guest.

"Heir to the Marquis of Bellingham, you know," she pointed out in a stage whisper to Lady Harrison, with a significant nod towards Lizzie.

Bertram had to consider the honours evened.

He and Winterborne assisted the Sutton ladies with their shawls and reticules. In doing so he passed near Horace, who was posing casually against the mantel.

"I say, any pretty chambermaids in the house?" his cousin enquired in a low voice, leering.

"If so, I shall warn my sister to keep them beyond your reach," he muttered in disgust. He was ashamed to acknowledge these three as relatives.

When they reached the front hall, Lord Carfax, warned by Braithwaite, was shepherding the slightly fuddled male Suttons out of the dining-room. Under cover of the chaos of servants carrying the Harrisons' luggage up to hastily prepared chambers, Lizzie slipped to Bertram's side.

"It was most unkind in you to draw your aunt's and Mama's attention to Claire at such a moment," she accused. "She will have to listen to recriminations on her single state all the way home."

"It was not my intention...," he began.

"And how dare you laugh at my brother," she interrupted, "when your cousin is not only a counter-coxcomb but a ramshackle rake. I heard what he said to you."

"Which makes you an eavesdropper, as well as a vulgar baggage," he responded irately. "The impropriety of your language is exceeded only by your impertinence."

"Hypocrite!" she hissed.

She flounced off to thank Caroline for her hospitality. Bertram watched her, frowning. He could not believe that he had been so undignified as to quarrel like a schoolboy.

It was also uncharacteristic. He could not remember

when he had last exchanged angry words with anyone, whatever the provocation, and the last few months with Amaryllis had been enough to provoke a saint. Now here he was, rebuking the manners of a chit in whom he had no interest, in defence of Horace, whom he despised.

He turned with relief to her sister.

"I must thank you for suggesting departure, Miss Sutton, though it deprives me of your company. May I hope to be permitted to call on you while I am in the neighborhood?"

"I'm sure Mama and Lizzie will be happy to receive you, my lord."

"And you?" he pressed.

She gave him a vague smile, as if her mind was suddenly elsewhere. "I rarely help to entertain callers," she murmured. "Good-bye sir." She turned away.

Bertram was speechless. As a snub it was a masterpiece, though he suspected she had not intended to be rude. An eccentric indeed! It was ludicrous of Caroline to expect him to court her. He had a very good mind to leave for London at dawn, only his aunt would take it as a deliberate affront and complain to his mother. Sighing, he went back to the drawing-room.

He spent the rest of the evening trying to avoid being forced into intimate conversation with Amelia. Not that conversation was precisely the word for it, since Amelia's repertoire consisted of "Yes, Cousin Bertram" and "No, Cousin Bertram." She appeared at the breakfast table in yet another pink muslin gown, shivering, and her mother proposed that she should spend the morning showing Cousin Bertram her sketchbook.

"I fear I shall have to postpone that pleasure for another time," said Cousin Bertram smoothly. "I promised Winterborne to ride over to Sutton's to see his new hunter."

"We must certainly pay our respects to the Suttons after interrupting their entertainment last night," said Lady Harrison, a hawkish gleam in her eye. "Amelia will enjoy driving in your curricle, Bertram."

Caroline came nobly to the rescue. "I quite depend on renewing my acquaintance with Amelia this morning," she lied. "She was just a little girl last time we met and here she is grown into a young lady. There will be plenty of time to visit the Suttons another day."

"Oh yes, Cousin Caroline, I should like it of all things," said Amelia timidly, grateful at being saved from a tête-à-tête with her terrifying male cousin.

Seeing Aunt Dorothy marshalling her forces, Bertram abandoned his ham and eggs and hurried out to the stables. His distaste for renewing his acquaintance with the peculiar Misses Sutton paled before his horror at the possibility of spending the day with the Harrisons.

=== 5 ===

THE TROUBLE WAS, Claire decided as she carefully trimmed a thorny stem, that it was impossible to tell what Lord Pomeroy was thinking. His polished politeness was distributed impartially, even to those harridans, her mother and his aunt, even to herself, an uninteresting spinster of uncertain years.

In contrast, Lord Winterborne's opinions could be read in his dark eyes, and fortunate it was that Mama was not given to reading people's eyes. He respected Papa's knowledge of horses; outside the stables he was indifferent to Sir James and held his sons in contempt. Lizzie amused him. Claire thought his opinion of herself was divided between pity and a mild interest. She was used to arousing the former. The latter, she hoped, was an offshoot of his growing interest in Lizzie.

It was warm in the greenhouse. She wiped her forehead with the back of her hand, trying not to touch her face with her muddy fingers, but not really concerned about the possibility. Mama had upbraided her for fifteen years for her lack of beauty, so it was scarce surprising that she was indifferent to her appearance. Edward was right in that she could have afforded decent clothes. She preferred to spend the income from her inheritance on this greenhouse, with its modern dry stove to encourage her roses into early growth. For Lizzie's sake she had stayed at home long after she was in a position to leave, but only her roses had kept her sane.

"So this is where you escape to every morning." Lord Winterborne filled the doorway, his shoulders a hairs-breadth from the jambs, his head slightly bowed to miss the lintel. "May I come in?"

"Come in? Yes... yes, of course," she stammered, taken aback by his sudden appearance and slightly resenting the invasion of her refuge. "But there is nothing to see here, my lord."

"On the contrary." He stepped in, smiling reassuringly. "Lizzie tells me you grow roses. They were my mother's favourite flower, though I am aware she was not alone in that preference. Whenever she was in London she would go to the Vineyard nursery to purchase the latest new variety. My father takes good care of her garden, but it does not thrive without her attention, I fear."

"I develop my own kinds," said Claire gruffly, busying herself with her roots and shoots.

"What are you doing now?" he asked, joining her by the bench.

She found it hard to believe that he was interested, but only moments earlier she had been comparing his candour with Lord Pomeroy's surface affability.

"These are the roots I was collecting the day we met," she explained. "I am trimming them and planting each in its own pot. Wild roses provide a hardier rootstock, and then I graft onto them."

"They look dead as doornails."

"Oh no, see how plump they are, and the new buds? They are in very good condition. Alfie buried them all in moist soil for me while I was confined to my chamber. Some of them were upside down, but they all survived."

"And each of these will grow into a new kind?"

"I wish they would! Very few prove worth keeping, even when you control the cross-pollination carefully, by John Kennedy's system. He was a partner at the Vineyard, you know, where your mother bought her roses. The Empress Josephine consulted Mr. Kennedy, even when her Napoleon was at war with England!" Embarrassed at displaying her enthusiasm, yet unable to resist his sympathetic interest, she looked down at her hands and muttered, "I sold one to Mr. Kennedy."

"One of your varieties? My congratulations, Miss Sutton, for I am sure it is a significant triumph. I must buy one for my own gardens. What is it called, Sutton's Special?"

"No! I am not so fond of that name." Her cheeks were hot and she kept her eyes fixed on her work. "It is a white bloom. I called it *Clair de Lune*."

"Moonlight and your name!" Lord Winterborne laughed, but it was a laugh of joy and admiration, not of scorn. "Uniting wit with skill."

"And luck." She looked up at him shyly and dared to ask, "Do you really mean to have one?"

"Certainly, and once it is flowering I shall boast to all my visitors that I know its creator. Oh, Miss Sutton, I knew there were hidden depths beneath that quiet surface."

Since she had no idea how to respond to such a compliment, she was pleased as well as dismayed to see Lord Pomeroy making his way towards the greenhouse. She pointed out his approaching figure to Lord Winterborne.

His lordship took her arm and turned her towards him. Then with one hand lightly holding her shoulder, he drew a pristine linen handkerchief from his coat pocket and gently wiped her forehead.

"Mud," he said succinctly. "Pomeroy would not understand the exigencies of your craft." His smile was conspiratorial.

Unaccountably breathless, she managed to smile back. Then she held out her filthy hands for his inspection, and they both burst into laughter.

Lord Pomeroy entered, his face a mask of polite enquiry. "Miss Sutton, Winterborne. Lady Sutton said I might find you here. I trust I do not intrude?" There was an edge to his voice.

Claire retreated behind her own mask, appearing totally absorbed in her potting though she was overwhelmingly conscious of the two large masculine presences. She sensed a tension between them that had not been apparent to her yesterday when they met in company.

"Morning, Pomeroy," drawled Lord Winterborne, "A glass house would be a poor choice for a romantic rendez-vous, do you not agree? Miss Sutton has been showing me her work."

Lord Pomeroy visibly relaxed. "Of course. Fascinating. You must tell me about it some time, Miss Sutton. For now, though, the sun is shining and I hope to persuade you to take a turn about the gardens."

Claire looked at him in surprise, then guessed the reason for his request. No doubt he wished to talk to her about Lizzie.

"Thank you, that will be delightful," she said uncertainly, hiding her hands behind her. "I shall be with you in a moment."

Lord Winterborne appeared to guess her dilemma, for he grinned at her and said, "Step outside with me, Pomeroy. We are crowding Miss Sutton."

She threw him a grateful glance and hurriedly washed her hands in a watering can, then put on her cloak.

The gentlemen were discussing horses when she stepped outside.

"I'll have Orpheus saddled and ride part of the way back with you," Lord Winterborne was saying. "I think you will agree that he is a magnificent beast. It is not easy to find a mount up to my weight. Ah, Miss Sutton, even this weak February sun strikes sparks of fire from your hair, but it brings little warmth. Have you no bonnet?"

"My cloak has a hood, sir," she said obscurely glad that she had never given in to her mother's insistence that she should wear a spinster's cap. "I am quite warm, though."

"Good. Then I shall leave you to show Pomeroy about your gardens. Your sister walked down to the village, I think, while I was engaged with your father?"

"Yes. I daresay you will meet her coming back if you go that way."

She took Lord Pomeroy's offered arm.

"You have no gloves, Miss Sutton," observed his lordship, sounding concerned. "Your hands will grow cold."

"Then I shall put them in my pockets. Let us go down this path. There is little worth seeing in the garden at this season, but I hope to find something to show you. I believe flowers bloom year 'round in Italy?"

"They do, especially in the south. They are not half so well appreciated as are English flowers in spring after a hard winter."

Claire had expected him to rhapsodise about the glories of a Mediterranean garden. His answer pleased her, as did his reaction to a fountain of golden forsythia. If he was merely being polite, at least his courtesy made her feel comfortable. With more confidence she showed him a patch of fragile Christmas roses. They strolled on into a formal garden surrounded by high, prickly ilex hedges. In a warm, sheltered corner a raised bed glowed with crocuses.

"The purple ones are my favourites," she said, stooping to touch one delicately. "See the contrast of the petals with the orange stamen. The colours are rich enough for a king's robes."

As she straightened, she saw Alfie racing towards them down the garden path. With his pale eyes staring, his carroty hair in spikes, arms windmilling, and mouth gaping for breath, he looked like a madman.

Lord Pomeroy put his arm around Claire protectively. Though she knew the boy was harmless she shrank back, afraid that in his urgency he would be unable to stop before running into them at full tilt.

He slid to a halt in a spray of gravel, his thin chest heaving as he struggled for air to speak.

"What is it, Alfie?" she asked soothingly. "Is Cook angry with you again?"

He gesticulated wildly.

"Horse!" he panted. "Master's big horse coming!"

Claire heard the drumming of hooves. Round the end of the

farthest hedge thundered a huge roan stallion, galloping straight towards them. Before she could react, Lord Pomeroy's strong arms swung her aside, dumping her unceremoniously in the middle of the crocuses. Alfie leapt to join her.

His lordship stood poised on the low stone wall in front of them. Realising it was trapped by the high hedges, the stallion neighed its fury and reared over him, eyes rolling whitely.

Claire huddled back, watching in helpless horror, sure he would be crushed beneath the iron-shod hooves.

Lord Pomeroy waved his arms and shouted. At the last moment the stallion swung aside and pounded away, just as a gaggle of stable hands ran into the garden.

Alfie plucked at Claire's sleeve.

"*Told* you, Miss Claire," he said proudly.

She took a deep breath and said in a remarkably steady voice, "Yes, Alfie, you told me. You warned us in time. Thank you." She turned to his lordship.

He was watching the men corner the stallion and calm him.

"A superb beast," he remarked in a conversational tone, no tremor betraying the fact that he had just risked his life. "I wonder what set him off."

Claire could guess what had happened. The breeze was blowing from the north. The horse, her father's best stud, must have caught the scent of the mares in season, which were pastured on the far side of the gardens. Some unfortunate groom's moment of carelessness had let him escape.

However, she could hardly explain this to so proper a gentleman as Lord Pomeroy.

"I cannot imagine," she said vaguely. Then, as he helped her down from among the devastated crocuses, she turned on him a gaze full of admiration and gratitude. "How very brave you were! He might have trampled us all."

"It was my pleasure, Miss Sutton," he responded with a nonchalant smile, for all the world as if he had just picked up her dropped fan. "I expect you will want to sit down after your fright. Allow me to escort you back to the house."

She would have preferred to return to the greenhouse, but after his heroic action she meekly accepted his solicitude and his arm.

He tossed a coin to Alfie with a "Well done, lad," and they turned towards the house.

Lizzie and Lord Winterborne were in the drawing-room with Lady Sutton. Claire had heard something of her sister's quarrel with Lord Pomeroy the evening before. Nonetheless, knowing Lizzie and beginning to know his lordship, she was not surprised by the unruffled politeness of his greeting and Lizzie's friendly reply.

Lady Sutton was looking complacent at having two eligible gentlemen in her drawing room. Claire made her excuses and fled before she drew down her mother's wrath upon her head by distracting either of them from Lizzie's side. She hoped Lord Pomeroy would not be offended at her failure to extoll his heroism in the incident with the stallion. Lady Sutton was perfectly capable of claiming that the whole situation was Claire's fault.

Now that she was on her own, she found she did feel a little shaky in reaction to the narrowly escaped danger. She lay down on her bed for a few minutes, but it was colder indoors than out and she soon grew restless.

Reluctantly she recognised that it would be rude to retreat again to her gardening; she ought to change her gown and go down. She looked through her wardrobe with a dissatisfied eye, then laughed at herself. Let only a gentleman display a chivalrous regard for her safety and she immediately wanted to dress up to impress him, like any young miss on the catch for a husband. She did not even like Lord Pomeroy particularly.

All the same, she put on her best lavender merino.

In her absence there had been an addition to the company. A young man lounged against the chimneypiece in a carefully casual pose. Claire was transfixed by his salmon-pink coat and pale peach pantaloons, which disappeared into matching boots with silver tassels. For a moment she did not even notice the ermine waistcoat.

Lord Pomeroy moved to her side.

"I believe you met my cousin Harrison last night, Miss Sutton," he said suavely.

Mr. Harrison bowed. Claire winced as he narrowly avoided putting out his eyes with his shirtpoints.

"I say, deuced happy to see you again, Miss Sutton," he assured her, waving a negligent hand to the imminent peril of a Dresden shepherdess on the mantel. "Fine day, what? Thought I'd drive m'sister over and see what Bertram's up to."

Claire realised that the inconspicuous Miss Harrison was seated by Lady Sutton. Her ladyship wore the gloating expression of a terrier shaking a rat, while the girl looked frightened half out of her wits.

"Good-day, Miss Harrison." Claire felt obliged to extricate the poor child from the interrogation. "It is kind in you to visit us when you spent yesterday travelling. I daresay you would like some exercise after being cooped up in a carriage. Do you care to take a stroll in the gardens?"

It was the only escape she could think of; she hoped Lord Pomeroy would not think her utterly lacking in sensibility to suggest returning so soon to the scene of their alarming adventure.

"Always best to get back on your horse at once if you're thrown," he murmured approvingly in her ear.

Mr. Harrison also approved. "Allow me to escort you, ma'am," he said offering his arm. "Bertram, daresay you will give your arm to m'sister."

For the first time Claire saw open emotion on Lord Pomeroy's face. He looked harried.

= 6 =

"SHALL WE GO, too?" Lizzie proposed to Lord Winterborne as Claire sent her a pleading glance.

"You are not fatigued after walking to the village already this morning?"

"I am not so poor a creature!"

"Then by all means let us go, if you feel able to control your levity so as not to embarrass Mr. Harrison. I must warn you that it will not be easy. Gardens are notoriously dirty places and God forbid he should soil those boots."

"Pink leather!" Lizzie dissolved in giggles again.

Her mother looked at her in suspicion. She tugged on his sleeve, hurrying him after the others before Lady Sutton could demand to know the source of her indecorous mirth.

As they left the house, her father approached from the stables and hailed Lord Winterborne.

"A word with you, my lord. If you will just step into my office, I won't take but a moment of your time."

"But I am presently squiring your daughter," pointed out his lordship coolly. "Later perhaps. You were saying, Miss Lizzie?"

Sir James looked thoroughly disconcerted. He nodded, and muttered, "Later then."

Without a backward glance, Lizzie and Lord Winterborne strolled on.

"Famous!" she crowed, scarcely managing to keep her voice low. "Perhaps that will convince Papa that his daughters exist. I wish you were my father, sir."

It was his lordship's turn to look disconcerted.

"I am not quite old enough for that honour," he assured her with a show of indignation.

Lizzie regarded him thoughtfully. "No, I beg your pardon, of course you are not. And Mama considers you of a suitable age to be my suitor. Perhaps the same sort of gentleman I should like to have for a father would make a good husband?"

"Undoubtedly. Would it serve to remind you that I am not yet in my dotage if you were to call me George?"

"But you are a peer!"

"Not I. My father is a peer, true, but I am a mere commoner until I inherit, which I pray may be many years hence."

"Truly? I expect Mama explained it to me once, for she sets great store by such things, but I do not often listen to her. Claire taught me better. I wonder where she is? I know she wanted me to help her entertain the Harrisons."

"They must have turned a different way. What do you mean when you say that she taught you better than to listen to your mother?"

"I had not thought you slow witted!" said Lizzie, surprised. "You have heard how Mama browbeats Claire. She endured eight years of such treatment before I was born and even then, though she was just a little girl, she vowed that I should not suffer so. You see, Papa wanted a boy. He blamed Mama when his first child was a girl, and she retaliated against Claire."

"So Claire tried to teach you to ignore Lady Sutton's reprimands."

"Yes, and she succeeded very well for though Mama irritates me, nothing she says hurts me. It is otherwise with Claire. For too many years she had no defence. If you were forever being told you were plain and totally lacking in countenance and charm, would you not be shy? And then Mama forced her to have a Season and blamed her for not attracting any offers. Now she is using that as an excuse to deny *me* a Season, which is why she is so anxious that I should bring you up to scratch."

"If she hears you calling me George, she will suppose me upon the point of a declaration."

"Yes, so I will do it. And you will call me Lizzie, of course. How surprised she will be when you leave without making an offer! She will scarce find time to ring a peal over me, though, for Claire and I shall go to London soon."

"Your sister has conquered her distaste for Society, then."

"Not really, but she will do it for my sake. After her dreadful Season, she developed a sort of shield of absentmindedness. And then her godmother left her enough money to escape from the family altogether. She has found life easier since, though she has stayed to keep me company."

"Still waters run deep," said George obscurely. "I was sure that there was more to Miss Sutton than met the eye."

"Claire is the most wonderful person in the whole world," Lizzie assured him. "I would do anything for her. I mean to get married as soon as possible so that she can retire to her Bumble's Green house and grow roses in peace."

"You don't hope to find a husband for your sister, then?"

Lizzie looked at George in surprise. "I never thought of the possibility! What a selfish ninnyhammer I am! Just because she thinks herself on the shelf and with Mama always calling her an ape leader, I never considered it. Only, she really is shy," she added anxiously, "and she says herself that her Season was disastrous. Do you think she can overcome that?"

"She will need help and encouragement."

"I shall help and encourage her! And you will too, will you not? You do like her, don't you?" Lizzie awaited his answer with bated breath. If he did not like Claire, she could not be friends with him, and he was a most comfortable person to talk to. She had never met anyone she liked better. Perhaps Mama was right for once and he would make her a good husband. He was not so *very* much older.

"I am beginning to conceive a great admiration for Miss Sutton," he said thoughtfully. "Yes, I will help you. How expert you are at drawing me into your schemes! You know, I believe this one also is best kept secret, if you can keep a secret from your sister."

"If it is to her benefit." Lizzie fell silent, pondering his advice.

They were strolling along a path bounded on one side by a hedge. Now they heard voices on the other side of the hedge, and as they drew closer to the speakers they recognised Mr. Harrison's.

"The young 'un's a pretty chit," he said, "but Cousin Caroline mentioned it's the old maid has the rhino."

Lord Pomeroy's voice followed, in a tone of icy contempt. "If I find you have made improper advances to either young lady..."

"No, no, assure you, coz. I know it don't do to treat respectable young women like serving wenches."

"Your manners towards serving wenches leave a great deal to be desired."

"There's no need to comb my hair with a joint stool." Mr. Harrison sounded injured. "It's marriage I mean by Miss Sutton. She may be an antidote, but the dibs are in tune and I can tell you, coz, I'm deep in Dun Territory."

Bursting with indignation, Lizzie did not hear Lord Pomeroy's response to this confession. George managed to hush her so that her outrage emerged as a hiss instead of the screech she had intended.

"What an odious, odious man!"

"Deplorable," agreed George.

"I must warn Claire to beware of him for I expect he is quite unscrupulous, whatever he claims. The trouble is, I daresay if I do she will think everyone who courts her is only after her money. I think I will not tell her. I shall just have to keep an eye on him myself. I don't suppose you...?"

"I am yours to command, ma'am," he sighed. "I shall endeavour to put a spoke in Horrid Horace's wheel."

"Splendid! I know she will be quite safe with you to look after her. You are prodigious obliging, my lord."

"George, remember?" He looked down at her, smiling but with a disturbing glint in his eye.

"You are prodigious obliging, George," she said obediently, as they rounded the end of the hedge.

Lord Pomeroy and Mr. Harrison were moving towards Claire and Miss Harrison, who stood looking at a flowerbed.

"Whatever happened to the crocuses?" Lizzie enquired. "They were so pretty and now they are crushed into the ground."

"I was just telling Miss Harrison," said Claire. She repeated the tale of the escaped stallion and Lord Pomeroy's swift, courageous actions.

His lordship came up in time to hear her last few words. Lizzie turned to him, reached up on tiptoe and planted a hearty kiss on his cheek.

"*Thank* you, my lord," she breathed, blue eyes shining.

Lord Pomeroy crimsoned, losing his usual air of imperturbability.

"It was nothing," he said gruffly, looking more embarrassed than gratified. "What an impulsive child you are!"

"No more impulsive in expressing my gratitude than you were in saving Claire, for you cannot have had time to think with Papa's stallion bearing down upon you. And I am not a child."

"Which makes your behaviour the less excusable," pointed out Lord Pomeroy.

Lizzie saw that Claire was distressed by this spirited exchange.

"I apologise, my lord," she said with stiff dignity, which was spoiled when she added, "I did not realise that gentlemen were so averse to being kissed."

Mr. Harrison snickered, George shouted with laughter, and Lord Pomeroy was surprised into a chuckle.

"It depends who is doing the kissing," he said wickedly. When she pouted, he added, "Come, let us cry friends, Miss Elizabeth. I cannot be heroically rescuing one sister and coming to cuffs with the other on the same morning. It is too exhausting by far."

Lizzie was incapable of holding a grudge. She took his offered arm, noting as she did so that Mr. Harrison was scowling at her. As they strolled on she mentioned this to her companion.

"Cousin Horace is as eager as Aunt Dorothy for me to marry poor Amelia," he explained wryly. "He imagines that while I might let a mere cousin sink in the River Tick, I am more likely to feel obliged to haul my wife's brother out."

"Would you?"

He raised his eyebrows at this. "Pray do not take offence again, ma'am, but you have a devilish blunt tongue!"

"And you ought not to use that word in the presence of a lady."

"*Touché*," he acknowledged, grinning.

"I suppose it was an impertinent question," she admitted. "However, if you did not want me to ask, you ought not to have told me about Horrid Horace."

"You are quite right, very bad ton washing the family linen in public," he said, with a puzzled frown, "and I cannot think why I did. Still, you deserve an answer, though it will scarce enlighten you. Since I have not the remotest intention of paying my addresses to Amelia, I see no need to make a decision as to Horrid Horace's fate."

"You are quite nice when you are not on your high ropes. Poor Amelia. I expect I had better look about for a husband for her as well."

"As well?"

"As well as for myself," she said hastily. Somehow she did not want to explain to Lord Pomeroy that she intended to try to find a suitor for Claire.

"I predict that it will not prove a difficult task to find a husband for you, provided you manage to keep your candour under control!"

Lizzie decided that this was the nearest she was likely to come to a compliment from Lord Pomeroy, so she accepted it gracefully.

"I shall be more careful in Town," she said, then added

with the devastating forthrightness he had just warned against, "You see, I should hate to disgrace Claire, but I do not mind in the least if people think Mama has brought me up badly."

To her delight, though he shook his head he laughed aloud.

Later, on the way back to the house, she whispered triumphantly to Claire, "I made him laugh aloud! He is human after all."

This opinion was confirmed some time after Lord Pomeroy and his cousins took their leave. Alfie bashfully approached Lizzie and Claire and thrust at each of them a small package wrapped in brown paper.

"Open now," he urged, his face pink with excitement. "Presents."

Each parcel contained a pair of gloves of York tan leather, warm and practical yet elegant. Before Lizzie could voice her fear that Alfie must have stolen them, he was eagerly explaining.

"Mr. Lord give me money," he said. "When I tell Miss Claire 'bout big horse. I want to buy presents for my misses, di'n't know what to get, so axed Mr. Lord. He di'n't mind, Miss Claire, honest. He went to the village with me an' help me choose. Said gloves is un—unceptable present for a young lady. They all right? All right, Miss Lizzie?"

"Perfect, Alfie," Lizzie assured him, trying them on. "Look, they fit beautifully."

"Thank you, dear Alfie," said Claire. "His lordship was right, they are quite unexceptionable and most welcome."

Alfie went off with a spring in his step, and they turned to each other.

"I saw these in the shop last week and coveted them," said Lizzie, "but I decided they were too expensive. How much did he give Alfie?"

"A shilling, I think. Lord Pomeroy must have paid the difference himself. Oh dear! He commented on my bare hands this morning!"

"It was prodigious kind of him," Lizzie said decisively, "both to Alfie and to us. You will not insist upon returning them?"

"No, I suppose not. Gloves are truly an unexceptionable gift from a gentleman to a lady, though it is perhaps a little premature after such a short acquaintance. But do we thank him for them, or pretend Alfie really bought them? What a dear creature Alfie is, to think of us. A shilling is a rare treat to him, after all."

"I shall embroider a neckerchief for Alfie. And I shall most certainly thank his lordship, for I suspect it will embarrass him which will be excessively amusing."

"How can you in one breath praise his kindness and in the next plan to embarrass him?" marvelled Claire. "I wish you will not."

Lizzie refused to be persuaded and went up to change for dinner feeling pleased with herself.

For a wonder, her mother was pleased with her as well. She bustled into the girls' chamber looking smug.

"You are managing them both very nicely, Elizabeth. I scarcely hoped that Lord Pomeroy would call on you so soon! That Harrison child is quite out of the running. There is nothing to recommend her at all, for she has no beauty and no countenance and I understand the family is quite to pieces. This competition between the gentlemen is most fortunate, but you must make a push to attach one of them soon, for there is no knowing how long they will stay."

"What do you suggest, Mama?" asked Lizzie. "Shall I trap one of them into compromising me?"

"Don't be vulgar, miss. All the same, there are ways to go about it without being obvious. Tomorrow we shall call upon Lady Caroline. Contrive to keep both of them tied to your apron strings until one comes up to scratch. Lord Winterborne is the better catch, of course, but Lord Pomeroy is not to be sneezed at."

"I should not dream of sneezing at Lord Pomeroy, Mama," Lizzie assured her. As Lady Sutton departed, satisfied, she added softly, "For teasing is much more fun!"

It was raining next day when the Sutton ladies set out to

visit Lady Caroline. Despite the weather, Lord Winterborne chose to accompany them, riding beside the carriage. Adducing this as proof that Lizzie had hooked his lordship, Lady Sutton was in a high good humour. She prattled on about ways to incite a gentleman to jealousy without giving him a disgust of one, until Lizzie could have screamed with vexation.

She was beginning to think that if one must use such underhand wiles to win a husband, she had rather do without one altogether.

The warmth of Lady Caroline's welcome formed a strong contrast with Lady Harrison's frosty greeting. At least, Lizzie noted, Lady Caroline welcomed herself and her sister warmly, while Lady Harrison thawed visibly at George's approach. She watched with interest the stratagems employed by the three older ladies, the end result of which was that George found himself in a tête-à-tête with the silent Miss Harrison, Lord Pomeroy and Claire were sent to the book-room to find a first edition of Gerard's *Herball*, and Lizzie herself was left without an admirer to hand.

Pleased to see her mother outmanoeuvred, she settled quite happily on a comfortable sofa and pulled out some embroidery from her reticule.

She was close enough to the ladies to hear their speech, yet far enough that they did not mind their tongues because of the presence of an unmarried girl. At first she was bored by a discussion of household matters. She had stopped listening, when she heard her own name.

Lady Sutton was delivering a strong hint that Lord Winterborne was expected to offer for her daughter's hand any day now.

"After all," she said, "what else should keep him so long in this part of the country?"

Lady Harrison responded by pointing out that at present her Amelia was engaging Lord Winterborne's attention, while Miss Elizabeth sat alone plying her needle.

Lady Caroline laughed. "George Winterborne has evaded

parson's mousetrap these many years," she said. "I do not look to see him fall so easy. He is a gazetted flirt, a breaker of hearts. He has been the most eligible gentleman on the Town these ten years and more, yet sensible mothers warn their daughters away. You will do well not to encourage yours to hope, ladies."

"But his attentions are most particular," stuttered Lady Sutton, looking uneasy. "I trust he is not the sort of rakeshame who would ruin a young girl of good family."

"No, rumour has never said that of him. Nor that he seduces the innocent of any class. And they say he never takes a married woman for his mistress. For all that, he has had more barques of frailty in keeping at one time or another than you could count in a month of Sundays."

"That does not signify," snorted Lady Harrison, "but I do not like to hear that he will raise a young lady's hopes only to dash them." She raised her voice. "Amelia, come here, pray."

Lizzie was very glad that she had not confided in George her conclusion that he might make her a good husband. She had only agreed to flirt with him to mislead her mother. How lucky that she had not fallen in love with him!

That being the case, she greeted him with her usual friendly smile when, released from Miss Harrison's side, he sat down beside her.

Lady Sutton immediately called to her. "Elizabeth, go and see what is become of your sister. She will be driving Lord Pomeroy to distraction with her foolishness, I wager."

"By all means, Miss Lizzie, let us go and find your sister," said George, rising with her.

"Winterborne," said Lady Caroline commandingly, "a word with you, if you please."

George sent Lizzie a comical look of impatience but bowed politely to his hostess and stood waiting until she joined him.

Though a sixteenth-century book sounded interesting, Lizzie had no intention of going in search of Claire, who would doubtless return when she was ready to do so. She did not want Lord Pomeroy to imagine that she was chasing him, though she hoped for a chance to thank him for the gloves. She left the drawing-room and spent several minutes studying the family portraits in the front hall, then slipped back into the room.

Lady Harrison was explaining her son's absence as due to the exigencies of his toilet.

"It sometimes takes him three hours to tie his neck-cloth," she said. "He has a reputation to uphold, for he is an acknowledged Pink of the Ton."

Lizzie could have told her ladyship something of Mr. Harrison's less savoury reputation. She held her tongue and moved cautiously in the opposite direction, hoping that her mother would not see her and demand to know Claire's whereabouts. She sank into a chair which she thought was hidden from Lady Sutton by the sofa where George and Lady Caroline were engaged in low-voiced conversation.

Again she found herself inadvertently eavesdropping.

"And now tell me," said George sardonically, "why I am suddenly an outcast and why you prevented me from going with Lizzie."

"You are an outcast because I revealed what a shocking flirt you are, so it is entirely your own fault. Never fear, your rank and fortune will soon return to the forefront of their minds, and they will dismiss my warning."

"And the other?"

"Now this is serious, Winterborne, and I must trust you to keep it in strictest confidence, especially considering your involvement in poor Bertram's loss. He must find a wife, soon, and I have persuaded him to pay his addresses to Miss Sutton. You will not wish to rob him of another bride! Not that I suspect you of casting out lures to the dear girl, for though I am very fond of her I am aware that in general she does not appeal to gentlemen."

"Then what makes you think Pomeroy means to court her?"

"Well, I am not certain, but he is looking for a quiet,

conformable wife who is beyond her first youth. He does not expect, after Amaryllis, to fall in love again. Besides, he dreads going on the Marriage Mart. You will not cast a rub in his way?"

"What a low opinion you have of me, ma'am," George drawled.

Lizzie was itching with curiosity and excitement. Who was Amaryllis, and what did George have to do with Lord Pomeroy losing her? Easy going as George was, she did not think she would dare ask him.

Did Lord Pomeroy really mean to offer for Claire? She could not guess. Was he good enough for her? That was for Claire to decide. Should she warn her sister of his possible intentions?

Sighing, Lizzie realised that she must keep the secret, for if Claire knew and then he did not ask for her hand, how horridly humiliating it would be!

== 7 ==

CLAIRE WAS BEWILDERED to find herself on the way to Lady Caroline's book-room with Lord Pomeroy. Her confusion was compounded by her inability to read his feelings.

"What exactly is this *Herball*?" he asked in his offhand way as they crossed the hall. "Caroline seems to think it something special."

"It is a botanical encyclopedia first published at the end of the sixteenth century. I shall be glad to see it, but you cannot be interested, my lord. I am sorry that you were dragooned into escorting me, for I am sure I can find it on my own. Pray do not feel obliged to stay."

He ushered her into a room lined with bookshelves, leaving the door open for propriety's sake.

"There is no obligation involved," he said politely. "Any man of sense must be interested in seeing a tome of such venerable age, especially in such charming company."

"Then if I were to persist in urging you to return to the drawing-room, I should be insulting you by suggesting that you are not a man of sense." Claire smiled at him, and to her relief he grinned. Lizzie was right, he had a sense of humour.

"I should call for pistols at dawn, ma'am, so I advise you to be seated while I hunt down our object. My brother-in-law keeps the place in good order, so all I have to do is find the section on agriculture. Here we are—subsection, horti-culture. I have it." He lifted down a huge, heavy book. "And I see why Caroline sent me with you. Lord, it weighs a hundredweight."

"You know your way about the library, sir."

"I do not spend all my time rescuing fair damsels from fire-breathing dragons. From time to time I open a book just to prove to myself that I can still read." Lord Pomeroy sat down on a sofa and balanced the volume on his knee. "Do join me, Miss Sutton. It is by far too heavy for you to hold comfortably."

Claire moved to sit beside him, uneasily aware of his closeness. As if he sensed her disquiet, he rattled on.

"In fact, I have been known to read an entire book upon occasion. At present, agriculture is particularly familiar to me. I left the diplomatic service some months since to take over running Tatenhill. I had a great deal to learn for I have never bothered before to concern myself with estate management. Do you enjoy country life, Miss Sutton, or do you long for the gaiety of London?"

"I have spent little time in London, my lord, but from what I have seen I prefer the country." Claire had the impression that he was slightly disappointed with her answer, though how her preference could concern him she had no notion.

"Of course, you are a horticulturist, and the gardens of London are for the most part scarce worthy of the name. Roses are your speciality, I collect? Let us see what John Gerard has to say about the rose."

He opened the great book and turned to the index. The print was clear, amazingly little faded with age, and as he turned the pages Claire saw that nearly every page bore beautiful woodcuts of the plants described. He found the rose, the first item listed in the Third Booke.

" 'The Plant of Roses,' " read Lord Pomeroy, " 'though it be a shrub full of prickles, yet it had bin more fit and convenient to have placed it with the most glorious floures of the world, than to insert the same here among base and thorny shrubs.' Very true. Ah, but see here his reason. 'Because it is the honour and ornament of our English Scepter. The Mahumetans say that it sprang from the sweat of

Mahumet.' Charming notion!" He skimmed through several more paragraphs, picking out lines which caught his eye.

Claire would have liked to read it more thoroughly, but he was already flipping backwards through the book.

"Wolfe's-bane, Crow-feet, Beares-eares, Fox-gloves and Oxe-lips. What wonderful imaginations our ancestors possessed."

"There is a modern rose called Seven Sisters," Claire said, "but many new ones are named after a person or place, like Fanny Bias and White Bath. I suppose they are rather dull." She did not tell him of her own rose.

Sometimes she regretted having given it such a ridiculously romantic name, for it turned a worldly success into a personal matter which she was loath to discuss. Lord Winterborne had appreciated it, but she was not sure that Lord Pomeroy would even be interested, though he would make a polite show.

He was reading again, something about a marsh weed known variously as Serapia's Turbith, Blue Daisies, or Hogs Beans.

"From elegant to commonplace to downright vulgar," he commented, and Claire had to laugh at the truth of it.

"Miss Sutton!" came a voice from the doorway. "I should know that enchanting laugh anywhere, I vow. What a delightful surprise." Mr. Harrison minced in, balancing with difficulty on heels some two inches high, encrusted with glittering stones. "May I beg your opinion on my footwear, ma'am? I think to revive the elegant fashion of the last century."

"From elegant to commonplace to downright vulgar," Lord Pomeroy whispered in Claire's ear.

Not wanting to hurt Mr. Harrison's feelings, she stifled a giggle before replying with tolerable composure, "Most unusual, sir. Our forebears wore such shoes for evening entertainments, did they not?"

"Very wise, Miss Sutton," his lordship murmured. "They might even go unnoticed if the crush were sufficiently great, though I fear that is too much to hope for."

"Yes, but one must not follow slavishly. Think how much more they will sparkle in sunlight," the fop declared.

"I wish I may see the riot in Bond Street when the horses catch sight of all that paste." This time Lord Pomeroy's voice, though soft, was all too audible to his victim, who glared daggers at him.

Claire wished she carried a fan with which to rap his knuckles. She had never before appreciated the value of that oddment of ladies' apparel.

"I expect they may become all the crack," she said, diplomatic if untruthful.

She wished she had not when Mr. Harrison, beaming, seized her hand and planted thereon a moist kiss. "Most kind, ma'am," he crowed, and sat down in a nearby chair.

Lord Pomeroy stood up, shelved the *Herball*, and began to wander restlessly about the room, while his cousin embarked on a long-winded and altogether inappropriate series of compliments. Claire soon lost her desire to laugh at his blatant disregard for truth. After all, if he was so lacking in taste as to wear those shockingly vulgar shoes, perhaps he genuinely admired her. She was vastly relieved when his lordship interrupted.

"Miss Sutton, I daresay you will wish to return to your mother. Allow me to escort you."

Gratefully she took his arm, and Mr. Harrison followed them out of the room. Somehow, the right moment to mention Alfie's gloves had not arisen.

Shortly after their return to the drawing-room, Lord Carfax came in to ask his brother-in-law's advice on some matter concerning his stables. The two went off, accompanied by Lord Winterborne. Mr. Harrison seemed glued to Claire's side, though she paid him little attention. He was not only ridiculous but also a bore.

Fortunately, Lady Sutton decided within five minutes of the gentlemen's departure that it was time to take their leave. The carriage was called for, and they set off for home.

No sooner had the carriage turned out into the lane beyond the gates than her ladyship opened fire.

"Claire Sutton, I declare you are the most provoking wretch alive! Here I come all this way to give your sister a chance to attach Lord Pomeroy, and what must you do but drag him off to bore him with your tedious herbs. And then, when Mr. Harrison singles you out, the prettiest young gentleman I have seen in a month of Sundays, you sit sullen and mute as a... as a..."

While she was searching for a suitable metaphor, Claire knocked on the carriage roof. When the coachman brought the team to a standstill, she opened the door and jumped down.

"It is a pleasant day," she said with outward calm. "I believe I shall walk home. Drive on, Johnson."

"As a toadstool!"

Walking away, she heard Lizzie's angry voice raised above the sound of the hooves.

By road it was a distance of some seven miles to Sutton's Stables. Claire knew a shortcut across the fields which would cut it to little more than four. A mellow wind was blustering from the west, bringing a breath of spring. Once she had left the lane, she took off her hat and enjoyed the feel of it blowing through her hair, blowing away her megrims with her hairpins.

For a couple of miles she followed a track across the hills, through flocks of sheep cropping the short, crisp grass. The Cotswold limestone made for dry footing and she walked swiftly, swinging her hat by the ribbons. She abandoned herself to the pleasures of the moment, tracing monstrous beasts in the racing clouds, watching a lapwing flap away with a mournful "peewit, peewit."

The going was more difficult when she descended into the valley. She had not put on walking boots for a morning call, and the fields were muddy. Her mood changed, and she could no longer forget her mother's scolding.

Every word stung, however hard she tried to ignore it.

Was she really tedious and sullen? Silent tears began to slip down her cheeks.

She had thought she was too old to cry. For Lizzie's sake she had hidden her unhappiness these many years, as best she could, though she knew that her sister guessed at it. Despising her weakness she wiped away the tears, but more took their place. She trudged on, a cold desolation in her heart.

"Miss Sutton!"

Orpheus cantered up beside her, and Lord Winterborne swung down from the saddle.

"I though I recognised you."

"I decided to walk," she mumbled, steadfastly gazing at the ground.

He put a finger beneath her chin and turned her face up to him. "Weeping," he said softly. "You are one of those lucky souls whose eyes grow more beautiful when they weep. They are like mountain lakes in the rain."

She felt her lips trembling and would not try to speak lest she break down.

He tucked her hand in the crook of his arm. "Come, let us walk together. I have been working Orpheus hard, and he will be glad of the respite. Not that I would insult him by suggesting that he needs it! He is a magnificent beast, worth every penny your father extorted for him. Spirited, yet docile too. See how willingly he follows behind us? But you must be used to the best mounts. Perhaps you and Lizzie will ride out with me one day?"

"We do not ride, my lord."

"Not ride? When your father owns the Sutton Stables? I beg your pardon, I daresay you do not care for horses."

"We have never had a chance to find out." Claire was glad to find that her voice was steady. "Papa considers the stables no place for a woman, and we have never been allowed near them."

Lord Winterborne fell silent. When he spoke again it was to change the subject.

"I believe I felt a drop of rain."

72

"I have felt several," Claire admitted. "I expect I ought to put my hat on, though it will probably be ruined. I have already destroyed a perfectly good pair of shoes with my stupid whim."

"What a pity that you are not wearing Horrid Horace's shoes. A mud bath could only improve them."

"I wish you will not encourage Lizzie to call him so, my lord!" she reproved, trying not to laugh. "It is all very well for you to do so, but she is all too likely to let it slip in his presence."

"You are right," he said meekly, "and I live in fear of her calling me George in company. That would never do. Unless, of course, I can persuade you to do likewise. Then instead of thinking her a forward chit, everyone will suppose that I am an old friend of the family."

"My lord!"

"George," he corrected.

"George, then." She laughed. "You are a wretched tease."

"That is better," he said approvingly. He took her hat from her, dropping Orpheus's reins, set it on her head, and again tipped her chin to tie the ribbons beneath.

Looking up into his dark eyes, she felt as if she were drowning. Then a large raindrop hit her nose, and she gasped in surprise.

"Hat or no, you are going to get very wet, Claire. I have no intention of enduring an unnecessary soaking, so I mean to ride. It would be unforgivably ungentlemanly in me to leave you walking while I ride, and you are too kind to force me to act so against my nature. Therefore you shall ride, too."

Before she could protest he lifted her onto Orpheus's withers, and before she had a chance to feel nervous he had swung up into the saddle behind her. His strong arm went around her waist.

"Remember, Orpheus and I are both gentlemen, you have nothing to fear. But I mean to canter, and you will be safer if you lean back against me."

With a little sigh she relaxed against his chest. Her hat

was knocked askew, and her cheek was pressed against the fabric of his riding coat. Once again she felt the beat of his heart, the rise and fall of his breathing.

Orpheus quickened his pace beneath them.

When they reached home, George helped her slide down near the front door before he went on to the stables. She stood bemused, watching his straight back and proud carriage, unconscious of the rain that fell in sheets now, until Golightly opened the front door and called her in.

"Why, you're soaked to the skin, Miss Claire," scolded the butler. "Let me take your pelisse afore you catch your death of cold."

Alfie entered the hall in time to hear his last words.

"You not going to die of cold, Miss Claire?" he cried, his face agonised.

"Of course not, Alfie," she assured him, but her teeth chattered, and she was shivering.

"Cold," he repeated, his expression paralysed by the effort of his mental processes. At last the idea emerged. "Take coal up to chamber," he said in triumph. "Tell Molly to light fire."

"Yes, Alfie, go at once." Lizzie flew in and ran to hug her sister, regardless of her wet dress. "Claire, I was so worried about you! Come up quickly and get into dry clothes. I gave Mama such a piece of mind that she went to bed with the megrim as soon as we reached home. You will be glad to hear that we are both impertinent, ungrateful hussies! I do not think there is the slightest chance that she will take me to Town now. Is it not wonderful? I had so much rather be with just you."

"You did not tell her our plans?"

"No, though it was monstrous difficult to hold my tongue. You are quite right that she will only try to throw a rub in our way unless we do not tell her until we are ready to leave. Oh, Claire, I am looking forward to it so, and I do love you!"

Once again Lizzie flung her arms round her sister and

hugged her hard.

Claire could not imagine why she had succumbed to the blue devils not an hour since. Lizzie, Alfie, and even Golightly cared for her. Her mother's animosity was insignificant, and soon she would be free of it.

She could not help wondering whether George had been moved by chivalry alone when he lifted her onto Orpheus's back. Was it possible that he, too, cared for her a little?

= 8 =

GEORGE, TOO, WAS pondering his feelings for the Misses Sutton as he rode 'round to the stables. The plain fact of the matter was that he enjoyed their company. He liked them in a way that he had not liked any female outside his immediate family for as long as he could remember.

Always the shadow of Danny's experience had come between him and the respectable young ladies he might have been expected to take to wife.

Now the shadow was lifted. That alone might account for the lack of cynicism in his relationship with Lizzie and Claire, and he might find that he looked on all women with a new eye. They were unusual young women though, unlike any he had ever met. For one thing, they never bored him.

Was liking and an absence of boredom sufficient ground for marriage? He had told his father he meant to look about him for a wife. He could imagine being happy with either of them. On the other hand, it would scarcely be fair to Lizzie to spoil her plot by offering for her after all, and the difference in their ages must be a disadvantage. Claire he ought not even to consider: he had as good as given his word to Lady Caroline that he would not interfere in Pomeroy's pursuit.

With a sigh of relief at this satisfactory reasoning, which left him free as ever, he dismounted and rubbed Orpheus's wet nose. His groom appeared from the tackle room.

"We'll be leaving this afternoon, Peter," he said. "Make sure that he's fed after you rub him down, though I don't mean to ride him and we go only as far as Oxford today."

76

"Right, my lord. I'll see to it the team's ready when you want 'em," the groom promised stolidly, with only a hint of a glance at the pouring rain outside. He was used to his master's restlessness and sudden decisions to move on.

George saw the hint and grinned. "Sorry to drag you out in this weather, but it's time to be off. Wrap up warm, and there'll be hot toddy at the Mitre when we reach Oxford."

He hurried to the house. The wind was blowing in gusts again, and he cursed as a flurry of rain bespattered his face. Nonetheless, it was time to go, before he found himself any more entangled in the lives of the Misses Sutton. The last thing he wanted was to raise any expectations he did not mean to satisfy.

He laughed aloud as he realised that that was precisely what he had been doing without qualm for the past decade. Truly Claire and Lizzie were different from the general run of females of their class! Well, he would see them in London.

Golightly met him in the hall and tut-tutted as he took the wet coat and hat.

"Luncheon will be served in the morning-room in half an hour, my lord," he announced.

"Thank you. Dry these as well as you can, will you? I shall be leaving for Town this afternoon. And send Slade to me now."

"Yes, my lord. A pity you must travel in this weather, my lord."

George realised that he would owe his host and hostess an explanation for his unexpected departure. And it must be good or Claire would be blamed, since she had been with him last. He racked his brains. It must be important enough that he had no choice but to leave, yet dull enough that he might have forgotten until the last minute.

He produced a sigh. "A legal matter," he said. "If one keeps one's lawyers waiting it always ends in disaster. Lord Carfax happened to draw my attention to the date. I have so enjoyed my stay here that I quite lost track of time."

"Precisely, my lord." The butler's tone suggested that his lordship deserved high marks for effort if not for truthfulness.

Slade's disapproval was more overt. He muttered ominously as he helped his master change out of his riding clothes.

"Can't pack that coat and hat damp, it'll ruin them. No time to clean the boots proper, let alone polish them. There's three shirts in the laundry, them girls are slow as treacle, besides three I've not yet ironed. Only five starched cravats."

"I shall go unstarched then," said George calmly. "Perhaps you would prefer to follow tomorrow with my wardrobe?"

The valet looked thoroughly offended. "I shall contrive, my lord, to be ready in time for your lordship's departure," he said with stern dignity.

His lordship departed immediately for the morning-room.

Lady Sutton and Lizzie were already there. The men of the family, after a hearty breakfast, generally made do with bread and cheese in the stables at midday. George wondered where Claire was, though he was unsurprised by her absence. Only her mother could have caused this morning's tears.

"I hope your sister has not suffered from her wetting, Miss Elizabeth?" he enquired, helping himself to a thick slice of cold roast beef and a piece of pigeon pie.

"I think not. She is not hungry."

"I must thank you, my lord, for rescuing the silly girl from the effects of her folly," said Lady Sutton ungraciously.

"*I* did not tell Mama you brought her home," Lizzie assured him. "She got it from the servants."

"Nonsense, Elizabeth, I saw it from the window," lied her ladyship. "You show a total want of propriety in supposing that any lady listens to servants' tattling. Obviously it is out of the question to expose your indecorous behaviour to the Polite World this spring."

George lost his appetite. It appeared to have come to open warfare between Lizzie and her mother, and he had no desire to find himself trapped between the battle lines.

Lady Sutton must also have heard that he was leaving. However, after her words to Lizzie about servants' gossip she could not admit it, so he was able to present his regretful explanation in due form. She glared at her undutiful daughter but accepted his apologies with a proper show of disappointment at losing the pleasure of his company.

"I must bid you farewell immediately," she added, pressing her hand to her forehead. "I feel one of my headaches coming on, I fear, and I shall be forced to lie down for the rest of the day."

George rose and bowed and expressed his hopes for her speedy recovery and his gratitude for her hospitality. As she tottered out, she passed near Lizzie and leaned towards her.

"You shall live to regret this day's work, missie!" she hissed.

Scarcely had the door closed behind her when Lizzie crowed, "I have begun to win! Now that I know that Claire will soon be gone and cannot be made to suffer, I can say what I think and Mama does not know how to answer."

"Abominable brat," said George through a mouthful of pie. His appetite had returned with his hostess's departure. "I hope I have not spoiled your plot?"

"Not in the least. It was splendid. Mama learned that you had brought Claire home—for which I must thank you— before she learned you were going. She was persuaded you had done it for my sake and that your reputation was much exaggerated. She told me to be prepared for Papa to call me this evening to tell me of your offer!"

George was tempted but decided not to enquire as to what she had heard of his reputation. Instead he asked, "And did you believe I had done it for your sake and was on the point of proposing?"

"Of course not! Why should you do anything for my sake? Even the plot, I am sure you joined in only because you thought it would be amusing. And you helped Claire because she was in difficulties and you are a perfect gentle-man. *Did* Lady Caroline exaggerate your reputation?"

"Since I've no notion what you overheard I cannot say, and true or not it is no fit subject for your conversation," he said repressively, thinking how unspoiled she was, how utterly lacking in vanity. Would London change her?

"No, I am sorry, you are right." Lizzie was penitent.

"You did overhear, I collect?" He grinned at her. "Surely Lady Caroline did not intentionally reveal my dreadful past to you?"

"No, I was eavesdropping. It is the best way to learn the truly interesting tidbits."

"Abominable chit," he said again.

"I daresay you are leaving because you cannot bear it here any longer?" she asked wistfully. "I do not mean to tease, but I do hope you will not cut us in London. Mama will definitely not be there."

"So I gather. No, I should not dream of cutting you in London, you mistrustful child." Too late he remembered her violent reaction to being called a child by Lord Pomeroy. However, she did not seem to notice. It made him feel old. "I shall be living at Bellingham House, in Berkeley Square. You must notify me as soon as you arrive in Town, and I shall be on your doorstep within the hour."

"Unless you are not at home when the message arrives," she pointed out.

"True. Now I should like to bid your sister farewell. Is she laid down upon her bed?"

"She said she was going to go to her greenhouse."

"In this—ah, the wind has shredded the clouds while my attention was elsewhere. Peter will be relieved. You'll excuse me, Lizzie. I shall see you again before I leave."

"Tell Claire that Mama has the headache and it is safe to come in." She smiled at him over the rim of her teacup as he left.

What a delightful girl she was, full of mischief yet devoted to her sister, always looking to protect her. If it were not for the sixteen years between them...but he would see her in London. If she had not fallen in love with some eligible young man by the end of the Season, perhaps he might try his luck after all.

Ragged clouds swept across the sky, now exposing now hiding the sun. The air was fresh and mild. Puddles glinted everywhere, and even the best gravelled paths were muddy. There would be another pair of spattered boots to be cleaned by the unfortunate Slade, who had never become accustomed to his master's disregard for his clothes.

George stood for a moment outside the greenhouse, watching Claire. Here in her own realm she moved with a sureness and grace which contrasted painfully with her awkwardness in her mother's presence. His lordship mouthed a silent curse at the absent Lady Sutton.

He knocked on the door. Smiling, Claire beckoned him in.

It was clear that she had come here while it was still raining, for wisps of hair clung in damp tendrils to her brow. The muggy warmth of the greenhouse had brought a rosy hue to her usually pale cheeks, and her lips looked invitingly sweet.

George reminded himself of his errand.

"I regret to say that I am come to make my farewells," he said.

The welcome died from her expressive face, replaced by the vague blankness that was her defence. George hated himself for driving her to that withdrawal.

"I thought..." she began hesitantly. "That is...was it something I said this morning? Or did?"

"Lord, no! Though I wager your mother will blame you, despite my attempt to persuade her otherwise."

"Then why...? You asked Lizzie and me to ride out with you one day!"

He was more than happy to see that indignation was overcoming her diffidence.

"It is most ill-bred in me to tell you this," he said, "but I cannot abide Lady Sutton's constant attempts to intimidate you and your sister. I feel that my presence sometimes exacerbates her rancour, so I have decided to rid you of that added burden."

Another lie, and he was not used to lying for the sake of tact. In general, he went his way with a blithe insouciance towards most people's feelings—another warning that he was right to be leaving.

Yet it was no lie after all, he realised, merely a reason that he had been hiding from himself.

"You will give me your direction in London?" he asked quickly. "I have not offended you beyond forgiveness?"

"No, how should you?" Her voice shook a little. "You are so considerate. I am not used to having my feelings regarded."

He took her hands, grubby as they were. "I know. Lizzie has told me something of your difficulties. I admire more than I can say the way you have taught and shielded her, allowed her to grow up uncrushed. You have been strong and successful, where I failed."

She looked at him in wonder. He let go her hands and turned away, leaning forward against her workbench and gazing sightlessly out into the garden.

"I have a younger brother, six years younger. When he was born, I promised my mother to take care of him. He little needed my protection, for my family was very different from yours, so I picked him up when he fell off his pony and took him to his first prizefight. He looked up to me, though, and I loved him as you love Lizzie. Only when the dragon came I had not built up my strength by endurance, as you have." He paused, hearing his voice shake as hers had.

"The dragon?" she asked quietly.

He glanced at her. She had gone back to her work, trimming stems and binding them together in the arcane mysteries of her craft, but he knew she was listening to every word. He was driven by a need to make her understand his weakness and her own strength. He began to pace up and down the narrow space.

"Danny joined the army and went to Portugal. After

Corunna he came home, wounded and with a Spanish bride. Both wound and woman put him through hell, and I will not apologise for using that word. I could not see how to help him so I stayed away, but there must have been something I should have done. There must have been something!"

"Perhaps not. How could you intervene between man and wife? But have you never seen him since?"

"She ran away and there was a divorce, a scandal in itself and of course rumours flew. Afterwards I went to him. He let me visit, but he never confided in me again, not until... He fell in love again, Claire, and he quarrelled with his beloved. And he told me, and I was able to make it up between them. *You* can imagine how I felt!"

"Yes, I think so." The faraway look in her grey eyes was not an escape but concentration upon an inner vision. "I am glad you told me. Is he happy now?"

"Very happy. He is to be wed in June." George felt as if he was relieved of a great burden. Her calm acceptance and undemonstrative sympathy warmed him. He sat down on an upended barrel and watched her hands.

Her long fingers with their oval nails moved with a delicate surety of touch. He wondered how it would feel if she touched him. He remembered the supple slenderness of her waist between his hands when he lifted her, the light pressure of her head resting trustfully against his shoulder.

The back of her neck was almost unbearably tempting.

"I must go," he said abruptly. "I want to reach Oxford tonight. I shall see you in London." As he left he ran one finger down the soft curve of her cheek in a gentle caress.

He strode back towards the house, unmindful of the puddles he splashed through. He had been too long without a woman. As soon as he reached town he would call on Suzette—or was it Annette? She would be happy to see him after his three-week absence.

The thought was uninviting. It must be time to find a new mistress, no difficult task, for his generosity was as well known to the ladies of the *demi-monde* as was his fickleness.

The devil of it was, he decided, that it was no mistress he needed, but a wife.

=== 9 ===

"WELL, BERTRAM?" LADY Caroline looked up from a letter as her brother joined her in the breakfast-room. "How goes the courtship?"

"I have not seen her since she was here three days ago." He helped himself from the variety of dishes on the sideboard and joined her at the table. "I've no intention of making a cake of myself by being too particular in my attentions before I have decided whether she will suit."

"Lud, sometimes I think you are a regular cold fish!"

"You know it is to be a marriage of convenience, Caroline. I cannot so easily forget the past."

"No, and I daresay I should think you a cold fish if you could. You cannot win, my dear. But tell me what you think of her. We dine with the Suttons tonight, remember."

Bertram groaned. "Truth to tell, her family must be the biggest obstacle—vulgar mother, impertinent sister, father who reeks of the stables, and the brothers do not bear thinking of."

"I doubt she will care to see any but her sister once she is married. You are dodging the point, however. What think you of Claire herself?"

"When she is on her own, and not absorbed in her wretched plants, she is well enough. No beauty, of course, but a coiffeur and a decent wardrobe must improve her looks. She is quiet enough, yet she has a certain humorous touch at times and I think her reasonably intelligent. An adequate companion for the country, but I do not mean to bury myself year 'round at Tatenhill. I must see how she goes on in Town before I commit myself."

"Claire would probably be quite content to be left alone in the country while you do your gadding about. It is not an uncommon arrangement."

"No, but I suppose I expect something more than that even of a marriage of convenience. I want a wife of whom I need not be ashamed before my friends, someone who can help me entertain, both in London and at Tatenhill. Perhaps when she is out from under her mother's thumb she will show more poise. Amaryllis always had such *savoir-faire*, even when I first knew her."

"Oh, if we are back to Amaryllis, I give up. Eat your eggs before they are stone cold. I must go and see my housekeeper."

"I shall drive over to the Suttons' early and meet you there for dinner."

"Very well, my dear. Remember that they dine early." Lady Caroline beamed her approval. She was about to leave when the door opened and Aunt Dorothy and Amelia came in.

"On the other hand," muttered Bertram, "perhaps I shall drive over this morning."

In the event, he spent the morning riding about the estate with his brother-in-law. He had always thought he had little in common with Lord Carfax, but now that he was forced to learn about estate management he found him both knowledgeable and helpful. He and his tenants had put into practice many modern agricultural improvements which had not yet found their way to Tatenhill. Somewhat to his own surprise, Bertram was interested.

He was also interested in the relationship between his sister and her husband. About to be leg-shackled, whether to Claire Sutton or some as yet unknown maiden, he wanted to see how others managed to live in wedded bliss.

The Carfaxes' marriage reminded him strongly of his parents': affectionate yet calm and undemonstrative. Caroline appeared to be happy, and Carfax never spoke of her with anything but praise for her common sense and good humour. It seemed to him an admirable relationship, and very much what he hoped for himself. He was not one for high flights of fancy or romantic notions.

He pushed away the memory of the pain he had felt when Amaryllis told him she had sold her engagement ring to buy necessities.

Though he doubted the Suttons would care, or even notice, if he appeared at the dinner table in his riding breeches, Bertram changed before setting out. His bottle green coat and buff pantaloons were moulded to his muscular figure with the perfection of fit attained only by London's premier tailors. His boots and hat, from Hoby's and Lock's respectively, shone glossy in the pale February sun. Pinkerton steadfastly refused to divulge, even to his master, whether he used champagne or some more recondite ingredient in the boot blacking. Whatever it contained, it was the envy of many an aspiring dandy.

Abel had the curricle ready. He was about to let go the horses' heads and jump up behind when Horace Harrison appeared, picking his way daintily across the stable yard.

"I say, coz, heard you was off to the Suttons'. Believe I'll come with you, pay my respects to the ladies."

"We dine there tonight, there is no need to go now." Bertram closed his eyes as he took in the full glory of Horace's costume.

He was wearing his jewelled shoes, and beneath his open greatcoat his waistcoat was likewise decorated with brilliants. As he had pointed out, they sparkled better in the sun than in candlelight. He looked like a jeweller's display case, except that Rundell and Bridge's, for one, would never be guilty of such a vulgar display, even had they been diamonds and not strass glass.

Abel loosened his grasp on the harness to gape at this apparition. The chestnuts shied.

In one swift motion Bertram brought them back under control. "Move to where they can't see you!" he shouted to his cousin.

Horace complied, hurrying past the restive beasts and

scrambling up into the curricle.

Bertram sighed. "I shan't need you after all, Abel," he called, and they rattled out of the yard.

"Devilish high-strung cattle," observed Horace.

"They are unused to such magnificence at midday."

"Good idea, matching weskit and shoes, what?" The man was impervious to sarcasm. "Wager Miss Sutton will like it. Prodigious complimentary she was when I showed her the shoes the other day."

Bertram's recollection of Claire's startled amusement was quite otherwise. He looked forward to seeing her face when she saw the waistcoat, and he would have wagered a good deal that forthright little Lizzie would be unable to control her giggles. His lips twitched, but he could only be glad that his cousin was such a clunch. At least there was not the slightest chance that Claire would favour his suit.

"You still mean to make up to Miss Sutton then?" he asked casually.

"Damme if I don't, though t'other one's more to my taste. I like 'em lively. Still, it's marriage we're talking about, not a roll in the hay, and the blunt'll make up for a deal of boredom."

"Lord but you're vulgar!" Bertram exclaimed, unable to keep silent while his possible future wife was traduced. "Miss Sutton is a lady, not a ladybird."

"That's what I just said," pointed out Horace sulkily, and mercifully fell silent for the next couple of miles.

It was nearly three when the chestnuts trotted up the Suttons' drive. Bertram stopped at the front entrance to leave his objectionable cousin, then drove 'round to the stables. Turning into the yard, he heard sounds of merriment.

In one corner, several stable boys with swinging shovels were jeering and whistling at something in their midst. From the height of the curricle seat Bertram saw that they surrounded a carrot-haired lad who stood holding a wheelbarrow. His face was screwed up in despair, his face blotched with tears, his clothes smeared with filth.

"The devil!" muttered his lordship, recognising Miss Sutton's servant.

He tossed the reins to an approaching groom, jumped down, and strode towards the derisive group. A flying clod caught him in the midriff. From it rose the distinctive aroma of horse dung.

The boys froze in appalled silence as he reached them. The only sound was their victim's sniffs.

Lord Pomeroy looked them up and down, one by one, then asked in an icy voice, "What is going on here?"

"He done ast for manure so we gi'en it 'im, my lord," one said sullenly.

" 'Tes only Alfie," explained another. "He's a nacheral. He don't know what's what."

"Sir James shall hear of this," his lordship promised.

They shuffled nervously, then the first one said, "T'master won't care. 'Tes only for Miss Claire's garden, nuthin' important, honest, my lord."

"He will care when I explain to him that his guest was, shall we say, caught in the crossfire."

For the first time they noticed the daub of muck besmirching his lordship's greatcoat, waistcoat, shirt, and pantaloons. Three of them melted away. The other two, visions of a whipping before them, hastened to apologise humbly.

"An' we'll clean off Alfie under t' pump," the larger offered.

"No!" wailed Alfie as the other snickered.

"No, indeed. Alfie is coming up to the house with me to have a hot bath. When he returns, the wheelbarrow will be full of manure, and the five of you," he looked threateningly at the stall where the other three huddled, "will be least in sight. Jump to it."

His horsewhip moved with astonishing speed. The two boys let out simultaneous howls and clapped their hands to their rear ends before setting to with their shovels. This time all the manure landed in the wheelbarrow.

Alfie blinked at his saviour, mouth agape.

"Come on, lad," Lord Pomeroy said kindly. "We both need to do a bit of cleaning up."

It was nearly an hour later that Bertram at last reached the drawing-room. He had considered sending his excuses by a servant and going home to change. However, the thought of what a servant would make of his story persuaded him to tell the young ladies his own version. Besides, Golightly had assured him that Lady Sutton was absent, and that his own clothes would be clean and pressed dry long before dinner time.

He was dressed in clothes borrowed from his host. Unfortunately Sir James, though almost as broad and preferring his garments loose, was considerably shorter. Bertram's wrists protruded from the cuffs, and his shirt showed a distressing tendency to escape from his trousers. No wonder he paused before entering the drawing-room and attempted to compose his features into his usual expression of affable calm.

Lizzie was seated facing the door. She looked up from her embroidery and went off into a peal of laughter. Bertram tried not to scowl at her.

"Lud, coz, you look like a scarecrow!" said Horace, shocked.

Lizzie rounded on him. "That's better than looking like a mannequin from a sequin manufactory!" she told him severely.

Bertram revised his opinion of her as Horace turned red and gobbled like a turkey cock.

Claire jumped up, dropping her book, and came towards him with both hands held out.

"Whatever happened, my lord?" she asked with evident distress. "We have been waiting for you this age. Golightly said only that you were delayed."

He took her hands, led her to a sofa, and seated himself beside her. "I have been slaying dragons again, ma'am," he said gaily, intent on reassuring her. "This time, in the form of five scrubby, grubby boys, and in aid not of a fair damsel but of your servant, Alfie. In the process, my clothes became...er, offensive, shall we say."

"Oh dear, I sent him to fetch manure from the stables."

90

She bit her lip, and he saw that her grey eyes were dancing. "Those horrid boys, I am so sorry, but how very kind of you to go to poor Alfie's assistance."

"I hope you whipped them!" said Lizzie, amusement replaced by indignation. "They pick on poor Alfie because he is a little slow. And we have not yet thanked you for that business with the gloves," she added inconsequentially, "which was equally kind."

"Not equally," he said, grinning at her, good humour restored by their obviously sincere gratitude. "The purchase of the gloves was my pleasure. I cannot say the same of the present incident."

"Gad no!" said Horace in horror. "Can't say I've ever come into contact with horse droppings, but I daresay it'll stain."

Bertram shrugged. "Golightly promised me the marks could be removed. I took the liberty, Miss Sutton, of requesting a hot bath for Alfie."

"Then I had best go down and make sure he bathes," Lizzie said, folding her needlework, setting it aside, and rising purposefully. Then she noticed the gentlemen's aghast looks. Again her laughter pealed. "Never fear, I do not mean to watch him at it!" she gurgled. "Only I must tell him to get into the tub or he will think it some new harassment." She hurried from the room.

"What a minx your sister is," Bertram said to Claire.

She smiled, but he thought there was something of sadness in her look.

"She will soon learn to curb her tongue in London," she said, "when she comes to realise that it is not only Mama who thinks her shockingly outspoken. I shall miss her frankness, I confess."

"I shall not !" Horace was still incensed at Lizzie's description of him.

"Doubtless she will not change her manner with her intimate friends," said Bertram, wondering whether he himself was to count among those continuing to be treated to her devastating candour. "By the way, Miss Sutton, have you learned yet where you will be staying in Town? I hope you will be kind enough to give me your direction."

She cast a dubious glance at Horace, and Bertram wished he had thought not to ask in his cousin's presence. Still, it could not be kept secret from him if he chose to find out.

"My lawyer has found us a house in Portman Square. It is a little out of the centre of things, I know, but otherwise it sounds as if it is just what we need. We left it very late, and London will be particularly busy this spring, I collect, because of the King's coronation."

"No knowing when that will be," Horace put in. "Prinny ain't going to set the date till they think up a legal reason to keep Caroline from being crowned queen beside him."

Bertram disliked gossip, and he found the subject of the relationship between George IV and his erring wife distasteful in the extreme. Nor was he happy that the Misses Sutton were to reside on the fringes of Society. That, together with their appalling mother, might well damn them in the eyes of the ton, and he could not marry a woman who was not acceptable to the best hostesses. He frowned.

"Does Lady Sutton go with you, ma'am?" he asked. "I believe there was some doubt."

"I am not yet certain, my lord, but I think not. She...my father cannot spare her for so long." She avoided his eye. "In fact she...she does not know yet that I have taken a house. I had hoped to keep it from her until we are about to leave."

"She shall not hear of it from me, nor from my cousin." He turned a stern gaze on Horace who looked puzzled but murmured assent.

He relaxed. It was unusual, to say the least, for an unmarried female under thirty to sponsor a girl in her first Season, but it could be passed off more easily than her ladyship's ill-breeding. He looked at Claire consideringly, wondering for the first time whether her single state was more due to her mother's vulgarity than her own oddities.

Lizzie hurried into the room.

"Claire, Mama is returned from the vicar's. Shall we go for a walk?"

Her sister glanced at Horace's shoes and Bertram's borrowed garments and shook her head regretfully. "Our guests are not dressed for walking," she pointed out.

Lizzie followed her glance to the glittering shoes and stayed there. She giggled.

"No, I suppose Mr. Harrison will not wish to risk soiling his finery. He may stay and entertain Mama, if he prefers. You will come, will you not, my lord?" She turned to Bertram.

"I, too, must pay my respects to Lady Sutton," he said.

"Fustian! I believe you are afraid to expose yourself to view less than perfectly dressed. You use your fashionable clothes as armour to hide behind."

"Lizzie!"

"Oh Claire, I'm sorry." She ran to hug her sister, then looked at Bertram and said stiffly, "I beg your pardon, my lord. I ought not to have spoken so."

Bertram accepted her apology with a cold nod, but the shaft had struck home. He was forced to recognise that to some extent his insistence on perfection of dress was a defence, a shield with a device which announced his identity so that no one need question more deeply.

"After I have greeted her ladyship, I shall of course be pleased to walk in the gardens with Miss Sutton," he said, with an ignoble feeling of having triumphed over Lizzie.

Judging by her grin, she considered the triumph hers.

She was not deterred from joining the outing, so they left Horace torn between sulks at being deserted and gratification at Lady Sutton's flattery.

They returned to the house just in time to change for dinner. Bertram was conducted to a spare chamber where his own shirt, waistcoat, coat, and pantaloons were laid out ready for him. Edward Sutton's valet fussed over him, assuring him that he personally had made sure that not the least stain remained.

"A shocking business, my lord, to be sure," he said. "I

understand Sir James has had the boys thoroughly whipped for their mischief."

"I have not told Sir James what occurred. How did he learn of it?"

"Why, I suppose one of the grooms, my lord.... Naturally everyone knows of your lordship's misfortune."

"Naturally," said Bertram drily. He had forgotten to allow for the rest of the world's love of gossip.

It was a relief to be properly dressed again. He was dismayed to realise how great a relief. Was his image of himself really so dependent upon his clothes?

It was in no very good mood that he went down to the drawing room, just in time for the announcement of dinner. With the Suttons, the Carfaxes, and the Harrisons, there were twelve at table. Bertram found himself seated between Claire and his cousin Amelia, and had to admire his sister's and his aunt's superior tactics. Lizzie was on the opposite side, some way down between Horace and one of her brothers. He surprised himself with a wish that she was next to him.

After passing the first course trying to extract a word or two from Amelia, Bertram turned with relief to Claire as the second course was carried in. His opening remark was interrupted by Sir James, calling loudly across the table.

"I say, Pomeroy, frightfully sorry about that affair in the stables. Tossing manure around indeed! Assure you the boys have been whipped soundly."

A startled silence fell on the company. Lady Caroline and Lady Harrison stared at their host, shocked at his breach of good manners in mentioning such a subject in polite company. Then Caroline glanced enquiringly at Bertram, hoping for enlightenment. As he shook his head in warning that the entire incident was equally unmentionable, Lady Sutton broke the silence.

"Of course the idiot will be turned off. We cannot have our guests subjected to such insult. I always told you, Claire, that no good would come of your championing an imbecile. He must go at once."

All eyes turned to Claire, but it was Lizzie who rose to her feet, her face blazing with anger.

"So he shall, Mama. He leaves tomorrow, with Claire and me, for London. And I shall have my Season despite anything you can do or say!"

She realised suddenly that everyone was gaping at her. She flushed, and Bertram thought he saw her lips tremble, then she fled the room.

Lady Sutton, her colour alarmingly heightened, was glaring at her other daughter. Bertram turned to Claire. Her pale face was blank.

"You will wish to go to your sister," he said quietly, pressing her hand. He stood up and pulled out her chair.

Her grey eyes glowed with fervent gratitude, and, wordless, she went after Lizzie.

Lady Sutton showed signs of intending to follow, but Lord Carfax, sitting beside her, spoke to her and she was forced to respond. Caroline made some negligent comment about the foibles of young girls and launched into a story of her own gaucherie at that age. The rest of the meal passed in uncomfortable avoidance of the slightest mention of the distressing incident.

The guests did not linger long once the gentlemen left their port. Lady Caroline insisted on travelling home with Bertram in his curricle, despite the cold.

"Well!" she said as they drove away from the front door. "What was all that about?"

Bertram told her. He described the simpleton's despair and the unintended damage to his apparel. He explained, insofar as he understood it, Claire and Lizzie's need for a London Season without their mother.

"And who can blame them?" he said. "I cannot think how you come to be on visiting terms with such people, Caroline!"

"In the normal way of things I am not. We have met them at other people's houses, of course, being neighbours, but

I have never before invited them. It is entirely for your sake, brother dear, and once you are gone I hope never to see them again."

"But you gave me to understand that you were well acquainted with Claire!"

"With Claire, yes, and with Lizzie to some extent. I buy all my roses from Claire, without ever seeing her parents."

"You buy roses from her? I had not realised her interest in gardening went so far! You have not been honest with me, Caroline. You are as full of mischief as Lizzie, I vow. Had I known the true situation, I'd never have started upon this damnable courtship."

"Well, you may drop it now," she said guiltily. "There can be no obligation upon you to call on them in London."

"True. Very well, I forgive you."

"And you will not tell Carfax?"

"If you promise you will never again embroil me in your nefarious schemes!"

=== 10 ===

Sir James, taking an interest in his daughters' welfare for perhaps the first time in his life, lent his aged travelling coach, a team of horses, and a groom to take them to London. He did not, however, go so far as to appear on the doorstep to wave farewell.

To Lizzie's disappointment, it was not the day after the disastrous dinner party. It did not take long to pack most of their belongings in a couple of trunks, but Claire's garden equipment had to be sent off by carrier's cart to Bumble's Green. It took most of the day to disassemble and crate the dry stove. Claire looked longingly at the greenhouse itself before deciding that it simply was not practical to ship all that glass.

Alfie was in ferment of excitement and had to be constantly recalled to the task at hand. By the evening Claire was exhausted.

"We shall go to bed early so as to be ready to leave early," proposed Lizzie. "And let's have our dinner on trays in our chamber. It may be shockingly cowardly, but I prefer not to face Mama at the table."

Molly, the chambermaid, brought up their trays one by one. As she set the second on the little table by the empty fireplace, she burst into tears.

"Please, Miss Claire, take me with you!" she sobbed.

The sisters looked at her in astonishment. Claire had never really noticed her before. She was a slight, pale girl of about sixteen who went about her duties as silent as a shadow, never drawing attention to herself.

"You want to go to London?" Claire asked kindly. "We had not thought to take anyone but Alfie."

"You'll need a maid, miss. I'll do anything. I'll cook and clean, and I'm good wi' hair, you can ask Doris, the parlourmaid, and even her ladyship says I set a neat stitch. And..."

"What of your family?" Lizzie interrupted. "Would they be willing to let you go?"

"I'm an orphan, miss. I don't have no one but Alfie. I takes care on him, like, see he gets his meals and his clo'es is clean and that. He'll be lost wi'out me. Please, Miss Lizzie, take me, too."

Claire and Lizzie looked at each other and nodded.

None of the family saw them off the next morning.

"I never imagined," said Lizzie, "that being disowned by one's family might give one such pleasure!"

The ancient carriage creaked down the drive, with Alfie perched proudly on the box beside the groom and Molly, quietly contented, inside with her back to the horses. Lizzie, seated opposite, opened her mouth to speak, then looked at the maid in dismay.

" 'Tend like I'm not here, miss," said Molly earnestly, catching her glance. "I wouldn't never tell anything I heared, honest, and I won't listen anyways. I'll just look out the window, quiet as a mouse. 'Tend I'm not here."

Lizzie was too eager to talk not to take her at her word. "I wonder why Papa lent us the carriage," she mused aloud. "To ensure our departure, perhaps. It is a pity that even his best horses cannot move it at more than a snail's pace, the great lumbering thing. Do you remember George's coach? With the blue leather seats? It was more comfortable than most chairs, and one hardly knew one was moving. Do you think George will come to see us in London?"

"Yes, I do," Claire said with certainty, "or he'd not have asked for our direction, and told us to expect him."

"Perhaps he was just being polite."

"I believe George—Lord Winterborne, that is—you really ought not to speak of him so familiarly, Lizzie. He seems to me to be a thoroughly sincere person. He is no diplomat, unlike Lord Pomeroy."

"You mean Lord Pomeroy sets tact above truth?"

"Well, that is an extreme way of putting it. I do not mean to accuse him of telling outright bouncers! But just because he, too, asked for our direction I do not necessarily expect him to turn up in Portman Square. Will you be disappointed if he does not?" Claire hoped that her sister was not developing a tendre for Lord Pomeroy.

"Yes, I should be sorry. I like him, for all he is so stuffy at times."

"He is certainly very reserved. He has been kind to me, chivalrous even, but I cannot feel comfortable with him, never knowing what he is thinking."

"I believe he is shy, like you. You would make an excellent pair."

"Oh, surely not!" Claire laughed. "Just imagine us at the breakfast table, neither speaking a word for fear the other does not wish to talk! You cannot be enamoured of him, though, if you think he and I would be a perfect match. I am glad."

"Enamoured of Lord Pomeroy?" It was Lizzie's turn to laugh. "Heavens no! If you and he would sit in silence, he and I would never stop brangling. Have you not noticed how we constantly come to cuffs? No, I had rather marry George—sorry, Lord Winterborne—for I can say anything at all to him, and he never turns a hair."

"Oh yes, he would make you a wonderful husband if you do not think him too old."

"I did at first, until I came to know him better. Now I think he is just the perfect age. However, it is not at all likely that he will ever make an offer."

"Why do you say so? He has been most particular in his attentions to you, Lizzie."

"Yes, but it is all a hum, to mislead Mama. It will not lead to anything more. I know I ought not to repeat what I have overheard, but when you went to the Carfaxes' book-room with Lord Pomeroy, Lady Caroline was talking about George. She told Mama that he is a gazetted flirt. He has broken the hearts of any number of young ladies. I do not mean to be caught in the same trap, I promise you, so I think of him as a very good friend and no more."

Claire was aware of a horrid sinking feeling which she could not explain. To be sure, she had hoped that something might come of George's apparent partiality for Lizzie, but there would be plenty of gentlemen in London seeking a bride. If George fought shy of marriage, it was nothing to her. In fact, it was better in a way, for if he wed someone other than Lizzie she must expect to lose his friendship.

"How very commonsensical you are," she said with attempted cheerfulness. "I am sorry that he has such a reputation, but it need not affect us as long as you are on your guard."

"I am glad you think he will visit us. All the same, I hope Lord Pomeroy will too, for I still think you and he would deal well together!"

Claire shook her head in amused disagreement, and the subject dropped.

They spent the night at the Catherine Wheel in Henley-on-Thames and arrived in Portman Square the next afternoon. Despite the short notice of their coming, the cook-house-keeper, Mrs. Rumbelow, had everything in readiness with welcoming fires in parlour and bedchambers. A short, round woman who moved with jerky efficiency, she also acted as caretaker for the owner when the house was empty, and she showed them around with proprietary pride.

As the lawyer had promised, the tall, narrow house was well suited to their needs. The basement, lit by windows high in the walls, was Mrs. Rumbelow's territory, and the attic was servants' quarters. In between, there were two parlours and a dining-room on the ground floor and three bedchambers on the first floor. All were sparsely but elegantly furnished, and spotless.

"I can see that you are an excellent housekeeper, Mrs. Rumbelow," said Claire approvingly as they finished their inspection of the third chamber and moved out onto the landing.

She beamed and curtsied jerkily. "Thank you, miss. There's a woman comes in to do the 'eavy cleaning and laundry and such. Being as you've brought your abigail and manservant, we won't need to 'ire but a girl for the scullery and a chambermaid."

"Six servants to wait upon the two of us!" said Lizzie in astonishment. "Surely we don't need so many, Claire."

"Molly is not really our abigail," Claire explained to the frowning housekeeper. "We are used to taking care of ourselves. We shall see if we can manage without any more maids."

"As you wish, miss." Mrs. Rumbelow was definitely displeased.

"If you and Molly find yourselves overworked, of course we shall hire more help," Claire hastened to assure her.

At that moment a squeal echoed down the uncarpeted stairs from the attic and Alfie came clattering down. His eyes were big with excitement.

"What is the matter?" asked Lizzie. "Never say there are rats in the roof!"

"Not in *my* house, miss!" said Mrs. Rumbelow, outraged.

"Don' care 'bout rats," Alfie told them. "Lots in the stables. Oh, Miss Lizzie, Molly says I c'n have a whole room jus' for me. With a bed in it! Can I? Can I, Miss Claire?"

"Yes, Alfie, I'm sure there is a room for you." Claire was filled with guilt as she realised she had no idea where the boy slept at home. The servants' living arrangements were her mother's responsibility, and her mother had never encouraged her to take an interest in managing the household. In fact, she thought bitterly, had she ever expressed an interest she would doubtless have been severely snubbed.

And here, within half an hour of stepping through the front door, she was already faced with questions to which she did not know the answers. Did they really need another two maids, or was it just that a larger staff would enhance Mrs. Rumbelow's status? What salary would she have to pay, and how much would their keep add to her expenses? The housekeeper's wages were included in the rent, but she had no notion what she ought to pay Alfie and Molly.

The first thing, she decided, was to see to their comfort.

"Will you show me your room, Alfie?" she requested. "I must see that you have everything you need."

Mrs. Rumbelow nodded approval, and Alfie beamed with pride as he ushered her up the narrow stair.

The next morning, Claire swallowed her pride and went to the housekeeper for advice. Her frank confession of ignorance won Mrs. Rumbelow over, and even elicited an admission that they might manage with just one more maid.

"And my niece Enid 'appens to be needing a position right now so with your permission, miss…"

For the next week Claire spent several hours every day learning the principles of household management from Mrs. Rumbelow. The housekeeper also proved a mine of information on fashionable modistes and inexpensive haberdashers, so she and Lizzie spent the rest of their time exploring these fascinating establishments.

Lizzie, showing an unexpected practical streak, refused to buy anything until they had thoroughly investigated both the latest fashions and the prices and quality of goods in the various shops.

"Then I shall sit down and make a list of just what we need," she explained, "so we shall not waste your money, for I can see it is all going to be shockingly expensive. But do you think, dearest Claire, we might afford a pair of comfortable chairs for the back parlour? The house is so elegantly furnished that there is nowhere to relax!"

"I have already consulted Mrs. Rumbelow," said Claire smiling, "and she says Tottenham Court Road is the place for furniture. I shall need all sorts of things for Bumble's Green, so it is not an extravagance. By the way, I received word from the caretaker there that my goods arrived, so I must go tomorrow and sort them out. Will you go with me?"

"I long to see your house, but I shall only be in the way

if you are arranging your gardening things. It will be a good opportunity to start on my lists. You will take Alfie to fetch and carry? If I decide to go out Molly can go with me."

They had taken Alfie on all their wanderings about the Town, and he had learned his way about the streets with astonishing speed, remembering the places they had pointed out to him. Since one of these was the livery stable in the next street, Claire gave him a note to take there requesting a gig and driver for the next day. It was the first time he had gone out on his own, and once again he was proud as a peacock. Alfie was enjoying Town life.

His mistresses waited anxiously for his return, and Claire noticed Molly hovering in the hall. While they had little fear that he would lose himself on so short an errand, if he succeeded they might send him farther afield, which could prove useful in the future. When he reappeared with a note from the stables promising a gig and driver for eight the next morning, Molly hugged him and Claire gave him sixpence. He went off happily to put it under his pillow.

Claire overheard Enid, the new maid, saying to Molly, "Well, I'll give yer this, 'e ain't bright but 'e's willin'."

Bumble's Green was a tiny hamlet some fifteen miles north of London, on the edge of Epping Forest. Claire had only seen her house twice, some five years earlier, when she had been in London to see the lawyer on receiving her inheritance. She felt a rising sense of anticipation as the carriage turned off the toll road, crossed the River Lea and rattled past Waltham Abbey. This was the place where she intended to spend the rest of her life.

The house was just as she remembered it, a small, square, two-storey building of red brick, built in the middle of the last century, set in the centre of an acre of land. She imagined the front garden overflowing with roses, saw herself growing old amid their beauty and fascination, the ladies of the ton driving out from London to buy her new varieties. For the first time the vision failed to satisfy. Would George Winterborne bring his wife to buy her roses?

She pushed the thought from her mind and stepped down from the gig, sending the driver 'round the back where the stables sheltered the kitchen garden from north winds.

The front door opened before she reached it, and she was warmly welcomed by the elderly couple who took care of the place for her. She never had sought a tenant, not wanting to envision strangers in her refuge. Only two rooms were furnished—the kitchen and a small back room where the couple slept. The latter had small, high windows and a large brass lock on the door. Mrs. Copple had a particular aversion to being, as she said, "murthered in me bed."

"You'll take a cup o' tea, Miss Sutton?" asked Mrs. Copple now. "It'll 'ave to be in the kitchen, I'm afeared. There's a spot o' mutton pie to your luncheon, but we wasn't expecting you so soon."

"Pray do not bother with luncheon, Mrs. Copple. I ate a hearty breakfast, not wishing to put you to any trouble. I should like a cup of tea though, and I expect Alfie and the ostler will like ale if you have some."

With her new understanding of household matters, Claire looked around the kitchen and saw a number of improvements that could be made, including a closed stove. However, the garden still held her chief interest, and soon she and Alfie were busy sorting out the pile of equipment and tools the carter had stacked in the little coach house. Then she walked about her property and chose the best spot to build a greenhouse. Before she realised how time was passing, the ostler returned from a stroll into the village and told her they must leave if she wished to reach home before dark.

No doubt he had found Bumble's Green lacking in attractions, for they reached Portman Square shortly after five, still daylight now that March had arrived. Claire paid him and trod wearily up the front steps.

Enid met her in the hall, her round face excited.

"There's visitors, miss," she hissed, gesturing towards the front parlour, "an' both on 'em's lords!"

Claire felt suddenly weak, overwhelmed with emotions she could not identify. She put one hand out to steady herself against the hall table, and caught sight of her grubby glove. She was wearing her gardening clothes, of course. She must change, and that would give her time to regain her composure. She started for the stairs.

It was too late. Enid had opened the parlour door and announced her return. Unwillingly she turned and entered the room.

The room seemed to shrink before her eyes as George Winterborne and Lord Pomeroy both rose with alacrity to greet her. She was used to seeing them in the more spacious rooms of country houses, and had never really grasped how big they both were.

"How happy I am to see you both, my lords," she said in a wavering voice, helplessly holding out a hand to each.

George was beside her in an instant, supporting her to a chair. She shivered at his touch.

"We startled you," he said in self-reproach, "and you are frozen."

Lizzie was kneeling at her side, drawing off her gloves and chafing her hands, her face anxious.

"Claire, are you all right? What is the matter? It is not like you to be so easily overset."

"I am more tired than I had thought," she said, feeling an utter widgeon. "I shall be quite all right in a moment. It has been a long and busy day."

"And we have been racketing about all week," added Lizzie.

"Drink this, Miss Sutton." Lord Pomeroy handed her a glass of Maderia. "It will soon set you to right."

"The colour is returning to your cheeks already," said Lizzie with satisfaction as she stood. "Oh Claire, is it not famous that they are come?" Her voice was joyful.

Claire nodded, aware that the gentlemen were grinning at her sister's exuberance. She sipped at the wine. She felt stronger by the minute, quite unable to account to herself for her momentary faintness.

George looked at her searchingly. "I see you are better, Cl—Miss Sutton." He glanced at Lord Pomeroy. "However, I believe it is time that we took our leave. May I call tomorrow to see how you go on?"

"Thank you, you are very kind, sir." She was shy with him, shyer than she had been since their first meeting. Yet, as he bowed over her hand, she was overcome with an urge to run her fingers through his crisp, dark hair with its sprinkling of grey.

He was a flirt, she reminded herself fiercely, and she was an old maid.

Lord Pomeroy took his place.

"I am persuaded, Miss Sutton, that fresh air without exertion will do you a world of good tomorrow. May I have the honour of driving you in the park if it is fine?"

From the corner of her eye, Claire saw George look startled and then sardonic. Wondering at his expression, she murmured a polite acceptance.

"Then I shall call for you at three, if that will suit." Lord Pomeroy's calm, smiling courtesy was soothing.

"Well, Miss Elizabeth," said George jovially, "shall we go along to keep an eye on your sister? I believe you will enjoy an outing in my high-perch phaeton."

"Oh yes, please!" Lizzie's blue eyes sparkled. "That will be beyond anything great."

"Three o'clock then."

Molly, who had been sitting in a corner quiet as a mouse to chaperone Lizzie, showed the gentlemen out. Lizzie peeked 'round the parlour door until the front door was firmly shut behind them, then she turned back to Claire.

"Whatever shall we wear?" she wailed.

Claire looked at her vaguely. "It does not signify," she said.

"Yes it does." Lizzie was indignant. "George and Bertram will not wish to be seen in the park with a pair of dowds."

"Lord Winterborne is too easygoing to mind what you wear, and Lord Pomeroy already knows me for a dowd."

"Fustian! Let me look at my lists. There must be something we can do to be ready by tomorrow. Ah, I know. We shall buy those shawls we saw at Waithman's. You remember, the cashemire? Fastened at the throat with a brooch, like the picture in *Ackermann's* that I showed you, they will hide the worst, and they will always come in useful in future. Then I'm sure George and Bertram will have rugs to keep us warm, which will conceal our lower halves! We will need hats, though. A neutral straw, I think, then we can change the trimmings to match anything. I saw just the thing in Cranbourne Alley at an excellent price."

Claire rose and hugged her, kissing her cheek.

"How very practical and ingenious you are becoming, dearest. But I do not need new clothes. Lord Pomeroy asked me to go with him only because I am the elder and he is too fastidious to ignore the niceties of convention. I confess I was surprised to see him at all, for I did not think him so taken with you as to disregard that dreadful scene! He might with perfect propriety have failed to call."

"He is not the least enamoured of *me*," Lizzie insisted. "It is *you* he is interested in. Are you not glad that he has not abandoned us?"

"Certainly. He is a courteous and considerate gentleman and must always be an acceptable escort for you." Claire wondered at her insistence, but was too tired to pursue the subject. "I shall go and lie down for an hour before dinner," she said. "Wake me if I fall asleep, for I missed luncheon and I am positively ravenous."

"So that is why you were faint," said Lizzie with relief. "I shall have Mrs. Rumbelow heat a bowl of soup and bring it up to you immediately."

As she made her way upstairs to her chamber, Claire considered this explanation with equal relief. How foolish of her to suppose that it was the sight of Lord Winterborne that had made her head swim!

=== 11 ===

LIZZIE SAT, CHIN in hand, gazing out of the window at the fading pink of the sky above the houses on the far side of the square. It was most satisfactory that her indecorous outburst at their last meeting had not caused Lord Pomeroy to abandon his pursuit of Claire. She flushed as she recalled how she had defied her mother and rushed from the dining-room. It was just the sort of ill-breeding he most deplored.

She must watch her step in future so as not to jeopardise Claire's chances.

Molly came in.

"I'll light the candles, miss," she said, "and build up the fire a bit. I took Miss Claire her soup. Fancy them two lordships coming to visit then!" She chattered as she bustled about the room setting everything to rights. "Lord Winterborne, he's right friendly, but that Lord Pomeroy, now, he's a proper gentleman. Allus polite an' never familiar."

At least Claire seemed to be warming towards Lord Pomeroy, thought Lizzie. She had described him as courteous and considerate today, instead of reserved and insincere.

She did not do him justice, though. He had been more than considerate to poor Alfie, and in that business with Papa's stallion he had been brave and chivalrous. Lizzie had not found him so very reserved. He seemed withdrawn and reticent at times, but she had laughed and quarrelled with him and knew him capable of frank sincerity.

He was as worthy of her sister's hand as any man could

be, and she resolved to promote the match. For some reason the decision brought her little satisfaction.

"Can I get you anything, Miss Lizzie?" asked Molly, pausing on her way out.

"No. No, thank you, I shall go up to change shortly." Lizzie knew Claire thought it ridiculous to change for dinner when it was just the two of them, but she enjoyed the ritual. She would enjoy it even more when she had some new gowns to put on.

March had come in like a lamb, but there was a chill wind blowing the next morning as they set out to do their shopping. They walked briskly along Oxford Street to Cranbourne Alley, which Mrs. Rumbelow had recommended as the best place for cheap bonnets and caps. Her delicately phrased warnings about the neighbourhood had passed right over Lizzie's head, and at ten in the morning none of the notorious lightskirts of nearby Seven Dials were in evidence.

Lizzie soon found a shop which sold precisely what she wanted. Leaving Alfie with strict instructions to wait outside, they stepped in.

The plain straw bonnet Lizzie had her eye on was carried off to the workroom to be ornamented with a wreath of for-get-me-nots and wide blue ribbons. Claire was more difficult.

"That Leghorn hat with the broad brim is perfect," said Lizzie. "You are tall enough to carry it off with an air."

"I do not need a new hat," Claire protested. "A new ribbon for this one will be enough."

"But…" Lizzie began to argue, then changed her mind. "But if you will not have one, then I shall buy two and you may borrow one this afternoon."

"Certainly you must have two, but the Leghorn will not suit you."

Foiled, Lizzie grimaced and chose a hat with a narrower brim. While Claire was looking out of the window to make sure that Alfie had not disappeared, she ordered a bunch of lilacs and a matching plume to be set to one side of the crown. They would go perfectly with the shawl she intended to purchase for her sister.

The milliner promised to have both hats at midday, so they summoned a hackney to take them to the City, to Waithman's on Ludgate Hill.

Mrs. Rumbelow had told them that Mr. Waithman, linen draper and member of Parliament for the City of London, had the best supply of shawls in the country. His prices were reasonable because he bought from the wives of merchants and soldiers, who came home from India with trunks full of the beautifully dyed and woven silks and cashemires to sell to him. Lizzie hoped that the particular ones she had in mind were still there, but there were hundreds to choose from and she was sure of finding something to match the new hats.

She was prepared for another battle with Claire, but her sister could not resist the soft warmth of the cashemire. She leaned towards a practical brown instead of the delicate design of lilac and silvery-green Lizzie had picked out.

"Think how well this will go with Grandmama's amethyst brooch," urged Lizzie. "You have nothing now to do it justice. This costs the same and will wear as well as the brown. Are you afraid of looking pretty?"

Claire smiled wryly. "Fine feathers do not make fine birds," she said. "Very well, I will take it. What have you in mind for yourself?"

Lizzie, with a triumphant grin, draped herself in a shawl patterned with a dozen shades of blue. "To go with Grandmama's sapphire," she pointed out. "After all, they are the only jewels we own."

"To match the sapphire or your eyes?" Claire teased.

"It was you who told me that blue is my best colour. We will take these two," she added to the shop assistant, quickly before Claire could change her mind. "Now let us go to the modiste and order some gowns, so that if George and Lord Pomeroy invite us out driving again we shall not have to hide beneath even the prettiest draperies!"

The package with the shawls, wrapped in brown paper

and string, was given to Alfie to carry. He followed behind them holding it gingerly in both hands, as if it contained the finest crystal.

Since Lizzie had very firm ideas about what she wanted, it did not take long to order two walking dresses, a carriage dress, and an evening gown. However, by the time her measurements had been taken it was growing late.

"I had hoped to explore Hatchard's book shop and Hookham's Library," she said, "but we must get home in time for you to eat before they arrive. It would be too dreadful if you swooned in the park."

"I can think of few things less likely!" Claire laughed. "Pray do not treat me like an invalid only because I felt a little faint yesterday."

"Then have we time to order your gowns now?"

"No, you are right. Though I am not an invalid, I am hungry. Let us go. We can go to the circulating library tomorrow, but pray remember not to display your interest in history in public. Mama is right about that, it would be fatal to your chances to be thought a bluestocking."

The sun had disappeared behind a pall of clouds and the wind had grown keener. When Lord Pomeroy arrived in Portman Square, on the stroke of three, he asked Claire solicitously if she thought it was too cold to go out in an open carriage.

"I have a fur rug in the curricle," he added.

Claire threw a mischievous glance at Lizzie but answered soberly, "I shall do very well, sir, with the rug."

"Then if Miss Elizabeth will excuse us, let us go at once before it grows any colder."

Lizzie helped Claire don her shawl and hat, fastening the amethyst brooch and tying the lilac ribbons. She thought her sister looked charming, and noted a glint of approval—and what she suspected might be relief—in Lord Pomeroy's eyes. He must have expected her to be shabbily dressed, so his invitation to drive in public with him argued a definite determination to court her. Lizzie watched wistfully from the window as he handed her up into the carriage and took his place beside her.

Before they drove off, George's phaeton pulled up alongside and he stopped for a word with them. By the time Molly showed him into the parlour, Lizzie had on her new finery and was ready to go.

"I take it you are no more deterred by the wind than is your sister," he said with a smile. "What a delightful bonnet, my dear, and the shawl intensifies the glorious blue of your eyes, as I am quite certain was your intention."

She laughed. "I mean to wear nothing but blue. However, I trust that you have a rug to cover my skirts, for my pelisse is two years old and looks it."

"Such vanity!" he teased, escorting her downstairs. "I fear there will be few to admire you, for the Season has scarce begun and the icy wind will deter all but the bravest."

They entered Hyde Park by the nearby Cumberland Gate. Though there were indeed few carriages to be seen, Lizzie thoroughly enjoyed the view from George's high-perch phaeton. The hood was up, protecting them from the worst of the wind. She chattered happily as they drove south, and he responded with his usual amused sympathy. He waved occasionally to an acquaintance. No one stopped to exchange greetings, all seemed eager to take a turn about the park and hurry home to the fireside.

They had nearly reached the ruffled waters of the Serpentine when Lord Pomeroy's curricle came towards them. Lizzie waved gaily, but his lordship and Claire were so deep in conversation that they did not notice her. She felt her heart give an odd little twist.

Of course she could only be glad to see them so much in sympathy. It must be the thought of losing her beloved sister that made her feel so peculiar.

George had fallen silent beside her. She glanced up at him and surprised a look of envy on his face. Even an incorrigible flirt, she supposed, must occasionally feel the want of a loving wife. She patted his arm sympathetically.

Startled, he looked down at her, then he smiled.

"You must have great faith in my ability as a whip. Had I jerked on the reins, we might have ended up in the Serpentine, not an inviting prospect at this time of year."

"My brother told me that you are a top sawyer, and a member of the Four-Horse Club, whatever that may be. He seemed to think it a great honour."

"It is, but even a member of the Four-Horse Club has been known to overset a high-perch phaeton. It is not the most stable of carriages."

"Then why did you ask me to drive in it with you?" Lizzie asked pertly.

"Because you are no timorous miss, and I thought you would enjoy it."

"I do, indeed I do, but I should have enjoyed it still more had I known from the outset that it was an adventure!"

"Minx."

He turned the phaeton to head for home. The hood no longer sheltered them from the biting wind, and he urged his team from a trot to a canter.

"One should never underestimate the ability of March to emulate January," he said apologetically. "If the weather ever improves, do you suppose your sister will like to ride in my dangerous vehicle?"

"I am sure she will. Just because she is quiet, it does not mean that she is poor-spirited."

"I did not mean to suggest any such thing."

Lizzie was surprised by the deep sincerity in his voice, quite unlike his usual joking manner. A little taken aback, she said in a deliberately bright voice, "Only do not tell her beforehand that there is anything out of the way about it, for if there is anything she fears, it is drawing attention to herself. I would not have her miss the treat for such a nonsensical reason."

He gave her a grin of complicity, but said drily, "I am persuaded that is one fear you do not share!"

Lizzie was glad of a hot cup of tea when they reached

home, and the gentlemen were warmed with a glass of wine. They sat in the back parlour, which had a wider fireplace. The men appropriated the new leather-covered armchairs, declaring them more fit for masculine use than the elegant but fragile Hepplewhite and Sheraton pieces.

As soon as her hands had thawed sufficiently, Lizzie took up her embroidery, a cushion cover for the new chairs. Lord Pomeroy admired the design of aconites and snowdrops.

"A delightful change from the usual roses," he said, then coloured slightly and glanced at Claire. "Begging your pardon, Miss Sutton! I've nothing against roses, I assure you."

"Embroidered roses cannot possibly be compared with the real thing," Lizzie asserted loyally.

"I wonder what would be your opinion of Miss Linwood's Exhibition," Lord Pomeroy said. "You have not heard of it? It consists of copies in embroidery of some of the paintings of the Old Masters. They are generally much admired."

"I have never seen the paintings, so I doubt I could properly appreciate Miss Linwood's work, though I should like to see it anyway."

"You must allow me to take you one of these days, first to the Royal Academy and then to Miss Linwood's in Leicester Square."

"I shall look forward to it, sir, but it will have to wait until I have some new dresses."

Lord Pomeroy laughed. "If it were anyone but you, Miss Elizabeth, I should protest loudly and say that you will do me credit whatever your dress. But I know your love of frankness, so I will say instead that I anticipate with the greatest pleasure seeing you in fashionable clothes."

"You are insulting, my lord," Lizzie pouted. "You mean, I collect, that I am not at present fit to be seen in your company?"

"If ever I heard such blatant fishing for a compliment!" he marvelled. "Wait a moment, let me see." He struck a pose. "Miss Elizabeth, your eyes are blue as the heavens above, your golden curls like a ray of sunshine brightening the day."

"Very nice. But I wish you will call me Lizzie. When I hear 'Elizabeth' I always think of Mama."

"Of course, Miss Lizzie."

"No, just Lizzie. I wish you will not be so formal!"

"I hardly think that will be proper," his lordship said stiffly.

She studied his face. Her suggestion obviously made him uncomfortable. Were appearances so important to Lord Pomeroy that he shied away from the merest hint of impropriety, or was it the suggestion of intimacy he shunned? She suspected the latter, but wondered whether he himself realised it. Of one thing she was sure: Claire was wrong in believing him insensitive. More likely, excessive sensitivity made him afraid of exposing his feelings.

She sighed.

"Lizzie, I'm sorry." He reached for her hand with a rueful look. "Of course there can be no harm in it. I am a pompous slowtop, or any name you wish to call me."

"Bertram will do very well." With a tremulous smile she put her hand in his, to be enveloped in his warm strength. For an endless moment her eyes met eyes as blue as her own. Then he let go her hand and she breathed again.

He stood up. "It is time I was on my way," he said in a neutral voice. "I shall call tomorrow, Miss Sutton, to assure myself that you have not taken cold from our drive. Or may I call you Claire, since Lizzie and I have just concluded a pact against formality?" He smile with his habitual charm.

Claire looked flustered. "If you wish, my lord," she faltered.

"Bertram," he corrected gently, raising her hand to his lips.

Lizzie looked away.

George also departed. He was going out of town for a few days, but he promised to call upon his return.

"Will you miss me?" he asked Lizzie teasingly.

"The sun will not shine while you are gone!" she exclaimed in a melodramatic tone, and they laughed.

Her prophecy was all too accurate. In the night the wind

died, to be replaced by a persistent, depressing drizzle that continued all week. There was no question of driving or walking in the park, and they took hackneys except to the closest shops. Bertram called twice but found them out. They were always shopping, for Lizzie was determined to accumulate a respectable wardrobe as quickly as possible.

By the time the sun came glimmering damply through the clouds, she knew she was ready for anything but a full dress ball.

At that point, she realised that Claire had not kept pace. The sum total of her sister's purchases was an umbrella, a pair of half boots, and two pair of woollen stockings.

"This is your Season," said Claire stubbornly. "I shall not need to dress up, since I am not looking for a husband."

Lizzie was dismayed. Her own words came back to her, that Claire was afraid of looking pretty, but she did not voice them. It was time to enlist George's aid. He had promised to assist her in helping and encouraging her sister to overcome her dread of the *beau monde*.

When George and Bertram appeared on their doorstep that afternoon, she blatantly wangled an invitation to drive out with the former.

"I shall not need to hide myself under a rug today," she announced gaily, twirling before them. Her pelisse of cerulean blue lutestring parted to reveal a tantalising glimpse of white jaconet and pale blue flounces. She had practised before a mirror.

She caught a look of dismay, quickly hidden, on Bertram's face as he turned to Claire and saw her still in her shabby, outdated costume. He was all politeness as he begged for the pleasure of her company, but enthusiasm was lacking. With renewed determination, Lizzie allowed George to hand her into his curricle.

"Not the phaeton today?" she enquired.

"I had hoped to have the pleasure of your sister's company today."

"Oh dear, I'm sorry," said Lizzie guiltily, "but I have to

talk to you. I daresay the curricle is better for that, as you will not need to concentrate so hard upon your horses."

"True." His lips twitched. "What is this matter on which you are so eager to consult me that you forced me to offer my services?"

"It is Claire. You saw her. She refuses to buy any new clothes. I am at my wit's end trying to find a way to persuade her without putting her on her guard."

"On her guard?"

"Yes, I cannot think it right to tell her that Bertram means to offer for her lest he should not come up to scratch. Which he may very well not if she does not buy some pretty gowns. He sets great store by such things, I believe."

"What makes you think that Pomeroy means to offer for your sister?" George was no longer in the least amused.

"I heard his sister telling you." Lizzie bit her lip. "I know I ought not to have listened, but I could not help it, honestly."

"And you feel that Claire will like the match?"

"Once she is better acquainted with him, how could she not? He is everything that is gentlemanly. At least, if he is an incorrigible flirt like you, I have not heard it."

"No, he has never been in the petticoat line."

"There is just one thing." Lizzie hesitated, then plucked up courage and rushed on. "Who is Amaryllis?"

"That I am not at liberty to discuss. No, I mean it, Lizzie. This once you will just have to curb your curiosity. Let it suffice that she is no impediment to a match between Pomeroy and your sister."

"Then it would be unconscionable to let a few yards of silk and satin stand in their way. Will you speak to her?"

George mused. "Yes, I think I see a way to approach the matter. You may not like it though, so I do not mean to tell you any more about it."

"You are odious," she said, but returned his grin with a pardonable feeling of smugness.

It was a balmy spring day, the lamb-like side of March in

evidence once more. Daffodils and the ton were both out in force. Lizzie was far more interested in the latter, and she noticed that they were not much less interested in her. They must suppose her to be George's latest flirt, she thought, until a disturbing notion crossed her mind.

Lady Caroline, fount of all wisdom, had also mentioned a staggering string of high-flyers who had lived under his lordship's protection. It was alarmingly possible that those high-nosed matrons and decorous misses thought her a barque of frailty!

Just as she reached that conclusion, George said with satisfaction, "Ah, that is what I was looking for. Courtney!" He hailed a gentleman who was riding alongside a barouche wherein sat a plump middle-aged lady and a slender young one.

The gentleman rode up. "Winterborne, good to see you."

George turned to Lizzie. "Miss Sutton, allow me to present the Honourable Archibald Courtney. Miss Sutton is Sir James's daughter, of Sutton Stables in Oxfordshire."

Sir Archibald bowed. "Happy to make your acquaintance, Miss Sutton. Had a couple of good hunters from Sutton Stables. Beg leave to present you to m'mother and sister."

He signalled to the coachman driving the barouche, who pulled up alongside the curricle. The ladies were introduced, and Miss Courtney fluttered her eyelashes at George.

The press of traffic forced them to drive on after the exchange of a few words. Lizzie looked back and saw Lady Courtney muttering in her daughter's ear. Warning her against George no doubt, she thought, and giggled.

George looked at her indulgently. "How much of that did you follow?" he asked. "My choice of Courtney to present to you, when he was escorting his mother, indicated to those watching that you are a respectable female whom they need not scruple to know. Now the business will go faster."

In the next hour, as they progressed slowly down the park and back again, Lizzie was made known to a bewildering number of strangers of both sexes and all ages. Despite

George's stratagem the ladies tended to view her with a certain suspicion, but the gentlemen were sufficiently admiring to raise her spirits.

"It's amazing what a difference a new gown makes, isn't it?" she said as the curricle swung out of the park onto Oxford Street. "You will speak to Claire soon, will you not?"

A few minutes later they pulled up behind a carrier's cart which stood unattended at the front door of the Suttons' house. A rawboned horse stood patiently between the shafts, head hanging, and in the back was a large object of indeterminate shape, swathed in Holland covers. The front door stood open, and from it issued the hoarse sound of men's voices.

"Ah, they have arrived," said George obscurely.

"What is it? I am sure Claire has not ordered anything so enormous except her new greenhouse. I hope they have not delivered that here instead of to Bumble's Green!"

"I believe you will find it is a little house-warming present."

"From you? What is it? It is certainly not little!"

"From Pomeroy and me. Come and see."

One of the ubiquitous street urchins had appeared to hold the horses. George helped Lizzie down from the carriage, and they went into the house. Two large men were wrestling a chair up the narrow stairway.

She clapped her hands. "Famous! It matches the ones we bought."

"We felt it was unsporting to condemn the two of you to the elegant chairs while we lounged at ease."

"It is very generous of you." Suddenly Lizzie was doubtful. "I don't know if Claire will wish to accept such a handsome gift. I remember she said gloves were unexceptionable, but furniture..."

"You cannot suppose that Pomeroy would lend himself to anything not perfectly proper."

"N—no, I suppose not." She looked at him in indignation as he roared with laughter. "I know that implies that I do not think the same of you. It is true, for I believe you might easily forget propriety if it interfered with generosity."

He took her hand. "Only the fiddling niceties of propriety," he said seriously. "I hope you know your reputation will always be safe with me."

"Oh yes, and thank you so much for the chairs, dear George. Never fear, I shall persuade Claire that would be the height of incivility to refuse them, so in future we shall all be comfortable together."

George took his leave, and Lizzie went to supervise the rearrangement of the back parlour. This took some time as her mind kept wandering.

She was not sure who perplexed her most. The chairs were such a *solid* present. Of course the oddity of such a gift would not deter George if he thought it would be useful, but it seemed an unlikely choice for a confirmed bachelor and womaniser. She would have expected something more frivolous.

And as for Bertram, he must consider himself as good as betrothed to Claire. Furniture was so very domestic.

She was glad when Claire came home to distract her from her reflexions.

= 12 =

GEORGE HAD NO intention of tackling the delicate subject of Claire's shabby and outmoded dress in so public a place as Hyde Park. Another week passed, therefore, before an opportunity arose to speak to her privately.

One afternoon, Lord Pomeroy suggested to Lizzie that he should take her next day to the Royal Academy and Miss Linwood's Exhibition. Lizzie accepted with alacrity.

"I hope you will join us," he said, turning to Claire.

"Thank you, but I must go to Bumble's Green tomorrow. Mrs. Copple writes that the materials for my greenhouse have been delivered, and I must be there to ensure that they build in the right place. There is no need to postpone your outing, though. I shall need Alfie, but Molly can go with Lizzie."

George spoke quickly, before Pomeroy could voice his evident discontent.

"I should like to see your Bumble's Green house. May I drive you there?"

Claire looked at him dubiously. "I shall leave early, there is nothing of interest, and I must be there all day."

"I look forward to learning all about the construction of greenhouses," he said glibly.

"What a rapper!" exclaimed Lizzie.

Claire laughed, but she accepted his offer. "I am willing to condemn you to a day of tedium because the gig from the livery stables is both uncomfortable and exceeding slow," she confessed. "I daresay it will take scarce half as long to get there with you driving, sir."

George noted with some amusement that Pomeroy was looking daggers at him.

"I wager I can do it in a third the time of a hired contraption," the younger man said challengingly.

"But not tomorrow," George pointed out, "since you are engaged to guide Lizzie's artistic education."

"That does not matter," said Lizzie, abandoning art without a second thought. "You ought to have a race. I will go with Bertram and Claire with you, George."

This proposal united the gentlemen.

"Take a female on a curricle race?" Bertram said, horrified. "You must have windmills in your head, Lizzie."

"Would it be so very unladylike?"

"Not merely unladylike but highly dangerous," George explained.

"Oh, then if it is dangerous, you must not race after all. Are you a member of the Four-Horse Club, Bertram?"

"No," he growled.

"A race would not be fair then, for George is. How odd, I had thought you a top sawyer too."

"Pomeroy is most certainly a top sawyer," George assured her. "To my knowledge he has been put up for membership more than once but has refused the honour."

"Why?" asked Lizzie.

Lord Pomeroy looked harassed. "Because I refuse to be seen wearing a waistcoat with inch-wide blue and yellow stripes!" he snapped. "I shall call for you tomorrow at eleven, Miss Elizabeth, if that suits you? Good day, ma'am," he said to Claire, and departed.

"Oh dear," sighed Lizzie, "he is miffed at me, and I do not even understand why."

"Don't take it to heart," advised George. "He simply transferred to you his annoyance with me."

"Why should he be angry with you?" Claire asked in astonishment.

122

George silenced Lizzie with a glance. "Perhaps he doubts his ability to best me in the race we shall not be holding," he suggested.

"I wish I had never said anything about speed!"

"Do not tease yourself, my dear. Men are odd creatures indeed when it comes to a question of sporting prowess. What time do you wish to leave tomorrow, taking into account the superior speed of my curricle?"

Claire smiled and shook her head at him. "Would nine be too early?"

"Not at all, ma'am. You must remember that at heart I am a countryman, not a Town beau. I shall see you at nine."

Lizzie went out to the front hall with him.

"Why did you look at me like that?" she demanded. "I do not believe Bertram is afraid of racing you, so why is he in a tweak?"

"Because I am to spend an entire day with your sister, goosecap. Chaperoned only by Alfie and Mrs.—er—Copple."

"You mean he is jealous? He is not angry with Claire, is he?"

"No harm done if he is," said George calmly, taking his hat, gloves, and whip from the hall table. "A little competition never hurt anyone."

Not that there was any real competition involved, he thought as he drove back to Bellingham House through the busy streets. He could not serve Pomeroy a backhanded turn by stealing another bride from under his nose. If the man only knew it, he was doing him a favour. Pomeroy cared about Claire's appearance. He, George, enjoyed her company whether she was up to her elbows in potting soil or wearing that enchanting hat with the lilacs which Lizzie had forced on her.

The feeling of calm was notably absent when George set out the next morning. In fact, there was a peculiar flutter under his blue-and-yellow striped waistcoat. It might have been caused by something he ate, but he was inclined to put it down to a perfectly natural apprehension at the prospect of taking to task a young lady over whom he had no possible claim to authority. She would have every excuse for taking umbrage, and the last thing he wanted was to be at outs with Claire.

He thought of Lizzie and squared his shoulders.

He was wearing his Four-Horse Club waistcoat, a flamboyant garment best reserved for meetings of the club, for two reasons: it would amuse Lizzie, and break the ice for a discussion of fashion with Claire. Why had he let Lizzie talk him into this? He might have been looking forward to a peaceful day in the country with a pleasant companion. Instead, Claire would withdraw behind her veil of abstracted indifference and likely never trust him again.

Her trust was disturbingly important to him. Perhaps it was best that he should lose it since she was to marry Pomeroy.

Lizzie came down to the entrance hall to tell him that Claire would be with him in a moment. She giggled when she saw the waistcoat.

"It is a bit bright, but nothing truly out of the ordinary. It does not begin to compare with the clothes Horrid Horace wears, or even my brother. Only someone as particular in his dress as Bertram could take exception to it."

"You do not think your sister will swoon at the sight?"

"No, she will probably not even notice. It seems excessively odd to me that Bertram should persist in his suit when she is so utterly uninterested in her appearance. Or his, come to that. You do mean to talk to her about it, do you not?"

"I do, though I cannot say I look forward to it."

"I am vastly obliged to you, dear George. Oh, here she comes. Look, Claire, George is wearing his Four-Horse Club waistcoat."

George turned to watch her coming down the stairs. She moved with unconscious grace, her tall, slender form floating down as if she weighed no more than a feather. The tips of her delicate, competent fingers grazed the bannister, and he shivered as he imagined them caressing his cheek, his back...

She flushed under his gaze and put up a nervous hand to

124

her hair, neatly coiled under the lilac hat. Her gardening clothes were half-hidden by the new Indian shawl. He wanted to assure her that she looked delightfully, but that would not suit his purpose. Either she would be reassured and so take his advice less seriously or, since he had complimented her on those garments before, she would think him mocking.

"Shall we be off? My cattle are champing at their bits."

"I am looking forward to the drive." She pulled on her gloves, kissed Lizzie good-bye, and wished her an enjoyable day. "It will be pleasant just to get out of the city," she continued as they went down the steps, "but I hope also to see for myself your prowess as a whipster. If there is a stretch of road where it may be done safely, will you spring the horses? Is that the correct term?"

"It is, and I will, if you wish it."

He handed her into the curricle, then took the reins from Alfie, who had been holding the horses, and joined her. Alfie hopped up behind, and they were off. George would have preferred to be alone with her, but if he had to have an audience for their coming conversation, a slow-witted lad devoted to his mistress could not be bettered.

"I have never been driven faster than a trot. I think I shall find it exhilarating."

"I never suspected you of sporting proclivities, Claire!"

"I'm afraid you think me a sad stick-in-the-mud."

He smiled down into her wistful grey eyes. "How could I possibly think such a thing of a woman as little bound by convention as you? And no, nor do I think you 'peculiar,' as your mother would have it. I can only wonder at your ability to tread the fine line between disregard for convention and outright impropriety."

"Even Mama never accused me of impropriety."

"Then I have no hesitation in pronouncing you not guilty."

They talked of commonplaces while he negotiated the busy streets of north London, until they passed the village of Islington and joined the Cambridge turnpike. A straight stretch of road lay ahead, devoid of traffic.

"Hold onto your hat!" cried George, and gave his team their heads.

They thundered down the turnpike, the light curricle bounding and swaying over the rough surface. George spared a quick glance at his companion, ready to rein-in if the slightest sign of alarm appeared on her face. She was pink-cheeked and laughing, eyes sparkling with delight. Reluctantly he returned his attention to the horses and checked their speed as the road narrowed and began to wind.

"That was marvellous," gasped Claire, out of breath as if she had been the one galloping. "Oh dear, I held onto my hat but all my hairpins have gone flying, as usual."

"Doubtless Mrs. Copple will have some," he said, clenching his hands to prevent plunging them into the mass of honey-gold silk flowing down her back. The journey was proving more trying than he had expected, and he had not even broached the subject of clothes. "I'm glad you enjoyed it, but a straight road with no obstacles is scarcely a test of driving skills. Which reminds me, you have not yet admired the waistcoat to which Lizzie drew your attention."

She glanced at the garment in question. "It does not seem to me remarkable, except as a testimony of your ability. I do not understand why Lord Pomeroy objects to it."

"As in behaviour, so in dress there is a fine line between the acceptable and the unacceptable, to the fastidious."

"To be sure. I hope I have taught Lizzie to choose what will at once suit her best and satisfy the dictates of fashion."

"Lizzie's new wardrobe is impeccable. It is a pity that you do not follow your own advice." Though he kept his eyes on a farm cart ahead, he sensed her immediate withdrawal. "For your sister's sake, Claire. Since you mean to chaperone her, your dress cannot but reflect on her. You have done so much for her already. Do not fail her in this small matter. Are you so set against it?"

"No." Her voice was uncertain. "I suppose it is just that I

have been told so many times that even in the most beautiful gowns I shall never be anything but plain."

"Your dear mama, I take it." He transferred the reins to his right hand and reached out to raise her lowered face to his. "You are not, ever again, to believe a word Lady Sutton says to you."

"Yes, my lord!" She looked surprised at the anger in his voice, but a glimmer of humour lit her eyes. "Not even that I am guilty of no impropriety?"

"I doubt she ever said anything so approving," he snorted, swinging the curricle past the cart, "merely implied it by lack of criticism on that count. It is not true that you are plain, even in your wretchedest gardening clothes. Nonetheless, I want to see you in a ball gown."

"There is little likelihood of that," she said bitterly. "I confess it had not dawned on me that my appearance must affect Lizzie. In any case it makes little difference. She has told me of your kind efforts to introduce her to your friends, but we have yet to receive a single visitor other than you and Lord Pomeroy, let alone any invitations. I was a fool to suppose myself capable of giving her the Season she deserves when I have no acquaintance in Town."

Aching to take her in his arms and comfort her, he managed to keep his tone light. "Then my efforts are not paying off. I must try something different."

"You must not think I do not appreciate it, but I do not understand why you are going to so much trouble for us."

How could she understand when he did not himself? He turned it to a joke.

"Let's call it an irresistible urge to spike your mother's guns."

A gurgle of laughter rewarded him. He smiled, more than willing to abandon the serious discussion which had landed her in the dismals.

" 'Tis a consummation devoutly to be wished'," she agreed.

"Hamlet, eh? I did not take you for a blue-stocking," he teased.

"Surely that is the sort of quotation everyone knows, and inappropriate besides, since Hamlet is talking of his own death, I believe. I cannot claim to be a blue-stocking, or even well-read, but one cannot spend all one's time in the garden, especially in winter. Books on gardening grow dull after a while."

"Never tell me your mama approves of you reading Shakespeare?"

"Heavens no, but Papa once saw *The Taming of the Shrew* performed, and he takes it as a personal insult if she says anything against the Bard."

The rest of the drive passed pleasantly and quickly in talk of the theatre, Shakespeare, and books in general. When they passed Waltham Abbey, they agreed that on some future, more leisurely, visit to her house, they might stop and inspect the magnificent Norman nave. George was glad to have laid the groundwork for a future outing in her company.

He also enjoyed the rest of the day. He was, as he had told Claire, a countryman at heart, and though he had never paid particular attention to gardens, either kitchen or flower, he found much to interest him.

He was especially glad he had come when a vociferous disagreement arose between the mason and the carpenter, come to put in the foundation and frame of the greenhouse, and the glazier. Glazed was the right word for the expression on Claire's face when the men started shouting at each other in a semicomprehensible Essex dialect. Alfie was putting up his fists, prepared to defend her to the death, when George stepped in. He silenced them with a look, and a few pithy, well-chosen phrases had them scurrying back to work.

Claire still looked shaken. George realised with a rush of tenderness that it was not only her mother's diatribes that overset her. She was sensitive to any display of animosity. He put his arm about her shoulders and led her towards the house.

"Come and sit down for a while. Mrs. Copple shall make

128

you a pot of tea. Those fellows know perfectly well what they should be doing, and I shall go back in a few minutes to make sure they are doing it."

"Thank you, tea does sound good." She was rapidly recovering her composure. "I hope you will join me?"

Claire was not in the least disconcerted at the notion of entertaining a gentleman in the kitchen. Nor was she put out of countenance by Mrs. Copple's tea, which arrived on the table very black, and very sweet, in earthenware mugs. While the housekeeper bustled about preparing their luncheon, they exchanged amused glances as they pretended to sip the treacle-like brew.

George gave up, hoping the woman would not be mortally offended.

"It's all very well for you," Claire whispered. "Gentlemen are not expected to drink tea. I shall have to finish every drop."

He grinned at her. "Be brave," he said. "By the way, I noticed your lad was ready to engage in a bout of fisticuffs just now. Inappropriate for the circumstances, but it might be useful some time if he knows how to handle himself. Should you object if I were to give him a few pointers?"

"Alfie? Do you suppose he could learn?"

"Bruisers are not generally known for their intellects. I spar regularly with Gentleman Jackson, and I'm sure I can teach him a few tricks."

"If you think it wise," she said doubtfully. "I daresay it would be good for him to be able to defend himself, as long as he understands that fights are to be avoided if possible."

"I shall impress that upon him. Well, there is no time like the present, but you must come and tell him to go with me or he will not stir an inch."

"I'll come at once."

"There'll be a bit to eat waiting for you around one, miss," Mrs. Copple promised as they went out.

"Thank you for rescuing me from that tea," Claire said as the door closed behind them.

"I hope that was not a sample of her cooking."

"If so, I shall hire a cook when I move here, or learn to do it myself!"

George nodded, keeping to himself his doubts that this would ever be her home.

After luncheon they left Alfie planting roses in the front garden and went for a walk in the Royal Forest of Epping. On the ancient hornbeams and beeches, strangely twisted after centuries of pollarding, buds were showing spring green, and nesting ducks quacked from the heathland ponds. It was quite different from Oxfordshire, Dorset, or Northumberland, and they found much to discuss. They agreed that walking gave an intimate view of the countryside which was missed on horseback or in a carriage.

By the time they left to drive back to London, George was convinced that Bertram Pomeroy must be touched in the upper works—for he had still not proposed to Claire.

== 13 ==

"MISS LINWOOD'S PICTURES are much more striking than the paintings at the Academy," said Lizzie decidedly.

"You cannot be serious in preferring embroidered copies to the original oils." Bertram's patience was wearing thin, his attention wandering from his horses.

"The colours are more vivid," she argued. "I could almost taste those grapes."

"How typical of a female. You are all Philistines at heart, I vow."

"You only admire the Old Masters because you have been taught to venerate anything ancient and Italian. It is not your own genuine opinion. Oh, look out!"

As they turned from Wardour Street into Oxford Street, a bleating flock of sheep on their way to Smithfield Market milled across the road. Before Bertram noticed their presence, his chestnuts were in their midst. The high-strung pair reared, and the curricle swung wildly to one side. Struggling to control them, from the corner of his horrified eye he saw Lizzie pitched out into the street.

She landed on top of a surprised sheep.

"Miss Lizzie!" shrieked Molly in his ear.

The horses were calmer now, shifting uneasily and rolling their eyes but no longer in a panic. Bertram glanced back at the maid, who was hanging on with grim determination and staring open-mouthed at her mistress.

Undignified but apparently unharmed, Lizzie scrambled to her feet. The sheep followed suit.

"You cow-handed cawker!" she stormed at him.

"Baa!" agreed the sheep and scuttled off.

"Get in," Bertram said, tight-lipped.

He was all too aware that the pedestrians on the pavement had turned from the shop windows to watch the comedy. The shepherd approached, waving his crook and screeching what sounded like Welsh curses, leaving the care of the flock to his black-and-white dogs. Beneath the horses' hooves a sheep with a broken leg struggled to rise.

Lizzie climbed up beside him and saw the injured animal.

"Oh, the poor thing! I must help it," she cried.

"No, you must not. You are going to sit looking unconcerned and twirling your parasol."

"My new parasol!" To his relief, Lizzie was distracted.

"Lawks, miss, them sheep's a-nibbling at it," came Molly's shocked voice. "The dirty beasts! I'll get it." She jumped down, seized the parasol, and whacked one of the animals across the back with it. "Scarper, you nasty creetur," she cried.

Bertram caught Lizzie's eye and she giggled. Unwillingly he grinned.

"Do you know what that nasty creetur said when I fell on it? I could swear it said 'Oof!' "

"What did you expect the poor animal to say? 'I beg your pardon, madam'?" Unable to resist the mischief in her face, he burst out laughing.

The shepherd glared up at him in a fury. Bertram tossed the man a sovereign. The efficient dogs had moved the flock past by now, its place taken by a swarm of gaping, pointing urchins. Molly handed Lizzie her parasol; she opened it and twirled it with a sweet, nonchalant smile.

Bertram urged the chestnuts onwards, fleeing the scene of the disaster.

"Can I stop looking unconcerned now?" hissed Lizzie as they turned up Wimpole Street. "My face is growing stiff."

"Yes, no one here saw me making a mull of it." He drew up at the side of the road and turned to her. "I don't know what to say, Lizzie. You were right to call me cow-handed."

132

"Oh no, for you handled them splendidly after they shied. I daresay they might have slaughtered the whole flock without your firm hand on the reins. Besides, it was my fault for provoking you. My wretched tongue seems to have a mind of its own."

"The fault was entirely mine. You are not hurt, are you?"

She wriggled experimentally and he found himself suddenly short of breath. Averting his eyes, he fixed his gaze on the nearest house, sadly disconcerting the lady descending the front steps.

"My shoulder aches a little," said Lizzie. "That sheep was quite solid, though much softer than the cobbles would have been. It is nothing to signify. I am sure a hot bath will put it to rights."

Bertram blinked and lost his breath again as a vision of Lizzie in her bath arose unbidden before his mind's eye. The disconcerted lady dashed back up the steps in alarm and slammed her front door behind her.

"The sooner I get you home, the better," muttered Bertram.

He drove the remaining four blocks in abstracted silence, and when they reached Portman Square Lizzie looked at him anxiously.

"I believe you are in shock," she said with a motherly air. "You must come in and have a glass of wine."

"I am quite all right," he responded, more brusquely than he had intended.

"Pray do come in," she insisted, "or I shall think you are angry with me for preferring Miss Linwood to Raphael."

"No, how can I be angry with a sincere opinion, even if I disagree with it? Perhaps I *am* in shock," he added with a wry smile, following her into the house. "I cannot recall ever having made such a cake of myself in public."

"Fustian! I was the one made a cake of, and I assure you I do not regard it in the least. Is the Madeira in the front parlour, Enid? Now come and sit down, Bertram, and I will pour you a glass. You see, I do not have your vast self-consequence, so an encounter with a sheep cannot dent it."

She laughed, but her words stung him a little. Then he saw that as she bustled about, taking off her modish pelisse and bonnet, she winced when she moved her left arm. He wanted to tell her to go and have a hot bath at once, but the words stuck in his throat. Instead he urged her into a chair, and handed her the wine she had poured him.

"I think you are more shaken than you will admit," he said roughly.

She looked up at him, her blue eyes huge with some unrecognisable emotion. Her rosy lips parted slightly and he leaned towards her. At that moment the door-knocker sounded.

"I'll see if miss is at 'ome," came Enid's voice.

The door of the parlour was open for propriety's sake, and Bertram shuddered as he listened to the caller's reply.

"Saw Miss Elizabeth drive up with my cousin," came Horace Harrison's confident voice. "Needn't fear that she won't receive us."

He appeared in the doorway, resplendent in mauve and gold, with Amelia trailing behind him, in pink muslin as usual.

"How do, Miss Elizabeth. Servant, coz." He glanced about the room. "Miss Sutton not here?"

Bertram saw Lizzie's instinctive protest at his presumption die as she noted Amelia's unhappy face.

"My sister is not at home," she said with a haughty mien worthy of a duchess. With equal graciousness she turned to Amelia. "I am happy to see you, Miss Harrison. Pray take a seat."

Horace cast a sly glance from his sister to his cousin. "Yes, do, Amy," he urged. "I must be on my way, came to see Miss Sutton, but I daresay Cousin Bertram will see you home right and tight."

Bertram concealed his impotent fury behind a mask of polite acquiescence. He could not bring himself to snub poor Amelia, especially in front of Lizzie. The day had been an unmitigated disaster.

He thought his cup of adversity was full, but it was about

to overflow. New voices were heard in the hall: Claire and George Winterborne laughing together.

"No, I shan't stay," said George.

Horace popped out of the parlour. "Miss Sutton! Well met. Came to call and found you out."

"Or perhaps I shall," said George.

So the wretch fancied himself as Claire's protector! Bertram silently cursed the name of Winterborne.

He sent a glance of appeal to Lizzie, and she shook her head slightly, merriment dancing in her eyes. He hoped that meant that she did not mean to reveal his clumsy driving to his rival. It was inevitable that she should tell her sister, if only to explain her sore shoulder.

Claire was pink-cheeked and gay. She greeted him with apparent pleasure, said a word of welcome to Amelia, and turned to Lizzie.

"Such excitement," she said. "I persuaded Lord Winterborne to spring the horses for a short distance, and we flew like the wind, I vow. He is truly a top sawyer."

"You must try if he will take you out in the high-perch phaeton," advised Lizzie demurely, avoiding Bertram's eyes.

He breathed a sigh of gratitude, knowing she was bursting to tell the tale of their adventure.

"Allow me to take your shawl, Miss Sutton," proposed Horace, his tone ingratiating.

"Thank you, but I believe I shall go upstairs. It has been a long day, and I am a little fatigued."

Since Claire looked anything but tired, Bertram could only applaud this masterly set-down. She was less in need of protection than Winterborne supposed.

He stepped forward, saying in a commanding voice, "We must leave Miss Sutton to her rest, Cousin."

Amelia jumped up as if he had addressed her. "Oh yes, so sorry, another time," she said breathlessly.

With Bertram's large figure towering on one side and George's bearing down on the other, Horace sulkily gave up and made his farewells.

In the bustle of general leave-taking, Bertram managed to whisper to Lizzie, "You will take proper care of that injury, will you not?"

"Of course, but it is nothing." She patted his arm in an oddly soothing gesture of reassurance.

The four visitors went down the steps together, but Bertram and George paused on the pavement and watched Horace and Amelia driven away in Lady Harrison's barouche.

"I don't care for that cousin of yours," said George with a scowl.

"Nor do I."

"Beg pardon." His grin was engaging. "A man ain't responsible for his relatives. It seems to me the best thing we can do is see that Claire and Lizzie get about a bit more, meet more people. I mean to write to my cousin Tilly to come up to Town and introduce them about. Is Lady Caroline expected in London this Season?"

"I believe she means to come later, when the date of the Coronation is fixed. Carfax will have to be here for that, of course. Daresay I could persuade her to come sooner."

"That's the ticket. How did Lizzie like the exhibitions?"

"She preferred the embroidery to the originals."

George roared with laughter. "An honest young lady, unswayed by accepted wisdom, or else she was roasting you."

"I should have laughed. The chit has an unmatched ability to ruffle my feathers." Bertram frowned. "What do you say to that curricle race we were talking of the other day?"

"You're on! Two days hence in the park? Eight o'clock?"

"That sounds all right. We'll meet tomorrow to settle the course? And not a word to the ladies." Bertram saw that Alfie, holding George's horses, was drinking in every word. "Hear that, lad? Not a word to Miss Claire and Miss Lizzie. We don't want them worrying," he added to George.

There was an infuriatingly understanding look in the older man's dark eyes as he nodded agreement.

Bertram wrote to Caroline that night. Though grateful to Winterborne for suggesting it, he was annoyed with himself for not having realised that the support of an established matron was needed to launch Lizzie. He was sure his sister would come if she possibly could. After all, Claire was in some sense already her protégée. He had no idea who George's cousin Tilly was, or whether she would be of any use, but Caroline had all the requisite connexions in the Polite World, and she was popular besides.

He only hoped she would succeed in persuading Claire to dress as befitted her future station. Until he saw her fashionably dressed and taking her place in Society, it was impossible to judge whether she was truly worthy of becoming his wife, and some day a countess.

On the other hand, he could not dismiss a vague uneasiness at the prospect of escorting Lizzie to the elegant entertainments of the ton.

On the morning of the race, veils of mist wafted about the trees of Hyde Park, and the sun was a pale disc in the hazy sky. When Bertram drove his four chestnuts up to the Grosvenor Gate, where they were to start, scores of spectators were already on hand. More arrived, in carriages or on horseback, at every moment. It seemed that half the male population of the town was eager to watch the match between the two notable Corinthians, and most of them had a stake in the outcome.

Bertram knew that everyone assumed he had a wager on with Winterborne. It was not so; the stakes in this contest were more subtle than mere money.

He was soon surrounded by a crowd of friends, offering advice and wishing him luck.

"I've laid a monkey on you, Pomeroy," cried one. "Fail me and I starve till next quarter day!"

"Take it easy 'round those bends," warned another. "Don't want to come a cropper."

"Lobcock!" snorted a third. "You don't need to tell Pomeroy that. Tell you what, if you win I'll give you five thousand for your cattle."

Bertram grinned and shook his head. Leaving the chestnuts in Abel's care, he went over to where Winterborne was talking to Lord Alvanley, who was to act as starter and judge. Lord Alvanley checked that they agreed on the course, then went off to clear a space for the start. George and Bertram shook hands and returned to their curricles.

As he drove up to the starting line, Bertram noticed Alfie standing under a nearby tree. He smiled to himself, wondering whether the lad understood anything of the sense of rivalry that had led to this meeting.

The course they had chosen was a little over two miles long. There were a couple of curves, but the significant difficulties were a right-angled turn down by the Serpentine and a hairpin bend up near the Tyburn turnpike. Bertram had no expectation of coming to grief at either, barring an unexpected flock of sheep, but he knew his opponent for a superb whip and he planned his strategy with care.

He let Winterborne take the lead as they galloped towards the hairpin. Both curricles rounded it safely and started along the long, winding track down to the Serpentine and along its banks. Bertram let the chestnuts have their heads, and they pulled up neck and neck with the other team. George looked over at him and grinned, saluting with his whip. As the right-angled turn approached, Bertram urged on his team, but try as they might they could not pull far enough ahead to take the inside. He had to drop back and let his opponent enter the last straightway ahead of him.

The sun broke through the mist. The chestnuts drew alongside the other curricle, then their noses were level with the opposing team's cruppers, their withers, their necks. Scarce a furlong remained before the finish line.

As they thundered onwards, Bertram glanced ahead. His eye was caught by a solitary female figure in blue, just beyond the main crowd. She was jumping up and down, trying to see the race, oblivious of the two men approaching her.

Bertram let fly the thong of his whip. The lead horses, unused to its sting, lunged forward, crossing the line less than a yard ahead of Winterborne's. Unaware of his victory, Bertram sprang down from the curricle, and forced his way through the cheering spectators. They fell back before the grim look on his face.

Lizzie was backing away from a pair of young bloods, alarm beginning to dawn on her face. Just as Bertram arrived on the scene, one of them grasped her arm.

A moment later he was lying flat on his back, looking surprised and fingering his chin. The second retreated as Bertram turned towards him.

"Terribly sorry...mistake," he muttered. "Beg pardon, ma'am!" Tipping his hat, he helped his companion to his feet and they fled.

"What," asked Bertram ominously, "do you think you are doing here?"

"Well, I could not see very much." The irrepressible chit was *smiling* at him. "But what I did see was vastly exciting. Did you win?"

Bertram looked blank. "I've no idea. I was too concerned at your danger to notice. What the devil do you mean by attending such an event? And on your own!"

"I am not on my own, Bertram. I am not a complete peagoose, you know. I brought Alfie."

"I suppose it was the half-wit who told you about this, against my direct orders. And where was he when you needed him?"

"You know he will not obey any orders except mine and Claire's, and ours he obeys absolutely. I told him to stay under that tree, and look, he is still there."

Alfie was indeed still stationed under his tree, watching them anxiously but not stirring from his post. Bertram realised that half the crowd, the half that was not dickering over wagers won and lost, was staring at them. Fortunately the more tactful gentlemen were restraining their brasher fellows from approaching him while he was engaged with a female.

He prayed that they were far enough distant not to recognise Lizzie.

"I must get you home at once," he said roughly.

To his relief Abel appeared, leading the chestnuts towards them.

"I must tell Alfie he can move," said Lizzie, "or he will stay there all day."

"Tell him he must walk home. Thank you, Abel," he flung at the groom, "you'll be walking home, too."

"Yes, m'lord. Congracherlations, m'lord!"

"I won, did I?" Bertram felt his ire beginning to fade. It did not for a moment diminish his intention of hauling Lizzie over the coals. He bundled her into the curricle and turned his tired team northward. "What do you think would have happened had I not reached you when I did?" he demanded.

"I don't know precisely," she admitted, "but I am very grateful that you came. You have not given me a chance to thank you. It was *splendid* the way you tipped that dreadful man a settler."

"I suppose your brothers are responsible for the boxing cant. It sounds ill on the lips of a respectable female, and any proper young lady would have swooned at the sight of fisticuffs."

"A proper young lady would have swooned on being thrown out of a carriage on top of a sheep," Lizzie retorted indignantly. "There is no pleasing you."

"It would please me if you were in future to avoid sporting occasions intended only for gentlemen."

"Those two rakeshames were not gentlemen! But you are right, I ought not to have been there. I had not realised it would be an exclusively male event."

"You cannot be expected to be up to snuff yet," he said grudgingly. "I am surprised that your sister did not forbid you to go."

She looked guilty. "I did not tell Claire. I suppose I guessed that she would not approve, and I thought it would be all right if I took Alfie."

"That knock-in-the-cradle is a totally inadequate escort!" Bertram exploded again. "I shall advise your sister to dismiss him and hire a competent manservant."

"He does his best," Lizzie said angrily. "He is devoted to us, and he does just what he is told. It is not his fault that he does not always understand. Claire would never dream of dismissing him."

Since Bertram knew this to be true, he glared at her and drove the rest of the way in silence.

When they reached Portland Square, he let her climb down without his assistance. She turned back to him, laying her little hand in its blue kid glove on the side of the curricle and looking up at him earnestly.

"I do thank you for coming to my aid, my lord," she said. "I hope you won."

"Abel says I did," he replied with a grin he could not hide. "You hurry in now before you are missed."

"I'm glad!" she crowed, and pattered up the steps.

He watched until the door opened, then drove homeward feeling baffled. She infuriated and delighted him. Somehow she managed to embroil him in her starts, when all he wanted was a quiet life. How right Caroline had been to propose the older sister not the younger as his bride!

That same day the second post brought a brief note from Caroline, and three days later Bertram paid a morning call on his sister at the Carfax townhouse.

"I was never so astonished in my life as when I received your letter," she greeted him.

"Why? I appreciate your faith in me, but you cannot have supposed that a gentleman could properly introduce a young lady into Society."

"I never thought Lady Sutton would be so tottyheaded as to let the girls go off to London on their own. I have not seen her since that dreadful party. But that is beside the point. You told me you were determined to drop the acquaintance."

"Was I so positive? I recall taking you to task for embroiling me in the situation."

"Don't quibble, Bertram. When you left Oxfordshire you meant to cut the acquaintance. What changed your mind?"

He shrugged. "I don't know. Perhaps curiosity to see how they went on without their abominable mother."

"And?"

"Lizzie is monstrous pretty in her new clothes. She is also as pert as ever, and as apt to fall into scrapes." He described the end of the curricle race.

"There is no mischief in her," said Caroline dismissively, "merely a liveliness proper to her age which will soon find its outlet in dancing till dawn, now that I am here. What of Claire?"

"She rarely retreats behind her shield anymore. She is pleasant and conversable and even witty upon occasion. Her dress, however, is still shockingly shabby and unfashionable. She has not to my knowledge bought a single new gown since they arrived in Town. I do not demand beauty, but I cannot marry a dowd, Caroline, for the sake of the family as much as because it offends my taste."

"That can soon be remedied. Is that all?"

"No, I must be certain that she is capable of behaving properly in Society. The Countess of Tatenhill cannot hide her head in the clouds every time she meets a situation she does not care for."

"I mean to bring her into Society, so you will have the answer to that soon. And if she passes that test you will propose, oh finical brother of mine?"

"Just as soon as Lizzie catches herself a husband," Bertram snorted. "I've no doubt Claire will wish the little wretch to make her home with us until then, and that I will not stomach!"

"Then we must find Lizzie a husband. It is a pity she has no portion."

"I suppose that as her brother-in-law it would be proper for me to provide something. I am more than willing to do it if it will persuade some unfortunate mooncalf to take her. But make no mention of it yet to your gossipmonger friends, for I must be sure first that Claire will suit."

"You are not the most impatient of suitors! You will be

glad to hear that Papa's health is much improved and he is therefore less likely to insist that you wed in haste. He is even thinking of coming up to Town for the Coronation, I collect. Mama writes that he has taken on a new lease of life."

"I am delighted to hear it, for many reasons, one of which is filial piety of course, but the greatest is that I shall not have to attend the Coronation in his place. I understand Prinny means to wear a thirty-foot train of crimson velvet emblazoned with gold stars and a black Spanish hat with white ostrich plumes. For vulgar ostentation our monarch cannot be beat!"

$==$ 14 $==$

CLAIRE WAS FEELING blue-devilled when the first items of her new wardrobe were delivered late one afternoon. A singularly persistent April shower had confined them to the house for most of the day, and their only visitors had been Horace and Amelia Harrison. Neither George nor Bertram had been seen for three days.

Lizzie had penitently confessed to her escapade in Hyde Park. Bertram had called that same afternoon, to make stiffly polite enquiries about her well-being. Lizzie, on her best behaviour, was demure and reticent, and Claire had to bear the burden of the conversation. He did not stay long.

Claire had hoped the quarrel would quickly blow over, as had their earlier altercations. She was sure Bertram had serious intentions towards Lizzie for, unlike George, he was no flirt, and there could be no other reason for his attentiveness to them both. He had not called since then, however. She was beginning to think the whole idea of giving her sister a Season without their mother's help had been an air-dream. Lizzie was philosophical about their failure to obtain a single invitation but Claire saw how sometimes, in the evenings, she would drop her embroidery in her lap and listen wistfully to strains of dance music issuing from one of the nearby houses.

The arrival of the new gowns was at once a welcome diversion and a reminder of George's promise to do something about their lack of acquaintance. She had done her part in ordering modish gowns. Was his mysterious departure from London something to do with his share of the bargain?

"Stop woolgathering, Claire, and come and try them on!" Lizzie pulled her out of her chair and they went up to her chamber.

To her surprise, Claire found that a pretty new gown was a very fair antidote to the megrims. Twirling in front of the mirror in a lavender jaconet morning dress trimmed with green ribbons, she wished George was there to see it. He would surely be pleased, though he had said he wanted to see her in a ball gown. That must wait until he had provided the invitation to the ball.

She was wearing the lavender jaconet next morning when Lady Caroline Carfax came to call. Lizzie was at the window, embroidering bluebells on a white muslin evening gown, when they heard a vehicle pull up in the square.

"It is Bertram, in an excessively smart landau. Claire, he has forgiven me at last. I mean to tease him about his sulks. Oh, who is that? Heavens, it is his sister!"

"Come away from the window. They must not see you peering into the street like a vulgar hussy. I did not know Lady Caroline meant to come to town. Are you sure it is she?"

"Yes. Bertram is knocking now. Oh, where is Enid? Shall I go myself? Suppose he thinks we are out?"

"How glad I am that I bought this gown before Lady Caroline arrived. I would not for the world have her see me dressed like a country bumpkin in Town."

A pattering of feet in the hall was followed by the sound of the front door opening. A moment later Enid burst into the parlour.

"It's 'is lordship, miss, wiv a grand lady. Bang up to the knocker, she is. Are you at 'ome?"

"Yes, yes, Enid, ask them to step in." Claire patted her hair anxiously. Though she had taken to plaiting it before she put it up, it was so fine that hairpins still tended to slip out. Scattered hairpins, she decided, were not so much a symbol of absentmindedness as an inescapable irritation.

She had insisted on buying a couple of caps, to make her look like a dignified chaperone, but the wisps of lace Lizzie had picked out for her did nothing to secure her hair.

Lady Caroline swept in with a rustle of silks. A comprehensive glance took in both girls and the room. Claire saw her raise her eyebrows briefly at her brother before she greeted them with every evidence of delight.

Bertram noted her changed appearance with astonishment swiftly turning to approval.

"You are in looks this morning, Claire," he said, bowing over her hand, too well-bred to comment on her clothes. His eyes strayed towards Lizzie.

"Are your chestnuts quite recovered, Bertram?" queried that damsel innocently. "I fear they must have been exhausted by the race."

"Not at all. Why should you think so?"

"We have not seen you since that day, and now you come in her ladyship's carriage. I suppose you have been confined to your lodgings for want of a team to draw your curricle."

"Lizzie!" warned Claire.

Her sister laughed. "Oh, I am just roasting him. I know very well that he stayed away because he was in a pet with me."

Claire turned to Lady Caroline and tried to distract her with a question about the health of her sons. Her ladyship answered politely, but Claire was certain she was straining her ears to hear the altercation behind them.

"Do those two always carry on like cat and dog?" she asked at last. "I have never known Bertram so easily discomposed. You must not think that he is not generally the most easygoing of gentlemen."

"He has never been anything but perfectly courteous towards me, ma'am. I fear my sister seems to have a certain genius for setting up his back."

"No matter. I daresay it will do him good to be put out of countenance for once. Still, enough is enough. I mean to take the two of you visiting with me, and he will be quite in the way. Bertram! You have served your turn and may take yourself off now."

146

To their surprise, he and Lizzie were grinning at each other. However, it was to Claire he turned with an invitation to drive in the park that afternoon.

"If my dictatorial sister does not tire you," he added solicitously. "I assure you my chestnuts are in fine fettle." The glance he threw at Lizzie was teasing, and she wrinkled her nose at him as he left.

Claire could not summon up more than a token protest at Lady Caroline's offer to make them known to her friends. It was easily overridden, without the least hint that they were in need of help. They hurried upstairs to put on their pelisses, Claire's a new one of green Circassian cloth with lavender embroidery, matching her gown. Adding the lilac-bedecked hat she felt prodigious fashionable, ready to hold her own with the tonnish matrons they were about to meet."

"Do watch your tongue!" she whispered pleadingly to Lizzie.

Skipping down the stairs, her sister nodded in jubilant acquiescence.

"We shall go first to visit a dear friend of mine," said Lady Caroline as they settled in the barouche. "I was at school with Anne, Lady Marchmont as she is now, and we correspond regularly. She is bringing out her eldest daughter this Season, so she will know who else is in Town at present."

Miss Marchmont's daughter was a lively brunette, with whom Lizzie was soon laughing merrily.

"May I hope you will bring your sister to a little party we are having tomorrow, Miss Sutton?" said Lady Marchmont with a fond glance towards the dark head and the gold, bent now over a fashion magazine. "Just an informal dinner and perhaps a few country dances later on. My Nell finds many of her contemporaries somewhat insipid, I fear."

Lady Caroline, looking distinctly complacent, whispered to Claire, "A very good start, my dear. I cannot deny that it is just what I hoped for."

They soon moved on to a round of calls that took them

147

all over the fashionable part of London. To Claire's relief, Lizzie's behaviour was perfectly unexceptionable, even when she found herself on the edge of a group of gossiping matrons with no younger companions present. She answered politely when spoken to and otherwise held her tongue. Two elderly ladies even complimented Claire on her pretty-behaved sister.

Gentlemen, relatives or suitors of the young ladies of the house, were on hand in several drawing-rooms. Lizzie had been introduced to one or two of these by George or Bertram in the park, and they hurried to her side now that she was under Lady Caroline's wing. Claire was amused by her demure composure, which dancing curls and dancing eyes rendered unconsciously flirtatious. She herself was glad to fade into the background, enjoying her sister's success without envying it in the slightest.

Lady Caroline left her card at a few houses where the ladies were not at home. These included Maria Sefton and Emily Cowper.

"They are the two best-natured of the Almack's patronesses," she explained to Claire at a moment when Lizzie was otherwise occupied. "Unfortunately, though we are of course acquainted, I am not on sufficiently intimate terms to ask for favours. I am sorry to say that I may not be able to procure vouchers for the two of you."

"I assure you, ma'am, that we do not aspire so high. Why, we already have five or six invitations, and all due to your kindness. I cannot thank you enough, for I confess I was quite in despair about poor Lizzie's come-out. I don't know how to thank you."

"I'd like to know what the world is coming to if country neighbours cannot lend each other a hand," said Lady Caroline comfortably.

Claire was itching to know whether Lord Pomeroy had anything to do with his sister's unexpected arrival in Town and still more unexpected assistance. If so, it must indicate a serious interest in Lizzie, and Lady Caroline's approval of her as a sister-in-law. She could not ask outright, though, and rack her brains as she might, she could come up with no subtle way of finding out.

Lady Caroline set them down in Portman Square. As they entered the front hall, Mrs. Rumbelow surged up from below, followed by Molly, Enid, and Alfie.

"Well," she demanded, " 'ow did it go then? These silly wenches din't think nuffink of it but I set 'em right. 'Aving lordships call is one thing, and very nice too, and I knows as 'ow it's all 'ighly respectable what wiv Molly playing gooseberry when called for. But 'aving a ladyship visit's summat else again, innit now? *That's* summat to write 'ome about, if you like!"

Claire laughed, and Lizzie skipped up to the housekeeper and kissed her round cheek.

"We've been invited to a dancing party tomorrow night!" she crowed.

They had just time enough for a bite to eat before Bertram arrived to take Claire driving in the park. Lizzie looked up from her embroidery to bid them good-bye.

"We could walk, if you would like to join us," he said to her uncertainly. "That is, if you have no objection, Claire? There is not room in the curricle for three."

"Lud, no, I'd not ask a Corinthian to walk! No, thank you, Bertram, but I must finish these bluebells. We are invited to the Marchmonts' tomorrow," Lizzie informed him with a carefully careless air.

Bertram looked smug, but his voice was equally casual. "The Marchmonts? I know Lord Marchmont slightly."

"Will you be there?" asked Lizzie eagerly. "It would be comfortable to have a friend present, though Miss Marchmont and I are in a way to be intimate already."

Bertram shook his head regretfully. "I have not received an invitation."

Claire was almost certain her suspicions were correct. Only with Lizzie did Bertram lose his stiffness, and Lizzie seemed to like him well enough. It would be a highly gratifying match for the daughter of an obscure country baronet, and with her lack of dowry she would be unlikely to find another as good.

Still, Claire did not mean to count her chickens before they hatched. Though Bertram unbent with Lizzie, it frequently led to quarrels. He might well not come up to scratch.

She enjoyed the drive more than usual. Not only was she conscious of looking her best, but several of the ladies she had met that morning deigned to acknowledge her. Mrs. Rumbelow was right, lordships were all very well in their way yet it took a ladyship to lend countenance to a young miss without the proper connexions.

Bertram's gratification at the greetings of her new acquaintances was evident.

"Might I ask whether you received any other invitations?" he enquired as they left the park. "I know that sounds shockingly impertinent, but I should not like to miss any occasion to which we have both been invited. As Lizzie said, you will be more comfortable with a friend at hand. At least, I hope you, too, regard me as a friend?" He pressed her hand.

Claire murmured a confused assent, and hastily enumerated their invitations.

When she and Lizzie arrived at the Marchmonts' next evening, she had to admit that he was right. Lady Marchmont greeted them kindly, but she was too busy with her score of guests to do more. Lizzie was welcomed rapturously by Miss Marchmont, and the two were soon surrounded by a circle of young gentlemen. Claire exchanged a couple of words with a mother and daughter she recognised, then, at a loss, she took a seat in an inconspicuous corner.

To her dismay, the next arrivals were Lady Harrison, Amelia, and Horace. Horace hurried to her side, dispensing fulsome compliments on her evening gown of sea green sarcenet. She was unable to reciprocate: his purple-and-orange striped waistcoat left her struggling not to laugh.

Claire was taken into dinner by a gentleman of middle years. He told her that had he known that launching a daughter meant doing the pretty to any number of tedious females, the chit might have mouldered at home for all of him. Since he then addressed himself to his food, without another word in her direction, she was given no opportunity to prove that she was not tedious. The only comfort was that his antipathy was clearly anything but personal.

Fortunately the youthful sprig on her right had better manners. Though clearly taken with a pretty young lady on his other side, he nobly did his duty by Claire during alternate courses, and she thought she kept him tolerably amused.

Claire's only pleasure for the rest of the evening was watching Lizzie dance. Horace Harrison joined her as soon as the gentlemen left their port, and did not stir from her side thereafter. He did ask her to dance, but she avoided taking the floor with him by pointing out that she was there strictly as a chaperone. Of course this meant that she had also to refuse the two pleasant-looking older gentlemen who asked her to stand up with them. Horace's presence at her side dissuaded anyone else from attempting conversation.

She was puzzled by his behaviour. She had attributed his frequent visits to Portman Square to his efforts to throw Amelia and Bertram together, but that did not explain his exasperating persistence that evening.

Lizzie's first ball was two days later. Neither she nor Claire had any fears of her being a wallflower, for several of the young men she had met at the Marchmonts' had come to call in the interim. Claire thought she looked utterly delightful in her new gown of lace over blue satin, and when Bertram came to pick them up he gazed at her as if he had never seen her before.

As he helped Claire arrange her shawl over her own new gown of figured silk, he murmured in her ear, "If I didn't know your sister for an imp of mischief I might take her for an angel tonight."

Lady Caroline awaited them in the carriage outside. As they drove through the gas-lit streets of Mayfair, Claire felt a rising sense of anticipation. She had hated every ball she had attended during her own Season, but now Mama was not there to denigrate her looks and her every action. Even if she did not dance herself, she meant to enjoy every moment of Lizzie's success.

"Remember you must not dance with any gentleman more than twice," she reminded her sister as they put off their wraps in the ladies' dressing-room. "If you cannot see me or Lady Caroline, go to Lady Marchmont. And you must not waltz until one of the patronesses of Almack's gives you permission."

"That may be never," Lizzie responded, "but there are so many other dances I do not mean to repine. I am so excited I could die!"

"Don't do that!" Claire kissed her and tidied her golden ringlets. "There, you are bang up to the nines, as Enid would say."

When they reached the ballroom, Bertram quickly put his name down on Lizzie's card for two country dances, before she was swept away by Nell Marchmont and their own group of beaux. He took Claire's card and studied it.

"May I beg the honour of the first waltz and the supper dance?" he requested.

"Oh, but I do not mean to dance, sir. I am here to chaperone Lizzie."

"Gammon," said Lady Caroline roundly. "I certainly mean to dance, though I daresay my poor feet will give out after a waltz or two. Bertram, you are not to disappear into the card-room after dancing with Claire. You must stand up with Cousin Amelia for at least one set, too."

Bertram groaned. "That will only put ideas into Aunt Dorothy's head," he protested.

"It would be excessively unkind in you not to," said his sister with considerable severity. "Claire, persuade this wretch he must do his duty by his cousin. I am going to speak to Mrs. Wrigley." She went off and was absorbed into a circle of chattering matrons.

"Pray do not let me keep you from the card-room, my lord," said Claire shyly.

"You must not let Caroline make you think me a hardened gamester! I mean to dance this evening, even with poor Amelia." He smiled ruefully. "However, between my terror of Aunt Dorothy and Amelia's terror of me, that is not likely to be a scintillating success."

"If Mr. Harrison asks me to dance, I shall have to do so," Claire pointed out. "It is only fair that you should ask Miss Harrison."

"I had not considered it before, but you are right. It is most unjust that a gentleman can choose his partners, while a lady must accept all comers or be thought ill-bred."

"It is possible for the quick-witted to think up plausible excuses, but I am not so ready of tongue, I fear."

"Say rather you are too honest. But I have a way to foil Cousin Horace. We must see that your card is full before he approaches you."

Bertram looked about the ballroom. Claire watched, fascinated, as he caught the eye of a fellow Corinthian and drew him to his side with a slight wave. Somehow, without overt persuasion, he had his friend begging to sign her card in no time. She graciously allowed him to engage her for the first dance, a quadrille.

"How did you do that?" she whispered to Bertram, as Mr. Ferguson cast a hunted glance at the door to the card-room.

"The art of the diplomat," he whispered, grinning. "I did learn the odd trick from my stint with the Foreign Office. Ah, Fergie, this is your dance."

Mr. Ferguson, a wiry gentleman in his late twenties, had only the sketchiest idea of the figures of the quadrille. Rather than suffer his bumbling, Claire hissed instructions at him at every turn, and they made it through without any major disasters.

"By jove, ma'am," he said, wiping his forehead, "if I always had a partner to coach me like that, I'd take to the floor more often. Always been afraid to make a cake of myself, don't you know. Have you any more dances free?"

She wrote him down for a simple country dance, then smiled as she watched him bolt for the card-room. She was looking around for Lizzie and Lady Caroline when Bertram came up.

"Sorry about that," he apologised. "I didn't realise Fergie was such a duffer on the dance floor. You are something of a miracle worker, Miss Sutton, to steer him through."

"I hope you too are a miracle worker." The successful outcome of the quadrille had boosted Claire's self-confidence. "I did not dare confess it when you asked me, but I have never actually danced the waltz. It was much frowned upon when I made my debut. I do know the steps," she hastened to assure him.

"We shall brush through," he promised, and led her out onto the floor.

As she might have guessed, considering his athleticism and his polished manners, Bertram was a superb dancer. Following his firm lead, she whirled about the room with never a hesitation.

The music drew to a close. Sweeping a curtsey to his bow, she smiled up at him as she fanned her hot cheeks.

"I never knew a dance could be so enjoyable," she said, slightly breathless from the exertion. "Thank you, my lord."

"Thank *you*, Miss Sutton." His blue eyes held an arrested look. "I have seldom had so light-footed a partner."

"I forgot that you must have waltzed with the ladies of Vienna," she said, suddenly shy. "A mere Englishwoman cannot hope to compare."

He laughed. "It is true that my duties at the Congress consisted largely of attending balls and fêtes, but one chose one's partner by nationality and likely knowledge of the current intrigue. Dartford, fetch Miss Sutton some lemonade, there's a good chap."

The gentleman he addressed, tall and lean, smiled and shook his head.

"Not until you have presented me to her, and I have persuaded her to grant me a dance."

His companion seconded his request, and soon both were inscribed upon Claire's card. It seemed that Mr. Ferguson had boasted of his quadrille, praising her to the skies, and mentioning also that she was connected with the Sutton Stables. Many of the gentlemen had bought hunters from her father. Once they had seen her waltz with Lord Pomeroy, her success was assured.

She was not so sought after as to be able to avoid Horace altogether, but she stood up with him for a country dance where they were apart more often than together. Lizzie and Bertram joined the same set. To Claire's relief, her sister remembered to address him as "my lord," and managed not to provoke him. Among the other youthful dancers, most of whom seemed to be either timid or coy, Lizzie's unselfconscious sparkle made her stand out, thought Claire fondly.

She was very tired by the time they reached home in the early hours of the morning. Her last thought before she fell asleep was of Bertram's kindness in ensuring that she, as well as Lizzie, should enjoy the ball. But it was with George that she waltzed in her dreams.

The house on Portman Square was besieged next day, by both Lizzie's youthful admirers and Bertram's older Corinthian friends. At times their little parlour was full to overflowing. Lady Caroline was there to lend Claire countenance, which she was particularly grateful for as Lizzie had dashed off to the Marchmonts' to discuss the ball with Nell. Even though few of the visitors stayed longer than the polite fifteen minutes, their coming and going lasted until midafteroon.

At last only Lady Caroline, Horace, and Amelia remained. "I must be off," said her ladyship apologetically to Claire. "I have an appointment with my dressmaker, who is an absolute tyrant. Amelia, do you care to go with me?"

If she meant to deliver Claire from the Harrisons, her effort was doomed to failure. Amelia cast a timid glance at her brother and still more timidly rejected the invitation.

"M'sister is hoping for a comfortable coze with Miss Sutton," explained Horace jovially. "Wants to chatter about the ball, I wager. Of course I shall stay to see her safe home."

Lady Caroline shrugged and took her leave.

Claire's skepticism about the silent Amelia's desire to discuss the ball was borne out when she retreated to a corner. Horace promptly dropped to his knees at Claire's feet and seized her hand.

"Must know I hold you in the greatest esteem, Miss Sutton," he announced. "Beg you will do me the honour to become my wife."

"Oh dear, Mr. Harrison," Claire heard herself babbling as she strove to withdraw her hand, "this is very sudden."

"Not at all. Been meaning to offer ever since Cousin Caroline mentioned your for—that is, since she introduced us. Love at first sight, and all that nonsense."

Claire succeeded in reclaiming her hand, stood up, and moved to the window. She tried to think of words that would, without trading insult for insult, make absolutely certain that he never repeated his proposal.

Bertram's curricle was outside, and a moment later Enid announced, "Lord Pomeroy, miss."

"What the devil are you doing on the floor, Horace?" enquired his lordship languidly. "Lost something? I daresay Miss Sutton will not mind if you continue to search while she goes to the park with me."

Red-faced and spluttering, Horace scrambled to his feet.

"No, no, it's nothing to signify," he muttered, trying in an irritated way to smooth the sagging knees of his mustard-yellow inexpressibles.

Suppressing a half-hysterical giggle, Claire hoped that at least he would be deterred from making a second offer by the damage to his nether garments.

"I'll fetch my parasol," she said gratefully. "Pray excuse me, Miss Harrison, a long-standing engagement."

As she hurried out of the room, Bertram winked at her. He was really quite human when one came to know him better, she thought.

She heard Horace's petulant voice behind her. "Amelia and I will walk with you, though I really ought to go home to change."

She continued upstairs to her chamber, secure in the knowledge that Bertram was more than capable of nipping his cousin's plans in the bud. Nor, with his exquisite courtesy, would he ever put her to the blush by referring to what had all too obviously been a proposal of marriage.

He had saved her from having to reply, but Horace would surely try again if he was after her fortune. She wished she could consult George on the best way to deter an unwanted suitor. She had not seen him for a whole week, and she missed him more than she cared to admit to herself.

She found her parasol, bonnet, shawl, and gloves, then paused to study her face in the mirror. The most beautiful girls only attracted George's passing fancy, and she was too old and too plain to aspire even to that brief happiness. She had dared to count him a friend, but he had been gone for a week, without a word. Had the gazetted flirt moved on to greener pastures?

=== 15 ===

"I AM NOT yet in my dotage," snapped Mrs. Tilliot. "Really, George, I have no need of a footstool, let alone another cushion."

"No, love, but you are cross as a bear with a sore head, so I know you are tired from the journey. Sometimes I cannot help wishing my ancestors had chosen to settle a little nearer London."

"Bah, four days on the road is nothing nowadays. I remember the first time I went from here to Bellingham with your parents. A good week's travel it was, and none of these newfangled springs on the carriage. Now, I can see you are itching to be off. I mean to retire early, so I shall see you at breakfast."

"Yes, ma'am." George saluted his elderly cousin with a warm kiss on her wrinkled cheek and went out, calling for his hat and gloves.

It was a balmy April evening, and he was brimming with energy despite the journey to Northumberland and back. He decided to walk to Portman Square. He had been gone for nine days; another quarter hour was neither here nor there.

Besides, it would take longer to have his curricle brought 'round.

When he reached the Suttons' house he was disappointed to see that no light showed in the parlour window. Surely it was too early for them to have retired. But of course, they would be in the back parlour, in those comfortable chairs he had persuaded Pomeroy to purchase with him. From one gentleman the gift must have appeared too particular. From two, it was odd but acceptable.

Strictly speaking, it was not proper for a single gentleman to call on single ladies in the evening. George had not done it before. To hell with propriety, he thought. He could not wait until tomorrow. He knocked.

No response. He knocked again.

The area door, down the steps to his right, opened and he heard Molly's soft country voice.

"There, I told you as it were our knocker. Go on, Enid, hurry up. She's just a-comin', sir."

Moments later the front door opened on a flurried maid, still adjusting her cap.

Beg pardon, sir. We wasn't expecting no one. Oh, 'tis your lordship! The misses is out. Gone to a grand ball, they 'ave. Second one this week.

So Bertram had summoned Lady Caroline and she was already at work, successfully. It was the only explanation. Feeling deflated, he cursed the ancestor who had planted the family's roots at the northernmost end of the kingdom.

"Do you know where they went?" he asked Enid.

"France... Spain... lessee... ah, 'Olland, it were. Lady 'Olland's dress ball."

"Kensington," groaned George. On the far side of Hyde Park and Kensington Gardens, and he was on foot. "Thank you, Enid," he said dispiritedly, and plodded off to find a hackney.

He had no idea whether he had been invited to the ball, but experience told him that whatever his reputation, no gentleman so eligible was in the least likely to be refused admittance. Such proved to be the case. The receiving line had already broken up, but a footman ushered him into the ballroom. He looked around for his host or hostess, to announce his presence, and spotted the youthful heir to the barony. The Honourable Henry Fox, down from the university for his mother's ball, was hovering close to a familiar figure: Lizzie, a vision in white crape embroidered with forget-me-nots.

He made his way to her side.

"Geo—Lord Winterborne! What a pleasant surprise! Are you a Whig? Mr. Fox has been telling me about his mama's celebrated political salon. Do you know Miss Marchmont?" She turned to the dark young lady sitting beside her. "We are the greatest friends."

"Chatterbox," said George, smiling at her. He bowed to Miss Marchmont, who fluttered her eyelashes at him with an experimental air. "I hope you have reserved a dance for me, Miss Elizabeth."

"Why no, for I did not know you would be here. But Mr. Fox has two. Perhaps he will give up one if you ask him nicely."

Mr. Fox stammered his willingness, overwhelmed at the attention from so notable a Corinthian. Then he stammered again as he tried to explain to Lizzie that he did not mean to suggest that he was happy to surrender the pleasure of dancing with her. George admired the way she extricated the lad from his involved explanation. He took her dance card.

"All your waltzes are free," he pointed out.

"I have not yet been given permission to waltz," she said sadly. "Claire does, though, so you must ask her. Here she comes. She was afraid you must be ill, when you were gone so long."

As George turned, a flood of warmth swept from his middle to the tips of every finger and toe and up to the top of his head. Claire had worried about him, his heart sang. He had not meant to distress her, had not thought to warn her that he was going out of town. For too long no one had cared about his comings and goings.

She was on Pomeroy's arm. He drew in his breath when he saw her, noting the dawning joy in her grey eyes, the smile that curved those delicate lips, the gleam of candlelight in her hair. She had never looked lovelier. Belatedly

he realised that she was also elegant, clad in flowing amethyst silk. He had always known that concealed beneath
the shapeless brown wool was a delectably slender figure.

"I always knew that you were beautiful," he murmured,
pressing her fingers to his lips, wishing her glove and her
companion to the devil.

Pomeroy glared at him as they exchanged polite greetings. George wondered what his face had revealed.

He waltzed with her, and she was light as a feather in his
arms. It passed in a dream, over before he had time to sa-
vour it. He watched her dance with other men, delighting
in her poise and grace even as he longed to challenge them.
Then he led Lizzie into a country dance, and she brought
him back to earth.

"Doesn't Claire look pretty tonight?" she asked. "I don't
know what you said to her about her clothes, but it worked.
I believe Bertram will come up to scratch after all."

She sounded wistful. George thought she must be wondering what she would do when her sister was married to
a man she was for ever at odds with. She must be wed by
then, and if none of the young sprigs had the wit to see
what a prize she was, then he would offer himself. He
would be able to watch over Claire then; he'd have some
right to intervene if Pomeroy did not treat her well.

George clenched his fists in helpless anger, to the alarm
of the demure miss with whom he linked his arm at that
moment. He did not believe Pomeroy appreciated Claire's
worth. He wanted a pleasant, peaceable wife, and that was
what he would get. Yet Claire was so much more.

George could not wish his brother's happiness undone,
but he could wish that Amaryllis Hartwell was not its cause.
It would be the act of a scoundrel to steal a second bride
from the unfortunate Lord Pomeroy.

Not wanting to draw the tattlemongers' attention to the
Misses Sutton, he stood up for a few dances with other
young ladies before he set out to walk back to Bellingham
House. Though tired by now, he was restless, his feelings

confused. It was not as if he was in love with Claire, after all, or he would scarce consider marrying her sister. He was physically attracted to her, and he had wanted to shield her ever since he carried her home to be met by her scolding mother. He enjoyed her company, respected her competence in her chosen field, and admired her successful protection of Lizzie. Anything else could be put down to the fact that she was the first available female he had met since changing his views on marriage. He clearly recalled his words to Amaryllis when she had asked why he was still a bachelor.

"With my brother's example before me," he had said, "I could not screw my courage to the sticking point. Now if you were to provide a pattern-card of domestic felicity, I might change my mind and stick my head into parson's mousetrap after all."

He had hinted the same to his father. He was ready to take a wife, and Claire fulfilled all the requirements. That was all there was to it. Doubtless once he started to look about him, he would find a dozen other suitable young ladies.

By the time he reached home he had persuaded himself that he was happy to have two charming friends in Claire and Lizzie. He would do his best to smooth their lives until they married, and then he would find himself a bride and settle down to produce an heir.

Mrs. Tilliot looked fit and spry as ever when he joined her at the breakfast table next morning.

"Did you see your Misses Sutton last night?" she asked as he kissed her cheek in his customary greeting.

"Yes, after walking over half London in search of them." He loaded his plate with eggs, kidneys, ham, sausage and sat down beside her as a footman brought in fresh toast. "They are less in need of your assistance than I supposed." He explained that Lady Caroline Carfax had already achieved their introduction to the ton.

"Caroline Carfax? Ah yes, Tatenhill's daughter. A ninnyhammer but a good-hearted girl."

"You know her?"

"You must remember, George, that poor Tilliot and I lived in London, and afterwards I spent every Season here with your parents. I knew Lady Tatenhill before her marriage, though her maiden name escapes me. Always shockingly high in the instep. So Caroline Pomeroy has done our work for us, eh?"

"So it seems, except that something Lizzie said makes me think they have no hopes of vouchers for Almack's."

"No? Then I shall have a word with Sally Fane."

"Lady Jersey? You know Silence too? You astonish me, Tillie."

Mrs. Tilliot snorted with laughter. "She always was a talkative creature, even as a small child. Yes, your dear mother and I knew little Sally's mama intimately. Ann Fane's father was a banker, you know, Robert Child. The poor dear had a difficult time of it, Countess of Westmorland though she became, until the Marchioness of Bellingham took her up. Ann inherited the bank, and her daughter owns it now, I collect, for all she's so set against the taint of trade. Explains her being such a high stickler, I daresay, that and her Gretna marriage. I've no doubt Sally... what's her name now?... will be happy to do me a small favour."

"Lady Jersey. Now I come to think of it, Jersey breeds his own hunters in Oxfordshire. He must know Sir James Sutton well, I imagine. I shall take you to call on her this morning."

"Lud, no. I am too old to be running all over Town paying visits. You shall go this morning and fetch your Misses Sutton to me, and while you are gone I shall make a list of people to invite to my at-home. It is by far the easiest way to advertise my arrival, and it will serve as a formal introduction for your Misses Sutton. None of your scrambling modern manners."

"Yes, ma'am," said George obediently, "but I beg you will not refer to them as my Misses Sutton. It makes me feel like an Eastern potentate with a harem."

"Not too far from the truth, if there is anything in the rumours by the time they reach Northumberland."

"Tillie, I am shocked! Besides, I have given up the muslin company since Daniel found himself a respectable match."

"No wonder you are so fidgety then. Go out and find yourself a high-flyer, boy."

George put his hands over his ears, grinning. "Scrambling modern manners and niminy-piminy modern tongues."

"Oh, be off with you!" ordered his cousin.

The Hollands' ball had not seemed the place to explain his absence to the Suttons. As he knocked on the door of the house in Portman Square, he decided not to tell Claire his reason immediately but to wait and see if she asked. He was in no way accountable to her. Besides, he did not want her to feel herself under an obligation because he had gone all that way just to do her a favour.

If she did not ask, Lizzie was bound to.

Claire was alone in the front parlour. She glanced up from her book as Enid announced, "It's 'is lordship, miss."

"George!" She smiled and held out her hand. "Come and sit down. Enid, send Molly down, if you please."

"Is Lizzie still abed?" he asked, his disobedient heart jumping as he took her hand in his. No gloves this morning. Her fingers burned him.

"On the contrary, she has already left for the Marchmonts'. There is more room for her admirers in their drawing-room."

Her soft laugh tore at his self-control. He wanted to cradle her in his arms, brush his lips across hers, teach her the meaning of passion. Molly came in. He sat down.

Tillie was right: he must find himself a ladybird.

"So Lizzie has collected a multitude of beaux, has she?" He forced his voice to display casual interest. He was not used to dissembling.

"Yes, but they are almost all boys, and half of them she shares with Nell Marchmont. There is little hope of marriage. Still, she is enjoying herself excessively."

"I am glad Lady Caroline has been so successful. I needn't

have gone all way to Northumberland." The words escaped him, half against his will.

"Is that where you were? What has your journey to do with Lady Caroline?"

"I went to fetch my Cousin Tillie, hoping that she might help you introduce Lizzie to the ton."

"Then it *was* a plot! I suspected it, but I did not like to ask Bertram. Was it your idea?"

"Yes." He tried to sound modest. "But Pomeroy's execution was better. He beat me in the curricle race, too."

"By a few feet. And Oxfordshire is closer by two hundred miles. It was your idea, and that is what counts."

"You are kind to say so, but you must allow Bertram credit for adopting my idea when he must have wished me at the devil for coming up with it first. On the other hand, Tillie vows she can obtain vouchers for Almack's for you."

"George! Lizzie will be *aux anges!*"

"And you?"

"It will be interesting to see what it's like."

"I somehow doubted that you would be overwhelmed at the honour," he said drily. "You must not tell Lizzie until it is certain. Will you come and meet Tillie now? I have strict orders not to return without you."

"I am expecting callers," she said with a doubtful frown.

Though he would have preferred to smooth away the wrinkles with his fingertips, he limited himself to words. "Unless you have promised to be at home, you need not let that concern you. You must learn that nothing increases interest like occasional unavailability."

"I find I enjoy entertaining visitors," she confided, "even though most of the gentlemen talk of nothing but horses. But I should like to meet your cousin, and I have no definite engagement until Bertram comes at four to take me to the park. Most people have left by then, you see, except Horace Harrison, who *will* stay on and on. Bertram protects me from his importunities. I daresay he feels in some sort responsible since Mr. Harrison is his cousin. I shan't keep you waiting above a minute."

She hurried from the room before George could demand details of Harrison's importunities. By the time she returned, he had recollected that it was none of his affair.

Mrs. Tilliot was favourably impressed by Miss Sutton.

"A delightful girl," she told George later. "I can't say I didn't have misgivings. However, it's clear she's not one of your lightskirts, and even if she had proved as vulgar as I feared I'd have done my best to establish her, for your sake. She confessed that her sister is a trifle outspoken, but I ain't mealymouthed myself. I don't pretend to know what you are about, but I like the girl and I'll do what I can for the two of them."

George was left speechless.

For his own peace of mind, he deliberately avoided Claire during the following week. It was not easy, for she spent a great deal of time at Bellingham House, helping Tillie prepare for her party. After losing the caterer's estimate, Lizzie was dismissed from this task, so he took it upon himself to keep a fatherly eye on her while her sister was occupied.

He was therefore extremely annoyed when, in the middle of the at-home, Lady Caroline took him aside to berate him.

"I don't know what you mean by giving a party in Claire's honour," she hissed. "It looks most particular! I warned you that Bertram means to offer for her."

"You are mistaken, ma'am," he responded coldly. "My aunt is giving the party to introduce Lizzie to her friends. If your brother chooses to interpret it otherwise, then perhaps a hint of competition will make him appreciate Claire better."

She flushed. "Just because he is not demonstrative, you must not suppose that he does not hold her in affection." Glaring at him, she flounced off.

As well be hanged for the deed as the appearance, he thought, and went to look for Claire. He grinned when he found her surrounded by fellow Corinthians, friends whom he had invited this evening but whom Bertram had originally presented to her in his absence. There was more competition here than Bertram had bargained for.

Claire smiled at him, but he decided against breaking into her circle. Instead he went to find Lady Jersey. The handsome, malicious leader of the ton was of an age with him, and she always enjoyed flirting with an attractive gentleman. Though it would be improper for him to request vouchers for the Suttons, there was no harm in turning her up sweet before Tillie approached her.

As duly noted in the *Morning Post*, on Wednesday, 25th April, 1821, Miss Sutton and Miss Elizabeth Sutton made their first appearance at Almack's escorted by Mrs. Tilliot and George, Lord Winterborne. His lordship had had too many flirts in his time for the latest to be worthy of a mention in the gossip column on the next page. Besides, it was filled with the names of those who, having unwisely visited Queen Caroline, had been crossed off Carlton House's guest list. Prinny, it was said, had taken to his bed at the news that his wife was still insisting on being crowned at his side.

George tossed the paper aside. He had derived much amusement from the evening.

There was Lizzie's *sotto voce* indignation when she found that this mecca of the Fashionable World was decorated without distinction and served an inferior supper. It had not prevented her jubilation when Sally Jersey, with a slyly inquisitive glance, presented George to her as a partner for the waltz.

There was Horace Harrison's vexed wail, "But they are *shockingly* outmoded," when he was turned away at the door for wearing turquoise trousers instead of the *de rigueur* knee-breeches.

There was Mrs. Drummond Burrell's horrified face when Tillie informed her that modern Society was utterly lacking in all the social graces.

Best of all, there was Pomeroy's annoyance that George, not he, had been instrumental in obtaining their admittance.

Matters came to a head between them towards the end

of May. George was on edge, increasingly disturbed by Pomeroy's slowness in declaring himself. Since he had maintained his self-imposed distance from Claire, never dancing with her more than once and escorting Lizzie more often, he failed to see why Pomeroy should be equally touchy. Be that as it may, when Gentleman Jackson paired them in a bout of fisticuffs in his saloon, they both waded in with uninhibited fervour.

They were equally matched. George had a slight advantage in height and reach, Bertram had comparative youth on his side. George emerged with sore knuckles and a sore face, satisfied that his final uppercut had left Bertram with a sorer jaw, though he'd not feel it till he awoke. He was annoyed with himself, though, for indulging in such a juvenile display of rivalry. Brushing aside congratulations and declining first aid, he summoned a hackney, since he had walked to Bond Street, and went home.

As he stepped into the imposing front hall of Bellingham House, Lizzie emerged from the drawing-room, looking back over her shoulder.

"Then we shall see you this evening, Mrs. Tilliot," she said, then turned her head and shrieked, "George! You've been in a carriage accident!"

She ran to his side, tenderly took his arm, and peered up into his face as Claire and Tillie followed her into the hall. The butler, two footmen, and three maids appeared from nowhere.

Claire hurried to George's other side and, ignoring his expostulations that he was perfectly all right, they led him to the drawing-room. On the way, they passed a large mirror, and he caught a glimpse of what all the fuss was about. His lower lip was split and swollen to the size of a damson, traces of blood from a nosebleed stained his upper lip, while his right eye was half closed, surrounded by a blotch of angry red which already showed signs of purpling.

His ribs began to ache as Claire and Lizzie deposited him on a sofa. Tillie took her first good look at him, moaned, and sank back on another sofa with her eyes shut.

Claire promptly abandoned him in favour of succouring the old lady. At that moment the butler appeared with a bottle of brandy.

"Jarvis, tell Mrs. Tilliot's maid to bring her sal volatile," ordered Claire.

To George's disgust, the brandy bottle disappeared again with the butler. However, a moment later it reappeared, clutched in the fist of a footman who bore in his other hand a plate with a slice of raw beefsteak on it. He was grinning. Slade, the valet, followed him with a bowl of warm water, clean white cloths, and a pot of salve.

"Your nose is bleeding again," announced Lizzie. "You are too big for that sofa. Lie down on the floor, flat on your back. Where's Jarvis? We need his keys to put down the back of your neck."

"I cannot drink the brandy if I am flat on my back," George mumbled through his swollen mouth, but Slade was on Lizzie's side, and he found himself examining the ornate plasterwork of the ceiling through the one eye now available to him. The beefsteak descended on the other eye.

Lizzie's blonde curls eclipsed the ceiling as she gently wiped his face with a warm, wet cloth.

"What happened?" she asked.

He gasped as Slade pressed a cold, wet cloth to his nose.

"Duthig," he muttered irritably. "It was odly a fredly batch."

"Best wait till his nose stops bleeding, miss," advised Slade. "Ah, Mr. Jarvis, may we borrow your keys?"

"Mrs. Tilliot's maid says she has no sal volatile, miss," the butler reported to Claire as an icy, jagged bunch of keys was forced down the back of George's neck.

Somehow he managed to turn his head a little to look suspiciously at his cousin. She threw him a large wink.

"Hartshorn, then, or whatever she uses," said Claire impatiently, chafing Tillie's hand.

"She tells me she don't have any remedies because her mistress never faints, it seems, miss. Might I suggest a drop of brandy?"

"An excellent idea," said George, scattering nurses, cloths, and beef as he surged to his feet. The keys slid down inside his shirt. "Thank you, Lizzie, thank you, Slade, I shall be much the better for a glass of brandy. Ouch!" The keys stabbed him in the back as he flung himself into a chair. He jumped to his feet again. "Slade, get these damn things out of my clothes."

"You had best see a doctor," said Lizzie anxiously, averting her eyes as the harrassed valet pulled the tail of his master's shirt out of his pantaloons. "I believe you are delirious. Do sit down and try to tell us what happened."

Claire, her arm solicitously about Tillie's shoulders, holding a glass of brandy to her lips, glanced at him. "Yes, do, George," she said. "You have frightened poor Mrs. Tilliot into a spasm, and I don't believe there is anything seriously wrong with you."

He tried to grin at her, unaware of the frightful grimace that crossed his battered face. "You have more sense than all the rest put together," he said approvingly. "It was just a boxing match at Gentleman Jackson's, a friendly meeting."

"If that was a friendly meeting I should hate to see the results of an unfriendly meeting," said Claire with asperity. "May I ask whom you met?"

"Lord Pomeroy."

"Bertram did that to you?" blurted Lizzie, aghast. "The horrid brute. I shall never speak to him again."

"You can come down off your high ropes, Lizzie. I tipped him a settler."

"I collect that means you rendered him unconscious. Gentlemen have incomprehensible notions of enjoyment." Claire paused as an abigail entered bearing a purple ostrich plume and a tinderbox. "Burnt feathers, the very thing! I see we are no longer needed here. I hope you will be well enough to join us this evening, ma'am. Come, Lizzie."

One-eyed, George watched her haughty departure. At the last moment she turned to him and said, "As for you, my lord, unless you mean to sport that face about Town, you had best rusticate for a while."

He could only hope he was right in thinking he saw a glint of amusement in her eyes.

"Not my best hat!" wailed Tillie. "Go and sew it back on again this minute, you silly girl."

"Whatever possessed you to sham a swoon?" George asked her.

"I don't know," she said airily. "At the time it seemed the right thing to do."

"I suppose as far as I am concerned the right thing—indeed the only thing—to do is take Claire's advice and rusticate."

The next morning he left for Dorset.

The countryside was very different from Northumberland's grandeur, with gentle chalk hills and wooded valleys. The Winterbornes had originated here, before Edward I sent them north to guard the border. Since 1300 the estate had been the residence of the eldest son, and George had lived there with his parents before his grandfather's death. It had been his since he reached his majority. He had introduced modern farming methods and built a new wing on the fifteenth-century manor, and now it was waiting to become a family home again.

He had not touched the old, formal gardens. The old-fashioned, sweet scented roses grew well here. He must send to the Vineyard Nursery for some bushes of *Clair de Lune*. Claire would tell him where best to plant them, laying out new flowerbeds and arbours.

Except that Claire would never see his gardens.

Everywhere he turned that first day he saw her face, heard her soft voice, longed to consult her on this small matter and that. He drank himself to sleep, and thereafter banished her from his mind with hard work on the estate all day and brandy in the evenings. He stayed two weeks, until every trace of the damage to his face had healed. Then he set out for Essex.

He passed through London, arriving late one evening, leaving early the next morning, seeing no one but Tillie.

His brother was glad to have his support for the ten days before his wedding. Their father came two days early. A long, wordless embrace ended the estrangement between the two, bringing unashamed tears to George's eyes. The next day their sister Mary and her husband arrived, and Tillie.

Amaryllis was stunningly beautiful as she walked down the aisle on Lord Bellingham's arm, in white satin with her copper hair gleaming through her veil. Standing with the bridegroom at the altar, George was not in the least surprised that Danny could not take his eyes off her. He doubted his brother heard a word of the Reverend Raeburn's short homily, devoted as it was to the joys of marriage (the vicar had recently married Amaryllis's former governess).

Yes, his new sister-in-law was beautiful. Perhaps it was understandable that Bertram Pomeroy, still dazzled by the memory of the woman he had been betrothed to for eight years, was slow to appreciate Claire's more subtle loveliness.

He would give him one more month, he decided. It was mid-June; the Coronation was set for the nineteenth of July; if Claire was still free on the twentieth he would offer her his hand and his heart, and be damned to altruism!

=== 16 ===

"IT'S MISS SUTTON'S man, my lord. Says he was told to take the basket to you, and he won't give it over."

Bertram groaned and opened his eyes. It was late morning on the day after the fight, but he still felt fragile. He moved his jaw with experimental caution and winced.

"Wha' say?" he asked Pinkerton through half-closed lips.

The valet repeated his announcement.

"Co' i'."

Correctly interpreting this as permission to admit Alfie, Pinkerton disappeared. Though Bertram had not the least desire to see him, he knew all too well that the boy's primary virtues were obedience and persistence. If put out, he would doubtless haunt the doorstep until he delivered his burden into the correct hands, and meanwhile Claire and Lizzie would be without his services.

Alfie trotted in and deposited a rush basket on the bed beside him. "I brung this, Mr. Lord," he said unnecessarily, beaming. "For you."

Bertram nodded thanks and dismissal, then wished he hadn't, as hammers started pounding behind his eyes. As he closed them again he saw his efficient servant lead the visitor gently from his chamber.

Pinkerton's soft footsteps returned, and he felt the weight of the basket removed.

"Wai'," he said. "Wha' is i'?"

There was a rustle of paper. "A punnet of strawberries, my lord. Must be early ones from Cornwall, and they're beauties if I may say so. Then there are two bowls," sniff, sniff, "one of gooseberry fool, if I am not mistaken, and one of restorative meat jelly. Most appropriate, my lord."

Tenderly touching his jaw, Bertram had to agree, but he wondered how the Suttons knew of his débâcle. He could not believe George had boasted of it, for however irritating, the fellow was a gentleman.

"Here's a note, my lord. I shall remove the victuals to the kitchen."

Bertram stretched out his hand for the paper and ventured to open his eyes again. It was bearable as long as he kept his head still.

"Dear Bertram," he read, "I was so sorry to hear of your indisposition. I made the fool and the jelly <u>with my own hands </u>(and Mrs. Rumbelow's help), and I went to the market at <u>crack of dawn </u>for the berries. Don't worry, I took Alfie with me. Lizzie."

Lizzie, of course.

The thought of her at Covent Garden Market among the foul-mouthed vendors, with or without Alfie, made him shudder. He could see the imp in her eyes as she wrote that, aware that he would disapprove. He did not know whether he was more impressed by her bountiful sympathy or her indiscretion.

She had surely not realised how her kindness might be viewed by the scandalmongers. Like the chairs he and Winterborne had given the Suttons, the gift would be perfectly unexceptionable from both of the ladies; from one, it was open to misinterpretation. At least she was not so lost to propriety as to deliver it herself!

What a confusing creature she was, dispensing her bounty in such a way that he must be as critical as he was grateful.

He heard the arrival of more visitors in the outer room: Fergie and Dartford come to commiserate, and to roast him on his defeat no doubt. They must not see Lizzie's letter. He thrust it under his pillow.

No sooner had his friends left than Lady Caroline appeared. He was not pleased to see his sister, since if she had heard of the fight the story must be the latest *on-dit*. He was still less pleased when he realised that Aunt Dorothy and Amelia were with her.

"What the devil?" he hissed as she bent over his bed of pain.

She shrugged helplessly. "You know what she is like. I could not stop her," she whispered.

Lady Harrison advanced majestically. "I have brought Amelia to soothe you in your affliction Bertram," she announced. "She shall brew you a posset with her own hands."

"But Mama, I do not know how to brew a posset!" blurted the unfortunate damsel.

"I daresay you have never been in a kitchen in your life," said Caroline soothingly. "And it is really not the thing for a young girl to be in a gentleman's bedchamber, or in his lodgings, Aunt, even if they are cousins."

"There can be no harm in it, since they are to be wed," said her ladyship.

Amelia rushed from the room in tears.

Bertram sat bolt upright. His jaw dropped, causing him excruciating agony which he ignored. "What did you say, Aunt Dorothy?" he asked, his voice icy. "I assure you I have not requested your daughter's hand in marriage, nor have I any intention of doing so."

"Amelia does not want to marry Bertram in the least," Caroline pointed out.

"It is in every way an eligible match," Lady Harrison said obstinately.

Forestalling Bertram's explosion, Pinkerton appeared in the doorway, wooden faced. "My lady, Miss Harrison asked me to inform your ladyship that she has gone down to the carriage."

With a venomous glare at Bertram, Aunt Dorothy marched out.

"I shall take the poor child in hand next Season," said

Caroline. "No more of that pink muslin, which makes her look quite washed out. Now, what is all this about a fistfight with Winterborne?"

"I am sure you know all the details," said her brother acidly, sinking back on his pillows. "Do go away, Caroline. I am feeling perfectly devilish."

"They are saying you quarrelled over Lizzie Sutton. I am trying to quash the rumours, of course, as is Mrs. Tilliot, and Lizzie carried it off with the greatest composure at the Eversleys' rout last night. George has gone out of Town."

"She's a brave little soul, isn't she? I can just imagine the old tabbies with their snide remarks."

"I know you were not fighting over Lizzie, but were you fighting over Claire?"

Bertram frowned. "I cannot believe he has serious intentions towards a plain female like Claire. His high-flyers have always been the most stunning creatures, his flirts, too, and he does not need her money any more than I do, unlike our obnoxious cousin Horace. It's more likely he is interested in Lizzie, as the gossips have it, for she is a pretty chit. Yet there is a sense of rivalry."

"I do not like to hear you call Claire plain, Bertram." It was Caroline's turn to frown. "If *your* intentions towards her are not serious, it grows late for finding an alternative."

"Oh, I daresay I shall marry her in the end, but you told me yourself that there is no hurry. I am enjoying the Season with no need to hunt for a bride, thanks to your brilliant notion, and as soon as we are betrothed there will be a thousand plans to make."

"All the same, you would do well to make more effort to fix your interest," said his sister, but his flattery achieved its aim and she ceased to press him.

He was able to continue evading the issue of his rivalry with George, since that gentleman remained absent. It was more difficult to explain to himself his lagging pursuit of Claire.

The best he could say was that he was resigned to marrying her. By now he was certain that she would make him a conformable wife. Her behaviour in Society was irreproachable, and when alone with him she was never less than pleasant. He was even growing almost fond of her. There was none of the rapture of his relationship with Amaryllis, but nor was there any of the hurt he had known when his lost love had disagreed with him, or the anguish of her final rejection.

Yes, he would marry Claire—sooner or later. In the meantime, he was comfortable in his bachelor quarters at the Albany. There were balls and routs and the theatre to attend, with her and her sister, more often than not. There were evenings with his friend, sometimes quiet, sometimes boisterous, and days out of Town attending horse races or prizefights. He even enjoyed an expedition to Waltham Abbey and Bumble's Green with Claire and Lizzie.

Time passed unnoticed.

This year the Season was prolonged beyond the beginning of June by the approaching Coronation. Prinny, assured that Queen Caroline would not take part, at last set the date. Instead of the usual exodus of the ton to their country estates, those who had not spent the spring in London were gathering daily in anticipation of the celebrations. Not a peer in the realm but meant to take his seat in Westminster Abbey on that day, for few indeed had been present at George III's coronation, three score years ago.

Daily Bertram scanned the *Morning Post* for the names of the latest arrivals. June was nearly over when the half-expected announcement caught his eye: the Honourable Amaryllis Hartwell, only daughter of Viscount Hartwell, was wed to Lord Daniel Winterborne, second son of the Marquis of Bellingham.

Expected as it was, the shock took his breath away. He stared unseeing at his plate of muffins and ham until Pinkerton asked anxiously, "Is there something wrong with your breakfast, my lord?"

"No. No, nothing. I am not hungry." He pushed his plate

away. At that moment the door-knocker sounded. "I am not at home this morning, to anyone."

He heard his manservant expostulating, then Caroline bustled into the room. After one look at his face she sat down beside him and patted his hand.

"You have seen it then, Bertram. You never did stop hoping, did you?"

"I don't know. I don't know what I think, I don't know what I feel. No, I don't believe I still had any hopes, or even that I still love her. I feel—blank."

She patted his hand again and reached for a muffin. "Of course you still hoped," she said, buttering it. "That is why you have been postponing offering for Claire. But it's over now. You cannot put it off for ever, you know."

He stood up and wandered restlessly about the room, picking things up and putting them down again, while she munched on her muffin and sipped the cup of tea unobtrusively provided by Pinkerton.

"You're right," he said with sudden decision. "If you will just go away and leave me in peace, I shall plan my proposal. Thank heaven she is of age, and I shall not have to approach her father."

Unoffended, Caroline finished the last bite and departed.

On his knees, he wondered, or should he just sit beside her? Horace had looked so undignified kneeling on the floor by the empty chair. He would talk of his esteem for her, the honour she would do him by accepting his hand. He had no intention of misleading her by offering his heart; she must know this was to be a marriage of convenience. Should he sit or kneel?

He knew he was procrastinating when he was unable to make up his mind on that simple point. At intervals throughout the day it nagged at him.

Whenever he thought about proposing to Claire, Lizzie's teasing face appeared before him. Except when he was actually furious with her, he had long since ceased to regard her as an obstacle to his marriage. Yet somehow she was involved with his unwillingness to declare himself.

That he was still unwilling he had to acknowledge to himself.

Among the next day's mail there was a letter from his mother. She had seen the notice in the *Morning Post*. Though she sympathised with him, she passed on an ultimatum. The Tatenhills would arrive in London on the seventeenth of July. After spending the next day recovering from the journey, his father would attend the Coronation. Another day of rest would ensue, then, on the twenty-first, Bertram was to present his betrothed to his parents.

There was nothing like a deadline to compose the mind, he discovered. He would propose on the twentieth.

He made a determined effort to distinguish Claire by his attentions, rather than treating the two sisters equally. In this he was not entirely successful. She was elusive, often spending the day at her house outside London, declining both his escort and George's.

George's behaviour puzzled him. His earlier absence argued indifference, yet now that he had returned he was as often as ever in the Suttons' company. Bertram knew he had introduced them to his father, the Marquis of Bellingham, come to Town for the Coronation. Possibly, as rumour had it, he meant to pay his addresses to Lizzie, yet rumour said the same of Bertram.

"Rumour," as Caroline assured her brother, "was ever a lying jade."

When Bertram asked Claire to suggest an outing, she generally consulted Lizzie, who chose Astley's Amphitheatre and balloon ascensions, Barker's Panorama, and a ride on a steam packet on the Thames. Though Claire enjoyed these, Bertram wanted to do something especially for her.

"No, don't look at Lizzie," he said one day. "What would *you* like to do?"

She looked at him doubtfully. "I should like to visit John Kennedy," she said, "but it would be the greatest bore for anyone else."

"John Kennedy?"

"The nurseryman who aided the Empress Josephine in

179

her rose garden. I have been to the Vineyard Nursery, but he is retired to Eltham, in Kent, and I cannot like to call on him on my own."

"Very proper. I shall take you. We might combine it with a visit to the remains of Edward II's palace at Eltham."

"That sounds delightfully Gothick," approved Lizzie.

Since he could hardly tell her that he had intended the invitation for Claire alone, Bertram resigned himself to another family outing.

John Kennedy proved to be a garrulous old man, delighted to receive visitors. Bertram was interested in his tales of crossing the British and French lines in the middle of war to advise Napoleon's wife at Malmaison. Then the talk turned to rose-growing, interspersed with stories about his twenty-one children. Lizzie grew restless, and Bertram found it difficult to maintain his expression of polite interest.

Mr. Kennedy showed no signs of flagging, and Claire was eagerly absorbing his every word. At least Bertram ventured to interrupt.

"We must be going, Miss Sutton, if we are to explore the palace."

"I'm sorry," she said, instantly contrite. "I forgot the time. Pray take Lizzie to see the palace and fetch me when you are done. Did you develop the Bullata, Mr. Kennedy?"

Bertram and Lizzie slipped out unnoticed.

"Now where is her sense of priorities," mocked Lizzie, "to set roses above a Gothick ruin, and a gardener above a lord."

Bertram laughed as they walked along the village street. He had been prepared to take offence at Claire's neglect, but Lizzie gave him back his perspective.

"I have a lowering feeling that she will not miss us in the slightest," he said.

"You did ask her what she wanted to do, and the palace was your idea, not hers. *I* am looking forward to it excessively."

Despite an argument over whether Edward II's murder was justified or not, Bertram thoroughly enjoyed the rest of the day. He had not realised that Lizzie's intelligence was as lively as her manner. Unlike most of her contemporaries, she had not merely read novels in pursuit of the Gothick, but was well-read in mediaeval history.

When he expressed surprise at her knowledge, she challenged him at once.

"You believed me an ignoramus, and now you suppose that I am a blue-stocking. It will not do to expose one's erudition, however limited, to the Beau Monde, but I thought you too understanding to scorn me for using the brain God gave me."

"I have always known Claire to be intelligent and well-informed. Why did I suppose that she had not brought you up the same? She has been a mother, and more than a mother, to you, has she not? What an extraordinary person she is."

"Ah, you do understand." Her blue eyes gazed up into his, losing their fire. "It was not easy. We tried to keep it from Mama, for reading too much was one of the imagined faults she saw in Claire. I daresay I have simply grown used to concealing it. I knew I could trust you, Bertram."

"Thank you for your trust in me," he said quietly, pressing the little hand that rested on his arm. "I did not mean to sound scornful. On the contrary, I can only admire you for studying voluntarily what I had beaten into me at school."

"No!" she said, her usual sparkle restored, "I cannot believe that you were ever anything but a pattern card of perfection."

"Toad-eater," he teased. "That's trying it on too thick and rare."

"I am merely extrapolating from the present to the past." She laughed, and he though he had never heard so enchanting a sound in his life.

=== 17 ===

"I'M WORRIED ABOUT Claire," said Lizzie as George's curricle turned in at the park gates.

"Well, wipe away that frown, or the world will think you at daggers drawn with me. Besides it does not suit your pretty face."

The world, or that part of it known to itself as the Polite World, was indeed abroad that sultry July day, seeking a breath of fresh air among the lawns and trees of Hyde Park. It was not, Lizzie acknowledged to herself as she bowed and smiled at an acquaintance, the best place for a serious discussion.

"She is unhappy," she persevered, waving to one of her youthful admirers with a shake of the head to hint that she did not want him to approach. She knew she was adding fuel to the rumours of an attachment between herself and George, but to seek a more private place would confirm them.

"What makes you think that?" His voice was abstracted as he negotiated a narrow gap beside the carriages of two dowagers who had settled for a comfortable cose in the middle of the way.

"Oh, a thousand things," said Lizzie impatiently. "Do you think she has found out about Lady Caroline meaning Bertram to marry her? Perhaps she is worried that he will not come up to scratch."

"Is she so very fond of him?"

George was tight-lipped, his face grimmer than she had ever seen it. Remembering the curricle race and the fist-

182

fight, she could not help wondering whether he might call Bertram out if he failed to propose. He was a very protective person, and having taken them under his wing he would not take kindly to anyone who hurt them.

"She likes him very well," she said judiciously, "but I do not believe she has a *tendre* for him."

"Then she is anxious to be married, no matter to whom?"

"Oh no! She has refused Horace Harrison at least three times, to my knowledge, and I think Lord Peter Dartford proposed, though she will not tell me. For all I know, she would refuse Bertram, but to realise that he has considered her as a bride and rejected her can only humiliate her."

"She would be mad to refuse him," said George harshly. Lizzie looked at him in surprise, and he smiled with an obvious effort. "Now you are going to tell me to wipe the frown from my pretty face lest the world suppose us at daggers drawn. No, I doubt she knows of Lady Caroline's plot, unless you have told anyone?"

"Of course not!" Lizzie was indignant.

"Of course not. I beg your pardon. You care for her too much to risk word spreading. Indeed, your concern for her is as admirable as hers for you." His smile this time was so warm that she blushed. "Then only you and I and Lady Caroline and Bertram know. It would not suit them any better than us to have Claire find out."

"I daresay you are right." She sighed. "All the same, she is unhappy, and I cannot discover why."

The conversation was halted by a group of three youths on horseback whom nothing would deter from accosting the object of their admiration. Lizzie duly fluttered her eyelashes at them, teasing one for his red-and-white striped waistcoat and another for the huge nosegay in his buttonhole, which he promptly presented to her. When they drove on, George was laughing at her.

"Do you enjoy having half the Town at your feet?" he enquired.

"Oh yes, it is famous fun, though it is not half the Town,

only a few gentlemen, most of them only a year or two older than me. And most of them admire Nell as much as they admire me. I daresay they think it safer. You must not think, though, that Claire is the only one to receive offers. I have had two or three."

"And refused them all."

"They were mere boys, and sad rattles besides."

"Then you have reconsidered the advantages of maturity?" George grinned. "I remember a time when you saw me in the light of a substitute father."

"You would make an excellent father," she retorted. "I wonder that you do not have a quiver full of children."

Bertram would have called her to account for the impropriety of that remark. George merely raised his eyebrows with an amused look.

"I am an excellent uncle," he assured her, "and I expect to have increased opportunity to practise the art now that my brother is married again. He and his bride are passing through London in a day or two, on their wedding journey, and I should like you and Claire to meet them. Can you come to dinner the day after tomorrow?"

"If they are half as nice as Mrs. Tilliot and your papa, we shall be delighted."

Claire had told Lizzie that, according to George, Lord Daniel Winterborne had had an unhappy first marriage and adored his new wife. Lizzie thought it a prodigious romantic story and was eager to meet the happy couple. She was not disappointed. Lord Daniel was very like his brother in appearance, but his face in repose was sad, even melancholy. When he smiled, which he did every time he looked at Lady Daniel, his expression lit with pure joy, while she had eyes only for him. They sat next to each other at dinner, and no one was surprised when the gentlemen rejoined the ladies within ten minutes of their withdrawing from the table.

Lizzie wondered wistfully whether she would ever find a love like that.

Except for the Suttons it was a family party, the marquis's

brother and his family making up the numbers to a round dozen. Lizzie was afraid that she and Claire might be regarded as intruders, but everyone was preoccupied with the bridal couple.

All the same, the invitation had most definitely been a mark of distinguishing attention. Was it possible that rumour had it right for once, and George wanted to marry her?

Lizzie lay long awake that night. Marrying George suddenly seemed like the answer to many of her problems. For one thing, she knew there would be no second Season for her. Claire had saved her income for years to give her this opportunity, and though she had said Lizzie must not marry where she did not feel a decided partiality, she longed to see her sister settled. And Lizzie could not deny that she did feel a decided partiality for George: she liked him better than any gentleman she knew except for Bertram.

Bertram? she thought, startled. Why had Bertram sprung to mind? Of course he and George were both very good friends. Bertram was younger and livelier, at least with her, but George was reliable, trustworthy, never miffed at her. Besides, Bertram was to marry Claire.

She could be comfortable as George's wife. She liked his family, and, though he had been roasting her when he suggested it, she had indeed come to realise the advantages of a mature husband. To be sure, she was not wildly in love with him, as Lord and Lady Daniel were, but perhaps she would never fall in love. The prolonged Season was slipping away, only ten days to go till the Coronation, and she could not wait for ever in the hope that she might meet someone to sweep her off her feet.

The Season was almost over, and neither George nor Bertram had proposed. Something must be done to force their hands.

That decision made, Lizzie fell asleep at last.

"Claire," she said thoughtfully the next morning at breakfast, "You do like Bertram, do you not?"

"Certainly. Now which are you going to have?"

"Which?" Lizzie's mind flew to George. Given an honest choice between him and Bertram, which would she have?

"Cherries, raspberries, or strawberries?" said Claire patiently. "You have been gazing at them these five minutes and more. It is not like you to be woolgathering when there is food in front of you."

"I cannot make up my mind, so I shall have some of each." She helped herself. "Really like him, I mean."

"Bertram? Very much more than I did at first. It takes some time to see past his reserve, but once one comes to know him it is clear that he is a kind, intelligent, and sensible gentleman."

"Good." Lizzie was much relieved. It would be a sorry thing to force her sister into a match with a man she held in dislike. "These cherries are heavenly. Pass the bowl, please."

Since she lacked the audacity to ask Bertram his opinion, she carefully observed his behaviour towards Claire over the next couple of days. His solicitude was obvious, and he even showed signs of resenting it when her attention was taken by any other gentleman. Lizzie decided he must be waiting to present her to his parents, whom she knew to be coming for the Coronation, to gain their approval before he proposed. The unknown Earl and Countess of Tatenhill must not be allowed to wreck her sister's future.

She set her mind to devising a plan, and soon had the first glimmerings of an idea. Unfortunately it meant tricking Bertram, forcing him into a compromising situation. Try as she might she could come up with no alternative. He was bound to be excessively angry with her, she thought unhappily. Perhaps she should wait and trust that everything would work out for the best.

With just a week left, Claire went to Bumble's Green, where she was having the house thoroughly refurbished in anticipation of moving in at the end of the month. She was often there these days, which had suggested part of Lizzie's plan. In her sister's absence, Lizzie went with a group of young people to a picnic in Richmond Park. Nell and Bertram and George were all present, and she managed to enjoy the outing despite the doubts and uncertainties plaguing her mind.

Bertram drove her home in his curricle. She was on her guard with him, and he seemed abstracted. Instead of their usual joking and occasional tiffs, they made polite conversation. Lizzie found it excruciatingly painful. By the time they reached Portman Square, shortly after six, all she wanted to do was to run up to her chamber and cry. However, she bit back the tears and invited him in for a glass of wine. Somewhat to her surprise, he accepted.

From the front hall they could hear Claire's voice in the parlour, raised in uncharacteristic indignation.

"I have told you time and time again, sir, that I cannot return your sentiments!"

Lizzie sped to the room and paused in the doorway. Claire was standing with her back to the window, a slender silhouette, with the evening light gilding her hair. Horace Harrison knelt before her, clasping both her hands. His lips were pressed to one, which she struggled to withdraw.

Setting Lizzie aside, Bertram advanced on his obnoxious relative. He seized him by the collar of his magenta coat and hauled him to his feet.

"This grows tedious," he said in a languid voice which failed to hide the steely undertone. "If I find you plaguing Miss Sutton again, you will have cause to regret it."

Lizzie stifled a laugh at the appalled expression on Horace's face as he gaped up at his large cousin.

"No, no, assure you, coz," he stammered. "Wouldn't dream of plaguing a lady. Honourable offer, and all that."

"The lady has rejected your offer in no uncertain terms. You will not approach her again on the subject."

"If you say so," Horace said sulkily, straightening his coat as Bertram released him. He turned to Claire with a stiff bow. "Pray excuse me, ma'am, I am expected elsewhere." He marched to the door, ignoring Lizzie. She heard him say

187

under his breath, "At least not when there is the least chance of you turning up, dear coz!"

Bertram, his arm about Claire's shoulders, was leading her to a chair. Despite her protests that she was perfectly all right, she looked pale. Lizzie hurried to pour a glass of Madeira.

"How came you to be alone with him?" asked Bertram gently.

"I gave the servants leave for the day since both Lizzie and I were out. Alfie was with me, of course, but I sent him on an errand as soon as we reached the livery stables. It is only just 'round the corner. Mr. Harrison was on the doorstep when I arrived, and he would not be denied."

"I hope he will trouble you no more, but if he dares you will tell me and I shall deal with him."

Lizzie's uncertainty fled. Horace had no intention of giving up his pursuit, and Bertram offered the only protection. He must marry Claire, and soon.

And she must marry George. After that dreadful drive home from Richmond, she knew she could not bear to live with Claire and Bertram once they were man and wife.

It would have to be Coronation Day, she decided. Not only would everyone be too occupied to notice her activities, but the day's schedule had been published in the *London Gazette*, so she knew just where everyone would be. The ceremony in Westminster Abbey was supposed to last from ten o'clock to about four, and only peers had been invited to the banquet in Westminster Hall afterwards. George and Bertram would surely go straight home to put off their formal attire. There each would find a note.

That part was easy. She was less sure how to lure Claire to Bumble's Green at the right moment. Her sister had mentioned giving the Copples leave to absent themselves for a couple of days to enjoy the festivities in the city. Though Lizzie would not have to think of a way to remove them from the premises, nor could she invent an urgent message from them requiring Claire's immediate presence. She puzzled over the problem for some time before abandoning it, hoping for a stroke of inspiration at the last minute.

After dinner she retreated to her chamber to write the notes to their lordships. "Dear George," she began.

It looked shockingly familiar, much more so than when she addressed him thus. She tore up the sheet and began again: "My lord." It was a bit formal, but she must hurry or Claire would be coming up to see what she was at.

"My lord, I am in a Dreadful Predicament. I received word of a Dire Emergency in Oxfordshire which requires my presence. Claire is from home, so I set out alone. My money was Stolen, and I am Stranded at an inn in the village of Colnbrook," (she had long since consulted a map) "with an angry Coachman and a Suspicious Landlord. Pray come to my aid as soon as you may!"

She signed and folded it, then started on the one for Bertram.

"My lord, Claire has been Kidnapped by a Villain." She thought of putting in Horace's name, but Bertram might see his cousin at the wrong moment. "He has taken her to her house at Bumble's Green. I beg you will follow at once with all speed and Rescue her from his Clutches!"

Again she signed and folded, then sat for a moment pondering. Bertram might wonder how she knew what had happened to Claire, but in the urgency of the moment he was not likely to stop to question her. It would serve. She dipped her pen preparatory to directing the two missives when she heard steps on the landing.

"Lizzie, are you unwell?" came Claire's voice at her door.

She shoved the letters under a book and turned.

"No, I was just dashing off a note to Nell to arrange a meeting for tomorrow. I shall be down in a moment. Is George already come to take us to the musicale?"

"No, but he will be here shortly."

"I am almost done."

To her relief Claire left. She retrieved the papers, scribbled "Lord Winterborne" on one and "Lord Pomeroy" on the other, sealed them, and hid them in an old reticule in her wardrobe. To justify her words to her sister, she then wrote to Nell. Somehow, lying to Claire was different from telling wild tarradiddles to their lordships. Feeling pleased with her preparations, she went downstairs.

Whenever she managed to get Alfie alone in the next few days, she coached him in the part he was to play. At first he was bewildered by the complicated instructions, then, when he understood, he protested.

"Miss Claire won't like it," he said obstinately.

"It is for her own good, Alfie. You must not listen if she tells you not to do it. She will be happy in the end, I promise. You must do just as I say and not listen to her."

By dint of much repetition his objections were dulled, and at last he was able to repeat Lizzie's orders without either mistake or remonstrance. It was none too soon. The Coronation was just two days away, and she still had no notion how she was to get Claire to Bumble's Green.

The night before the great day was made hideous every half hour, from midnight on, by the ringing of bells and roaring of cannon. It seemed an odd way for the King to attempt to endear himself to his subjects. Lizzie slept through much of it, but her dreams were troubled.

When she awoke it was nearly noon, and she was ready to abandon the entire project. Its impropriety and under-handedness preyed on her mind. She was not sure she wanted to be George's wife, or anyone's, and she was still less sure that Claire wanted to be Bertram's. She did not dare imagine what the gentlemen would think of her trickery. Perhaps they would never forgive her, and they might blame Claire, too. Perhaps they would refuse to be pushed into marriage, and she and Claire would both be ruined. The horrid possibilities seemed endless.

Fate took a hand, removing the last difficulty. Claire came into Lizzie's chamber looking exhausted, pale, and with dark smudges under her eyes.

"I cannot bear it any longer," she said, distraught. "I must get away, be alone."

Lizzie pulled her down onto the bed and hugged her. "You look as if you have not slept a wink. Those dreadful guns!"

"They were just the last straw. Do not ask me to explain, Lizzie, but I must be alone. I am going to go to Bumble's Green for a day or two, while the Copples are away. I must be back by the day after tomorrow, for I do not care to offend the Tatenhills by missing their dinner party. Do you think Lady Marchmont will allow you to stay with Nell?"

Lizzie's doubts flew away as the last pieces of the plan fell into place.

"Of course. She likes me, and Nell will be delighted. You are not leaving this minute, are you? I shall need Alfie to take a note to the Marchmonts."

"Not for at least two or three hours. I must write one or two notes myself, excusing myself from engagements, so do not send Alfie until I am ready. And then I shall have to pack some clothes, and talk to Mrs. Rumbelow." She passed a weary hand across her forehead.

"Claire, you are not ill, are you?"

"No, I just need time to think." She tried to smile. "We have been gadding about so these last months that there is never a moment to spare. Don't worry, darling, I just need a little peace and quiet."

Lizzie hugged her again, remorseful. "It is my fault you have been burning the candle at both ends."

"Nonsense. I have enjoyed every minute." Claire stood up. "I'll send Molly to help you dress."

An hour later Alfie was sent out to deliver several notes. Though he could not read, they had developed a system of symbols for the houses he was sent to most often. Having learned them he never forgot, and he had never made a mistake. Unknown to Claire, he had nothing for Lady Marchmont: the note he carried to her house was directed to Nell and said nothing of significance. He did, however, call at Bellingham House and the Albany.

As soon as he returned, Lizzie went down to the kitchen where Claire was consulting Mrs. Rumbelow.

"There is no objection to my staying with Nell," she said, which had the merit of being true, since Lady Marchmont had no knowledge of the proposed visit. "Unless you need me, I shall leave at once."

"Of course, love. I shall send for you as soon as I return to Town. Here are a couple of sovereigns, for I am sure you have run through your pin money long since."

Lizzie flung her arms about her sister. "I do love you, Claire," she murmured. Catching Mrs. Rumbelow's skeptical glance, she added indignantly, "And that is not creampot love but appreciation of your thoughtfulness."

"I know it," said Claire, laughing. "Oh, you had best take Molly with you. Lady Marchmont will expect you to have a maid, I make no doubt."

Taking Molly on her adventure played no part in Lizzie's plans. She was about to protest that she could perfectly well share Nell's maid, but she paused to consider. Perhaps it would be just as well to have company while she journeyed to the inn.

"I'll see you in a couple of days then," she said, kissed Claire, and skipped upstairs to tell the girl to pack up a few clothes.

Alfie fetched a hackney for them, another job he had grown very good at in the city. The driver and his horse were both thin and lugubrious. The former eyed Lizzie doubtfully when she said she wanted to drive out towards Kew. However, she was wearing her prettiest carriage dress, a delightful midnight blue confection, and a respectable abigail accompanied her. He whipped up his nag.

It was hot inside the hackney, and the ancient straw on the floor smelled most unpleasant. Molly, disappointed at not going to stay in a "real lord's house" and apprehensive about the plan unfolded to her, snivelled in a corner. By the time they reached Kensington, Lizzie was ready to scream. She signalled to the driver, and when he stopped she jumped out.

"Gettin' down 'ere?" he enquired hopefully.

"No. I mean to ride on the box with you. It is horrid

inside." Lifting her skirts, she scrambled up beside him before he found the wits to object. There was not the least chance of anyone seeing her in that disgraceful position since the entire Beau Monde was at or hovering near the Coronation. "Let's go. Can your horse not go any faster?"

This was to become a constant plea as they left the city behind them. The bony creature kept stopping to grab a mouthful of leaves or grass as they passed.

"'E's a Lunnon 'oss," the driver explained uneasily. " 'E don't unnerstand this 'ere countryside, no more nor do I."

"I'm sure the poor beast is happier than he has ever been in his life," said Lizzie, "but I wish he would hurry up."

At last they reached Kew. The driver's relief was evident, until Lizzie informed him that she had not said she was going *to* Kew but in that direction.

"Pray let us go on to Colnbrook," she coaxed.

"This 'ere's a Lunnon 'ackney. Out you get, missie, and that'll be a crown 'ere and another fer me journey back, that's 'alf a sovereign."

Eyelashes fluttering, Lizzie played her trump. "Oh, but I have no money on me, for fear of being robbed. I am to meet someone at the inn in Colnbrook who will pay you a whole sovereign, or perhaps even two."

"I orter know better'n to pick up a swell mort!" he said in disgust, shaking the reins. "Colnbrook? That'll cost yer four guineas, that will."

The horse reluctantly abandoned a particularly succulent tuft of grass and plodded on.

At that speed, Lizzie thought drearily, George would reach Colnbrook hours before she did. He would decide it was a hoax, turn around, and go home. And then she really would be in the predicament she had invented!

= 18 =

MRS. RUMBELOW WAS bemoaning the waste of a good saddle of mutton she had "bought special acos o' the Coronation, like." Claire listened with half her attention and what patience she could muster.

"You and Enid must eat what you can, then make the rest into potted meat," she suggested at last. "I shall be back the day after tomorrow. I really must go and pack now."

She went slowly upstairs, housekeeping problems already forgotten. She had told Lizzie that she was not ill, and strictly speaking it was true, yet she was not well. No doctor was needed for diagnosis: she was suffering from lovesickness.

Her simmering unhappiness had reached a climax yesterday, when George took her to Westminster to see the preparations for the Coronation. The mingled joy and torment of being with him was more than she could bear.

Before he left—before that shocking fight with Bertram, she had been able to take pleasure in his company, enjoy his friendship, with scarce a second thought. She knew herself ineligible, for her petty fortune could not tempt him, so she had guarded her heart. Her defences were not proof against the unexpected sight of his battered face. Aching to hold him, to soothe his hurts, she had instead been curt, derisive even. She had told him to rusticate and he had obeyed, and the pain of his absence had taught her that she loved him.

If he had stayed away, time might have healed her wounds as they had healed his. He had returned, more charming, more considerate than ever. She had retreated, escaping to her

194

house to prepare it for the long-awaited day when she could remove thither permanently, the day she now dreaded.

They had gone yesterday to Westminster. A marvelling crowd was examining the wide, covered walk between the Abbey and the Hall. Blue-carpeted, it was raised three feet above the ground to improve the view of spectators willing to spend up to twenty guineas to watch the procession from the gaily decorated stands. George traded shamelessly on his rank to obtain entrance into the Hall.

"I shall attend the ceremony in the Abbey," he told Claire as they entered under the thirty-foot triumphal arch. "Only peers are invited to the banquet though, and I'll be damned if I'll sit in the galleries watching my father guzzle."

"You mean they built all those galleries just so that people could watch other people dining?" she asked in astonishment.

"There will be more ceremonies. The challenge of the King's Champion, for instance. He is to ride in on a white charger, borrowed for the day, I collect, from Astley's Amphitheatre."

Claire laughed. "I hope it will be aware of the dignity of the occasion and not try any circus tricks. That table on the dais with the scarlet and gold drapery must be for the King."

"Did you hear that he is making all the Privy Councillors wear Elizabethan dress? White and blue satin, with trunk hose. For the first time, Father is glad to be a member of the Opposition."

"He is a Whig?"

"Yes, and I mean to follow in his footsteps. I trust you do not favour the Tories?"

Claire was baffled by this question. It was asked in a jocular way, yet there was something in George's dark eyes that said her answer mattered to him.

"I believe reform is overdue," she said hesitantly.

"That's my girl!" He touched her cheek lightly, then turned away to point out the musicians' gallery above the triumphal arch, leaving Claire shaken and confused.

George, too, was ill at ease. She had a horrid feeling that he was trying to think of a way to say good-bye. After the Coronation celebrations were over the ton would be leaving London for their country estates, and she knew that he always preferred the country. By the next time he came to Town she would be settled at Bumble's Green.

"How does your redecorating go on at Bumble's Green?" he asked, as if he had read her mind. "I trust you have not aped our monarch's preference for red and gold. It is a trifle hard on the eye, is it not?"

"It goes well," she answered as they left the Hall through a side door. "It will be ready next week for the furniture to be delivered, or so the painter promises." She hoped he would request an invitation to inspect the house, but he said nothing to the purpose as he escorted her, with his usual solicitude, through the crowd to the curricle.

As they drove back to Portman Square he waxed eloquent over the beauties of Dorset in summer. Claire wanted to cry.

She had once thought that he might offer for Lizzie, but he had not yet done so. Bertram might be ready to come up to scratch now that his parents had arrived. Why else should Lady Tatenhill have invited the two of them to dinner? Claire wondered if Lizzie would have him. She had turned down a number of unexceptionable offers but she might prefer life with Bertram, despite the inevitable discord, to retiring with her sister to Bumble's Green.

It was even possible that Lizzie was nursing a secret *tendre* for Bertram. She had asked so earnestly whether Claire cared for him, and with her lively temperament she did not dread argument. Claire could not imagine quarrelling with the man she loved.

"You are quiet today," George had said as he helped her down from the curricle.

"So are you," she had retorted.

Their eyes had met and held for an endless moment, then she had turned and hurried into the house.

As she packed a pair of bandboxes, she tried again to decipher the secret message she had read in that long look. Nothing but her imagination, she decided sadly.

"Miss Claire, Miss Claire!" Alfie panted up the stairs, his red hair standing on end in its usual disarray. "All the gigs is hired out today acos o' the Crownation. There's only a chaise left an' they says it's old as Paul's steeple. Who's Paul?"

"They mean St. Paul's Cathedral, I collect," Claire explained absently, " the old one before the Great Fire, for the new one has a dome. I shall have to take it. Carry these down, if you please, and then run back to the stables for the chaise."

She was following him down when a knock sounded at the front door, and Enid popped up from the kitchen to answer it.

It was Horace Harrison. He saw her on the stair, and it was too late to retreat.

"Miss Sutton," he said, with an elaborate bow which put his eyes in danger from his shirtpoints. "My cousin is safely ensconced in Westminster Abbey, so I am come to assure you I have no intention of trifling with your affections. I beg you will listen to my suit."

"Pray do not, sir!" Claire was acutely conscious that Enid and Alfie were listening avidly. "I am on the point of departing for the country."

"Then you must allow me to drive you. You will be more comfortable in Mama's barouche than in any hired vehicle. I do not pretend to be a top sawyer like Bertram, but I am generally accounted a fair whip and will engage not to overturn you."

Claire was tempted. Horace was bound to make another offer, but that seemed easier to cope with than an endless journey in an ancient chaise. He would be seated on the box, not inside the vehicle with her, so he must wait until they arrived to propose. In fact, she owed it to him to depress his pretensions thoroughly, for Bertram's interruptions had never allowed her to complete her rejection in no uncertain terms. Alfie's presence would ensure that he did not go beyond the bounds of propriety.

"Thank you, Mr. Harrison," she said tiredly, suppressing her misgivings. "That is very kind of you. I am ready to leave at any moment."

If Horace had exaggerated in describing himself as a fair whip, at least he had a realistic view of his own abilities. He never raised his team's gait above a trot, slowing to a walk around corners. The barouche, though old-fashioned, was indeed comfortable, and Claire managed to doze, rousing now and then to nod and smile when Horace called her attention to what he considered interesting landmarks. There was little traffic, a holiday having been declared in honour of the Coronation. The peaceful greenness of the countryside was soothing to her tattered nerves.

It was nearly six when they reached Bumble's Green. The new rose-garden glowed in the golden light, and a light breeze wafted the fragrance to Claire as the carriage drew up before the house. She knew she had been right to come. Here in the quiet of her own home she could sort out her feelings and regain her composure.

"Will you come in for some refreshment before you leave, Mr. Harrison?" she invited unwillingly. She had no hope that he would decline. "It must be in the kitchen, I fear, for the other rooms are not yet furnished. Alfie, take the carriage 'round to the stables if you please, then bring my things in."

The lad hurried to obey. He seemed oddly excited, pink-cheeked and muttering to himself, casting puzzled glances at Horace and shaking his head. Claire watched him with a frown and resolved to ask what was troubling him as soon as she had disposed of her unwanted suitor.

She led the way into the house and down the passage to the kitchen. They passed the door of the Copples' bedchamber, where she would be sleeping, and she smiled as she noticed the key in the big brass lock. No doubt Mrs. Copple had intended to leave her valuables safely shut up and then had forgotten to remove the key.

Horace Harrison, in his celestial blue coat, orange waistcoat, and huge topaz pin, looked thoroughly out of place in the kitchen. He sat stiffly on the edge of a chair at the scrubbed white-wood table, watching in astonishment as Claire lit the new Rumford stove and set a kettle to boil.

"My dear Miss Sutton," he protested, "when we are married you will have servants to do such tasks."

"I have said I will not marry you," she pointed out, "and I have servants of my own. They happen to be absent." In truth she was rather proud of her skills and annoyed with him for not appreciating them.

Horace rose, took a large handkerchief from his pocket, and spread it on the spotless flagstone floor. The moment for his proposal had arrived. Fortunately, so had Alfie. He walked jauntily into the kitchen, looking smug and jingling something in his pocket.

"Been't you tired, Miss Claire?" he enquired with a strange grimace contorting his flat features.

"Yes, I am, Alfie. I shall just prepare something for Mr. Harrison to eat before he leaves, and then I believe I shall lie down."

Horace picked up his handkerchief with a sulky air and sat down again. Claire went to the larder, where Mrs. Copple had left bread and cheese and fruit for her. She prepared a simple repast and made a pot of tea.

Alfie was sitting in a corner, whistling tunelessly. His blank face encouraged Horace to try again, though he did not go so far as to kneel. When Claire joined him at the table with a mug of tea, he pushed aside his plate, already half empty, and reached for her hand.

"Mr. Harrison, pray watch what you are about!" she exclaimed.

It was too late. The tea spilled down her gown and she jumped up with a cry of vexation.

"Humbly beg your pardon, ma'am." He drew out his handkerchief again and made futile motions at her skirt.

She backed away from him. "You must excuse me, sir, while I change. And I beg you will not expect me to entertain you further this evening, for I am exhausted. I am grateful for your kind assistance in bringing me here, but I must insist that you believe I have no intention of accepting your hand in marriage, now or ever. I wish you a good journey back to London."

That covered everything, thought Claire as she hurried out of the kitchen, and she hoped he had the grace to take no for an answer. She had been a fool to let him come here.

The door to the bedchamber was open. She went in and closed it firmly behind her, then looked for her bandboxes. They were nowhere to be seen. She had never really inspected the room before. It must once have been a storeroom, judging by the small, high windows above the huge oaken wardrobe. The bed was also huge and looked excessively lumpy. The bandboxes were not in the wardrobe which the Copples had emptied for her use. Nor were they under the bed.

She went back to the door and opened it, meaning to call Alfie to bring her luggage. Horace was just outside, raising his hand to knock. She stepped back in alarm, and he followed her in.

"Miss Sutton, you cannot mean it. You are angry with me, but I shall prove my love. And besides, you will be ruined if you do not marry me," he ended on a more practical note as he clutched her in his arms and aimed a kiss at her lips.

"Release me at once!" Claire struggled to avoid his wet mouth, which landed on her temple. He was stronger than he looked, and he was bearing her back towards the bed. "Alfie, help!" She kicked at his shins.

He let her go with a howl, just as Alfie dashed in. Her bodice had caught in Horace's brooch. The fabric ripped as Alfie pushed Horace away, and for a moment she was too busy pulling the torn garment together to realise that Alfie had put his boxing lessons from George to good effect.

Horace lay stretched on the floor on his back, motionless.

"Alfie, you are wonderful!" she gasped, kneeling beside the victim to see how much damage he had sustained.

The boy bolted through the door and slammed it behind him. Claire heard the key turn in the lock.

"Alfie, what are you about?" she called, jumping to her feet and running to the door. "Unlock it at once, and bring me my bandboxes."

"Can't, Miss Claire!" wailed the unhappy lad. "Miss Lizzie said lock you in wi' the gemmun an' don't listen."

His footsteps died away down the passage.

Feeling faint, Claire sank down on the edge of the bed. He had misunderstood something Lizzie had said, but once he had got an idea into his head he would not budge an inch. She contemplated a night spent fending off Horace's advances and shuddered.

=== 19 ===

BERTRAM CONSIDERED GEORGE IV'S coronation ostentatious in the extreme. It discouraged him that the First Gentleman of the Realm, who had spent several fortunes promoting the arts, should display such a vulgar want of taste. He had only attended because the Earl of Tatenhill insisted it was his duty to be present.

He watched his frail father droop in his heavy velvet and ermine robes, glad that he and his mother had at least persuaded him not to attend the banquet following the six-hour ceremony.

His mind wandered to the proposal of marriage he would make to Claire tomorrow. The prospect disturbed him. He told himself he was being ridiculous, that she would suit him in every way, and she must be grateful to receive so flattering an offer. There should be advantages to having a grateful wife who would not scold or tease, not that Claire was given to scolding or teasing. That was Lizzie's way. All the same, if it were not for his father's command, he would not be making an offer.

His eyes returned to the earl, who was limping up to the throne to kiss the monarch's left cheek. The business was nearly over.

At last the tail end of the procession left the Abbey. It was well after four. Judging by the crush of spectators fighting their way to the exits and the roar of the crowds outside, he would be lucky to reach home by six. He must change before he went to White's for a quiet evening with his cronies, the last he would enjoy for some time now that he was about to become betrothed.

He waited until the worst of the crowds had gone, then strolled back to his lodging in the Albany. Pinkerton gasped with dismay at the sight of his master's creased coat and limp cravat.

"I've laid your evening clothes out, my lord. Your lordship's bath will be ready in ten minutes. Oh, here's a note came for your lordship some hours past. Miss Sutton's lad brought it, said it was urgent. Allow me to relieve your lordship of his coat."

Bertram glanced at the note, recognising Lizzie's hand. He set it on his dresser and submitted to Pinkerton's aid in easing out of his coat. What ailed the chit now? he wondered.

"Don't say they are crying off from dinner with the earl," he muttered.

"My lord?"

"Nothing. My bath, if you please." He reached for the note with one hand as he pulled off his neckcloth with the other. Scanning it rapidly, he paled. "Hell and the devil confound it! Pinkerton!" he roared. "My riding clothes, quickly. I shall have to do without the bath. No, I'd best drive. Tell Abel to put the chestnuts to the curricle, and send word to Mr. Ferguson at White's that I shan't be able to join him. Hurry, man!"

Twenty minutes later, Bertram took the reins from Abel and stepped up into the curricle.

"You want me along, m'lord?" enquired the groom.

"No. Yes. No. Can you keep your mouth shut?"

"Mum's the word, m'lord."

"Jump up, then."

Abel scrambled to his perch as the carriage dashed off down Piccadilly.

"The Bath road, m'lord?" he ventured to ask as they left behind them the noisily celebrating crowds in Hyde Park.

"The Bath road. How many inns are there in Colnbrook?"

"Least half a dozen, m'lord. 'Tis a long stage but lots o' folks stop there."

"Damnation, that's what I thought. Why the devil did the ninnyhammer not give me its name?"

"Miss Lizzie in a bumblebath again," opined Abel.

"How did you guess? No, don't tell me. I'll be damned if I know why she expects me to rush to the rescue."

If Abel had an answer for that rhetorical question, he kept it to himself. Though his lordship drove at a furious pace, the groom was not worried, for this time his master wanted to arrive in one piece.

The extraordinary sight of a London hackney carriage, with a very tired horse, standing in the yard of the first posting house in Colnbrook advertised to Bertram that his quarry was here. The sun was setting, he noted worriedly. Even if they set out immediately he could not return Lizzie home before dark.

"Take care of 'em," he ordered, tossing the reins to Abel. "I'll hire a pair to go back and you can bring the chestnuts tomorrow." He strode into the Cross Keys.

The sound of raised voices led him through the door on his left, into the coffee-room. Lizzie stood in the middle of the room, her bonnet dangling from her fingers, the cynosure of the fortunately few customers. She was engaged in a spirited argument with a stout couple who must be the landlord and his wife, and a small, grubby man Bertram had no hesitation in identifying as the hackney driver.

"I *swear* you will be paid," she said passionately, then caught sight of Bertram. Her mouth fell open.

It was extraordinary, he mused, how pretty she was even when she was gaping. It suddenly dawned on him to wonder how she had managed to send Alfie back to London with the message.

"Bertram!" she squealed. "What on earth are you *you* doing *here*?"

The trio assailing her turned as one, their expressions changing as they took in the immaculate Corinthian with his eyebrows raised in supercilious enquiry.

"How much?" he drawled, ignoring Lizzie.

The driver scuttled forward. "Two guinea the flash mort promised me, guv," he whined, "but I orter get four, all this way outa Town."

"The young miss wants a private parlour," explained the landlady in a conciliatory tone.

"An excellent idea. See to it." He tossed a couple of coins to the driver. "Come, Elizabeth."

Moving in a dazed way, she took his offered arm and they followed the innkeeper to a private parlour. Bertram nodded approval, though the room was sadly beneath his usual standards.

"Tea and biscuits for the young lady," he ordered, "and a heavy wet for me. I'll want your best pair put to my curricle shortly."

"No!" said Lizzie, recovering her voice. "I'm not going anywhere with you. How in heaven's name did you find me?"

Bertram shut the door in the fascinated landlord's face.

"You wrote to me," he reminded her, leaning against the table and enjoying her flashing eyes and pink cheeks.

"I did not! At least, not telling you to come here. Oh no, Alfie must have made a mistake and delivered George's note to you!"

"I hope you are not suggesting that I read a letter addressed to Winterborne. I have it here." He passed it to her and watched the dawning realisation on her face. "Come now, Lizzie, tell me what this is all about," he said gently.

"You will be excessively angry with me," she said in a muffled voice, turning her back on him but not before he noticed the agitated clasping and unclasping of her hands.

"To my extreme astonishment, I find I am not angry at all, only curious."

"You are supposed to be at Bumble's Green, locked in with Claire for the night so that you will have to marry her," she confessed, her voice unsteady. "George was meant to come here and compromise me so that he would have to marry me."

Bertram's hands tightened on the table's edge until his knuckles showed white. "Are you so very much in love with George?" he managed to ask past the strangling sensation in his throat.

"No, but you were to marry Claire, and I knew you would not want me to live with you. I had to marry someone. Oh, everything has gone wrong!" she wailed, and burst into tears.

Lizzie crying—bright, cheerful Lizzie crying—he could not bear it. In two strides he had her in his arms, and once she was there it seemed only proper to shower her face with kisses.

At first she strained away. Aghast at his own actions, he was about to let her go when he felt her arms creep up about his neck. His heart jumped as he saw the wonder in her tear-drenched blue eyes.

"Bertram?" she said hesitantly.

His answer was to crush her lips beneath his own.

"Ahem!" said the innkeeper appearing behind her. "Tea, my lord. Your lordship's groom has picked out a team for your return to Town." He set a tray on the table.

Bertram found himself standing by the window smoothing his hair with a nervous hand, while Lizzie hid her scarlet cheeks at the other end of the room.

"Thank you," he said, clearing his throat. "I shall call if we need anything else."

"Certainly, my lord." The landlord bowed his way out.

"Will you have some tea, Lizzie?" Bertram asked, his voice unnaturally calm, ingrained good manners coming to the fore.

"Yes. No. I don't know. I don't care. Oh Bertram, I am sorry I tried to compromise you, even if you were supposed to be George, and it is kind in you to pretend you...you like me a little, but I know that I am for ever driving you to distraction. You need not marry me. Claire will not mind, she need never know what happened."

"You forget, my love, that by now Claire must be thoroughly compromised herself." Somehow she was in his arms again. It felt most natural. "Besides, I find that I was

206

paying court to the wrong sister all this time."

She hid her face in his chest. "You need not pretend, honestly. I brought Molly, so I am not really compromised at all."

"Little widgeon, have you not heard what I am saying? It is you I want to marry, though I must admit to being taken by surprise myself. Somehow I must have fallen in love with you in between our quarrels. But I forget," he stiffened, feeling cold all over, and his arms dropped to his sides, "perhaps you do not want to be my wife. There is no reason why you should not make your home with Claire and Winterborne." He stepped away from her, turning his back to hide his wretchedness. "What a coxcomb I am to suppose that you return my feelings! You need not make any more excuses, your maid is chaperone enough."

"Bertram!" The desolation in her voice tore his heart. "I do! I do want to be your wife. I have been wondering all this time why it made me so miserable that you meant to marry Claire, when you would be such a perfect husband and I want her to be happy. It was jealousy. What a cat I am!"

"Coxcomb and cat, perhaps we are well matched." He turned again to find her holding out both hands to him. He took them and held them tight, drinking in the sight of her. "Such a very pretty little cat, even with your hair all awry."

"You should look at yourself in the mirror," she retorted. "I am shocked that you should go about with your neckcloth in such disorder."

"I tied it in an almighty hurry, and it has been through a deal since," he said, happy to see her recover her spirits. "Come and rest your dishevelled head against my disgraceful cravat, little love."

He led her to a sofa by the fireplace and pulled her down beside him. When her blonde curls were tickling his chin in a satisfactory manner, he disturbed her again to kiss her ear.

"Much as I adore you," he said seriously, "and though I recognise that I might never have realised it without your muddled intervention, I want to do the thing properly. I want to introduce you to my parents as my betrothed, and have the banns read, and wed you before all the world in St. George's, Hanover Square. I don't want anyone to be able to say there was anything havey-cavey about our wedding."

"I should like a big, fashionable wedding," she said agreeably, snuggling closer, "as long as it is soon." She sat up suddenly, bumping his chin. "But suppose Lord and Lady Tatenhill don't like me! That is why I went through all this instead of waiting for you to propose to Claire. I was afraid the earl might forbid you to marry her."

"They will be too pleased to see me betrothed to take exception to you, unless you are particularly outspoken when you meet them!" He grinned at her indignation. "Perhaps we had better present them with a *fait accompli*. I shall send a notice of our engagement to the *Morning Post* tomorrow. Oh lord, it is nearly dark! I must get you back to Town at once. Caroline will have to take you in if Claire is not at home."

"Just when I was perfectly comfortable," mourned Lizzie. "Bertram, do you think you ought to go to Bumble's Green and make sure that Claire is all right?"

"No, minx, I do not. George is perfectly capable of taking care of her, and I have a feeling he will be delighted to do so. Come now, let me put on your bonnet."

Naturally, the face turned up to his called for a kiss, so it was some minutes later that Molly was summoned from the kitchen to accompany her mistress back to London. Bertram demonstrated his prowess as a top sawyer by driving the admittedly sluggish job-horses all the way with the reins in his right hand.

His left arm was elsewhere.

=== 20 ===

GEORGE WAS PREPARED to swear that the Marquis of Bellingham, tall and dignified in his robes with his coronet perched
on his white hair, had winked at him as he passed out of
the Abbey in the monarch's train. His father had little liking
for solemn ceremony and was outraged at the cost of the
Coronation when the common people were suffering. Nonetheless, he meant to attend the banquet afterwards. Not for
the world, he said, would he miss the sight of Lord Howard
of Effingham, a choleric gentleman, riding his ill-behaved
horse into Westminster Hall in the middle of dinner.

The thought of the banquet made George realise that he
was ravenous. He fell in with a couple of friends as the
spectators filtered out of the Abbey, and he persuaded them
to go with him to Long's ordinary for a rump and a dozen.

Full of beef and oysters, he walked home through the dark-
ening streets a couple of hours later. Ahead of him the sky was
brightened by the fireworks in Hyde Park. The citizens of London were always as ready for a celebration as King George was
to provide a spectacle. He wondered whether Claire and Lizzie
were watching from their window.

As he stepped through the front door of Bellingham House,
Jarvis materialised at his elbow with a silver salver.

"A letter, my lord, brought round by Miss Sutton's lad several hours since. Urgent, he said it was." The butler's voice was
reproachful. He had taken a liking to the Misses Sutton.

George took the note and went into the drawing-room.
Tillie was reading a Minerva Press novel she had borrowed

from Hookham's. He kissed her and enquired after the adventures of the heroine, with which she had been keeping him up to date.

"Never mind Fidelia, you provoking boy," she said. "What does Lizzie's note say? I have been on tenterhooks. Indeed, I was tempted to read it, and had it been in Claire's writing I should certainly have done so, for if *she* claimed urgency I'd not hesitate to credit it."

He opened the paper, read it, and frowned.

"She claims Claire has been abducted by a villain and taken to Bumble's Green. What the devil is the chit up to? Supposing it to be true, how should she know where they went?"

"And who is the villain? How intriguing! It sounds like a Cheltenham tragedy."

"A Banbury tale, more like. However, there may be some kernel of truth, and I shall have to investigate." He strode to the chimneypiece and pulled the bell rope. The butler popped in so quickly that it was plain he had been hovering just outside. "Jarvis, tell Slade to set out my riding clothes, and send to the mews to saddle Orpheus and bring him 'round immediately." He shook his head ruefully. "I shall feel a proper nodcock riding *ventre à terre* to Portman Square to find them sitting at the dinner table."

The only light visible at the Suttons' house was in the basement. Impatient, George hitched Orpheus's reins to the railing, ran down the area steps, and hammered on the door. Enid greeted him with surprise.

"There's no one 'ere but me and Auntie, my lord," she said. "Miss Claire went off to Bumble's Green wiv Alfie, and Miss Lizzie's gone to stay at the Marchmonts'."

"Miss Claire went to Bumble's Green? What time was that?"

"I dunno. What time did Miss Claire leave, Auntie?"

Mrs. Rumbelow heaved herself out of her chair and came to the door while George fumed at the delay.

"Musta bin nearer four than three, my lord," she decided. "There weren't no carriages at the livery when our Alfie went 'round. Then that Mr. 'Arrison come by, and Miss Claire drives off wiv 'im."

So the villain of the piece was Horace Harrison. A tuppenny-ha'penny rogue, but George did not like to think of Claire alone with him and only Alfie along to play propriety. Where Lizzie's note came into the picture he could not guess.

Before the last light had faded from the western sky, a full moon rose, so he made good time though the branching, twisting River Lea prevented riding cross-country. As he passed Waltham Abbey, he heard a clock strike ten. Late enough for his poor darling if she was fending off Horrid Horace's advances, but not so late that he could not return her to Portman Square in time to save her reputation. She had ridden Orpheus with him before.

Was that the moment when he had fallen in love with her?

The fragrance of roses met him as he turned into the drive. Claire and roses—she should grow them by the acre in Dorset, and his mother's garden in Northumberland would thrive at her touch. His decision was made. Pomeroy had left it too late and was about to lose another bride to a Winterborne.

The only visible light shone from the kitchen window, and George remembered that most of the house was not yet furnished. Avoiding the square of lamplight, he led Orpheus 'round to the stables. Even the sight of Lady Harrison's barouche and pair could not deter him from seeing to his mount, but never before had that noble creature's care been so skimped. No more than three minutes later he strode into the kitchen.

Alfie was sitting at the table, his carroty head pillowed on his arms. He looked up sleepily; his face was tear stained. Whatever mischief was brewing here, the lad seemed to be an unwilling accomplice.

"Where is Miss Claire?" demanded George harshly.

Alfie burst into fresh tears. "Oh, Mr. Lord," he sobbed, "she's in the Ockles' room. I din't want to, honest. Miss Lizzie told me to."

"Told you to do what?"

"She said I mun lock Miss Claire in wi' the gemmun. She said it'd make Miss Claire happy in the end."

George seethed with anger. What kind of rig was Lizzie running? If any harm came to Claire from this night's doings it must all be laid to her account.

"Show me," he ordered.

Alfie wiped his nose on his sleeve, picked up the lamp, and led the way, snivelling. When they reached the door to the Copples' chamber, he produced a large key from his pocket and unlocked it. George opened it and stepped in.

His gaze fell at once on the bed, where his beloved lay bathed in moonlight pouring through the high windows.

"*Clair de lune,*" he murmured.

He glanced about. There was no sign of Horace. He went 'round to the other side of the bed, stepping softly, and even peered under it. Nothing. He opened the wardrobe.

The unfortunate Mr. Harrison blinked up at him. A large handkerchief stopped his mouth, and he was bound hand and foot with strips of white material. The topaz in his neckcloth winked in the flickering lamp light.

George guffawed. He could not help himself. Somehow his fragile Claire had overcome this sorry fop, tied him in knots, and deposited him in the wardrobe, a most fitting place. He roared with laughter.

Suddenly the light dimmed. As George turned, he saw the door closing and then he heard the key turn in the lock.

"Damnation!" he swore. The confused half-wit was still carrying out Lizzie's instructions, and now he had a third fish in his net.

"I fear it is not the least use calling him," said a soft voice behind him.

Woken by his laughter, Claire was sitting up. The moonlight was bright enough to see the drowsy droop of her eyelids, and that she was smiling at him. He shut the door of the wardrobe on the pop-eyed Horace and went to sit on the edge of the bed. She slipped her hand into his. His pulse quickened.

"You were laughing," she said wonderingly.

"At your erstwhile suitor, my darling. I found I had been worrying about you quite unnecessarily. How did you manage it?"

"All I did was tie him up and put him in there. Alfie tipped him a settler before he locked the door."

"Somehow, on your lips boxing cant has a delightful ring," George mused, studying her mouth.

"I had to tear a perfectly good lawn petticoat to tie him up with."

He was amused at her indignation—until he noticed her ripped bodice.

"He tore your dress!" he cried, outraged.

Her clasp on his hand prevented his jumping up to wreak vengeance on Horace. Her other hand, which should have risen in automatic modesty to cover her breast, instead touched his lips.

"Hush," she said. "It was an accident. It caught on his pin." Unexpectedly she giggled. "That was when I kicked his shins, and then Alfie hit him."

Breathing hard, he gathered her into his arms.

"You'll have to marry me," he muttered into her ear.

"Do you mind?" she asked, but her arms were about his waist.

"There is nothing in the world I want more." He pulled back a little to look into her eyes, silvered by the moon. "I love you, Claire."

She sighed. "I did not dare to hope. Only there is one thing, George..."

"What?" A sense of foreboding clutched at his heart.

"I love you, too. And I do not want to share you with...with ladybirds, or even with innocent flirts."

"You shall not. You are all I want or need. I promise you that since I first met you not even the fairest Paphians have tempted me. I know, for I went looking."

"Why?" She was puzzled.

With a groan of remembered frustration, he pulled her closer. "Because I wanted you so much, and I could not have you. It's going to be a long night, beloved, but we shall be married tomorrow."

"I want you, too, George. At least, when you touch me I feel shaky inside." Her voice was shy, trembling with emotion, with suppressed passion and, he thought, with fatigue.

"We have the rest of our lives before us." He rocked her gently. "I cannot believe you are going to be mine. Try to sleep now, so that the morning comes sooner."

"I will lie down, if you will hold me. Don't let me go." Already her eyes were closing.

He was filled with wonder at her sweet surrender. She dared to trust him, this girl, this woman betrayed by her own parents from whom she should have learned to trust.

George was woken by tentative knocking at the door, the sound of the key turning, the light of a lamp. He was lying on his side, his left arm flung across Claire's back as she lay face down beside him. They were both fully dressed and on top of the covers, and he was damned if he was going to pretend he had been sleeping on the floor.

He blinked at the light and groaned.

"Pomeroy! What the devil brings you here?"

"Lizzie," said Bertram succinctly.

"I warn you, I shan't let you call me out."

"I don't mean to. I'm going to marry Lizzie. She had sudden qualms about whether Claire would want to marry you."

"Oh yes, she does. Don't you, my love."

Claire stirred. "George?" she asked sleepily, then turned and buried her face in his shoulder.

He held her close. "So this is Lizzie's doing?"

"Yes." Bertram looked about for a chair, then sat down on the edge of the bed. He explained Lizzie's plot, how it had gone awry when Claire interrupted the writing of the notes and they had been addressed wrong. "But I find it is Lizzie I want to marry after all," he ended simply. "And I have suspected for some time that you were head over ears for Claire. Only after Amaryllis and your brother, I could not give her up to you."

214

"Why do you think I did not declare myself long since?" George demanded. "I meant to give you until tomorrow to make up your mind."

"I meant to propose to Claire tomorrow. Lizzie's fiasco has saved our bacon at the eleventh hour."

"You love her?"

"I am besotted with her, or I should be at home beating her. You do not know the worst—she forgot to tell Alfie to release you in the morning. I had a devil of a time getting the key off him." He handed it over.

"Thanks, but I regret to inform you that *you* do not know the worst either. Your charming cousin is in the wardrobe." Grinning in satisfaction as Bertram's jaw dropped, George explained Horrid Horace's presence and his current predicament. "So I'd be grateful if you'll take him with you," he added.

"By all means." Bertram took the lamp to the wardrobe, opened it, and stared down in disgust at his miserable cousin. "You mean to stay here, then?" he threw over his shoulder as he dragged the miscreant out and untied him.

"Yes. Claire is exhausted. You don't happen to be acquainted with any archbishops, do you?"

"As a matter of fact, I do. An uncle of mine, devilish chap. He's in Town for the Coronation. I'll get you a special license first thing tomorrow."

"I'd appreciate it. Now remove your cousin, if you would, and close the door behind you, there's a good fellow."

Bertram departed with a wave, followed by a hobbling Mr. Harrison.

George dropped a tender kiss on the top of Claire's head and went back to sleep.

If you would like to receive details of other Walker Regency Romances, send for your free subscription to our Walker Regency Newsletter,

"The Season"
Regency Editor
Walker and Company
720 Fifth Avenue
New York, NY 10019

FIC
DUN

Dunn, Carola.

Two Corinthians

$19.95